Time passed: the ship gained velocity. The warnings grew more sharp, more dangerously worded.

The warnings ceased.

One of the destroyers, a dark-hulled, slender weapon invisible in the dark of space, opened fire. A laser beam sparked dimly, barely to be seen glinting against the stars. Cliffs smiled. They were firing warning shots.

Two more shots flashed forth, each slightly more bright than the last. as the gunners aboard the Destroyer narrowed the margin by which they permitted their beams to miss. The light that Cliffs and her pilot saw was only photon leakage from the tightly focussed beams. The same beams, taken head on, would have vaporized large segments of the ship, killing all aboard.

One shot. That's all it would take. This thing isn't armored.

REVOLT

AND

REBIRTH

by Jefferson Swycaffer

Book 3
Tales of the Concordat

Cover illustration by
Hanzo

New Infinities Productions, Inc.
P.O. Box 657
Delavan, WI 53115

REVOLT AND REBIRTH

The New Infinities Productions logo is a trademark owned by New Infinities Productions, Inc.

The "BSM" logo is a trademark belonging to Berkley Publishing Corporation.

First Printing: December 1988

Printed in the United States of America

Distributed to the book trade by Berkley Sales & Marketing, a division of the Berkley Publishing Group, 200 Madison Avenue, New York, New York 10016

9 8 7 6 5 4 3 2 1

I S B N : 0-425-11343-4

New Infinities Productions, Inc.
P.O. Box 657
Delavan, WI 53115

Dedication

This book is for Maximilien Robespierre,
who was devoured alive by the revolution he
led;
for Sergei Prokofiev,
whose musical revolution triumphed in great
artistic joy;
and for *William H. Stoddard*,
who has yet to make up his mind.

Acknowledgment

Several of the concepts and nomenclatures used in this story are taken from the Imperium™ and Traveller® games, published by Game Designers' Workshop and designed by Marc W. Miller, to whom all my thanks for his kind permission regarding this use.

Anarchy, anarchy! Show me a greater evil!
This is why cities tumble and the great houses
rain down.
This is what scatters armies.
> — Sophocles, *Antigone*

The Dream of Reason produces monsters.
> — Goya, *Caprichos*

Sterner than Hope, gentler than Duty.
> — Anon.

We are a race inured to endless slaughter;
   we must endure.
We shall freedom gain, swords in our hands.

We seek a peace contrived by our own forging;
   we will attain triumph.
Our victory shall free us.

Death on all sides harries us;
Foemen seek our lifeblood;
Winter darkly closes in.

We strive; we will secure us;
Our lives are our own now,
and forever shall be ours.

Come, saying after me:

We are a race who march with strides of titans;
   we shall endure.
Triumph shall come to us, whose cause is true.

(We are a race whose battle deaths are many;
   we shall endure.
Triumph, be thou kind.)

— Szentellos,
After Revolution.

1

I feel such woe when I contemplate the future, but it is as nothing to the grief I know when I remember the past.
— Appollonia of Archive

The revolutionary leader Szentellos caught the military leader Petrosius by surprise in an empty alleyway. He held Petrosius' arms clamped tightly below the elbows, and, with his flat, bony hand, he covered Petrosius' mouth.

"Petrosius, harken to me." Szentellos spoke in a harsh whisper, binding his captive in his thin, powerful arms. The way was narrow, and it cramped them both so that he easily constrained Petrosius' struggles. Yet Petrosius fought on, trying to reach either his foe, his sidearm, or his personal emergency screamer, a device which could have the alley swarming with battle robots from the sky in only five desperate seconds. Szentellos' strength was more than his equal and quickly overmastered him.

And it was a commoner who held him. He lurched, hammering his captor harshly against the wall. The grip that held him never faltered. In the darkness, their sounds of struggle were lost amidst the roars and rising thunders of traffic over the city and the planet that were Archive.

"Only listen. All I ask of you is that you listen."

Petrosius relented, ceasing his useless, frantic struggles. He nodded once, curtly.

"I speak honestly," Szentellos whispered sharply. His voice was thin and brittle yet desperately strong. "The time has come. Do you hear me, Petrosius? The time has come."

Petrosius, held and bound, made no response.

"The Empire is dead, but the Emperor still lives. Billions grind to surfeit him with pleasures, while an economy that once fed the stars now barely holds one world together. The Empire has collapsed, but the task of rebuilding is denied even a beginning. The time has come. Will you help me?"

And with that, he sprang back, releasing Petrosius and allowing the leader to see his face.

Breathing heavily, they regarded one another. The dim alley light showed Petrosius little more than the silhouette of his assailant: a high forehead, overshadowed by two tall, unruly tufts of stiff hair, and a huge, ax-bladed nose. But he sensed the commoner's tension, strength, and wiry-muscled resolve.

"What do you want?"

"I want to talk treason with you because you are the lord Emir of the sky, commander of the Belt, and I need your help."

"Treason?"

"The Emperor must die. His personal control must be distributed, not among his Sultans, but among the people. His excesses must be abolished."

Petrosius breathed out a long, unhappy sigh. "You're real. I didn't dare dream that you were."

Szentellos paused. "I am . . . real? What do you mean?"

"There have been rumors of a revolution. I would have joined it, but I never knew how."

Szentellos nodded. "I had hoped you felt this way. We plot revolution in a world that has never known freedom. And there are many of us. I, personally, am both the greatest and the least of our cadre. And we cannot succeed without you."

Petrosius shook his large, handsome head. The darkness shadowed him but could not hide the glinting of distant light reflecting from his uniform and his decoration. His voice was accustomed to giving orders, yet it now showed stress. "I've wanted to join you now for perhaps a year, perhaps two. But the reports, the word. . . . You're so shadowy, so secluded." His shoulders slumped.

"There are planets out there, burning. Burning because no one knows how to get food to them with the lines shattered and the networks toppled. The Emperor is aware of the chaos —

how can he not be? What action will he take? He. . . ."

"Petrosius. We are going to win." Szentellos voice was sharp. "Our victory is going to cost us. But we are going to win."

"And you want my help?"

"We need it."

Petrosius closed his eyes and fought not to weep. "You have it. To stop this insanity, I will do whatever you require."

"Eventually you will be asked to betray the Belt for us. We cannot win our victory on the ground, only to look for death from the skies. The weapon-laden Belt above us is our greatest fear. More: you will need to get us past the robots."

"But who are you?" Petrosius insisted. "Why have I sought for you and never found you?"

"We are many, and subtle. I will name you a name: the Sultan Thendall."

"He's with you? Biogenesis and Implants?"

Szentellos smiled wanly in the gloom. "No: only Thendall himself. How much manipulating of the Biogenesis labs could he do without being caught? We cannot afford to be caught . . . not this early. Years of preparation will be called for."

"I'm yours. I will work by your side."

"Come then. I will show you a secret way, and we will take oaths to the death of the Emperor Arcadian."

Szentellos led Petrosius along the alley and through a covered way descending through the wall and into deeper darkness. Petrosius' feet stumbled along the steep, downward-sloping ramp, his arms groping ahead uselessly. Several times dizziness assailed him, and he understood that his senses were being manipulated by projectors aimed at his skull.

Not if his life were to depend on it could he manage to backtrack his way out of the labyrinthine cellar through which he was led. All that he knew for certain was that he had descended a great distance and now was climbing. Soon, when he felt he could stand it no longer, he was allowed to stop. A chair brushed the backs of his legs, and he gratefully sat.

A light came on, showing him the interior of a high room inside a nobleman's house along the palace ridge. The ceiling was vaulted and bare; the floor was inlaid with rich golden woods. Through tall windows he saw the speckled night over Archive, and the steep hills falling away in darkness to the rich black sea.

At a table, Szentellos sat, his hands supporting his chin, his attire all decorative rumples of black and grey.

The other man at the table was Thendall, the Sultan of Biotechnology in the Emperor's hierarchy of centralized command.

Thendall, a study in brown-haired and clean-cut gentility, smiled wryly, as if at a joke that only he understood. His face was handsome, clever, and witty.

Are we, then, to form a Revolutionary Council? Two noblemen, led by a commoner? Petrosius flinched and thought of planets burning, planets dying, planets crying out for the help that he knew how to give but was forbidden to deliver.

"Sultan," he bowed to Thendall.

"Emir," Thendall bowed back.

The two of them looked over to Szentellos, who slowly began to paint for them the picture of their upcoming struggle.

∞

Lyra stretched and contracted, her head tossed back, her side glued to her sheets by the sweat of her passion. Under the probing caresses of her lover, a little pang of apprehension arose to alarm her. "Oh. Don't do that . . ." she murmured, the passions at odds within her. Instantly, Basil ceased his probing and gently, so gently, made as if to withdraw. Lyra, contrite now that her fears had been dispelled, knew that she could trust him, and the knowledge felt as good as his touch. Hugging the soft creature, she pulled him to her and took his love.

At length, after she had spent herself and after she had slept, she managed to drift to a languorous semi-awareness. Basil lay beside her, asleep, warm, his fur matted with their mingled sweat. Lyra ran her eyes over the soft length of his form: face down, head averted, strong back rising and falling with his gentle breath. He wasn't human; he was better. He was a Verna, and he was hers.

She wanted to see his face; she made a little

cooing noise. Basil awoke at once without moving. Within an instant, he had placed himself in his surroundings, not in the slow and groggy state that Lyra had, but fully awake and fully aware. He turned his large head to her, his expression inquiring.

White as snow, white as ice, his fur was soft and luxuriant. Atop his head, two sharp ears swiveled forward, attentive, gentle. Lyra feasted upon the sight of his impossibly huge, liquid eyes: darkest black pupils surrounded by large, light-brown irises that seemed, of themselves, so loving, so obedient. She gazed over his stretching muscles and at his wriggling, tiny stump of a tail.

Others tended to see comic, jester's faces on their Vernae; they wanted to ridicule the smile as that of a simpleton. But Lyra knew differently. Her Verna, Basil, was noble and thoughtful.

Her father, the Sultan of the Palace, ranked high on Archive and stood almost in the very shadow of the Emperor. But he had tendered Lyra only the smallest of pittances to spend upon a servant. "Buy a Verna if you must," he'd told her, "but be sure to get a used one. And no gladiatorial models, either!"

How surprised he would be to discover that she had found a prime gladiatorial-class Verna within the reach of her funds. Basil was a lover and a fighter, a sex-model and a combat-model. It had been to her new slave, then, and not to any of her human friends — mere acquaintances, she thought roughly; she had no friends — that she had sacrificed her virginity. She had not been disappointed.

She rose then and showered, signing to Basil not to follow her into the rising steam. "Your turn next," she said, and slid the pane shut. Through its transparency she could see Basil turn and sit, dreaming whatever wordless thoughts were his. He didn't stare at her while she showered; what human would have had the decency?

He'd been affordable, at the bright stables kept by the Biogenesis Sultanate: Basil was defective. What accident of genetic mixture, what computer flaw, had left him with a bright, clever mind yet incapable of speech? Incapable, in fact, of verbal reasoning at all? He was dangerous, the attendants had hinted, because he could only operate on emotional levels. But Lyra, emotional herself this day, had seen a way of buying her heart's desire without specifically thwarting her father's demands.

Basil was far from a mindless drone. At worst, he was like a clever animal: he understood what she meant by the tone of her voice, even if the words were beyond him. Lyra, luxuriating in the shower, knew that he was a more intelligent thing by far than a mere beast. He was an alert, aware, and gentle thing, lacking language but knowing love.

An hour later, the mists cleared from her brain by a heady dose of sobrietants, she rode up through the vast, ornately decorated corridors,

16

halls, and galleries of the Emperor's palace to her father's apartments. The night's pleasures and exertions had already begun to recede in her memory, dreamlike. Was it wrong to have done what she had? But it had been glorious; her face and neck flushed from the warm memory of it.

She entered her father's suite unaccompanied, striding boldly within, unbidden, as the door, recognizing her, swung itself open. She found the Sultan in a drawing room, deep in thought.

"Daughter? Pet!" He bounded from his chair to greet his darling Lyra. "How are you? Did you buy a nice domestic? What color fur does it have? How old is it?" He gestured her to a seat in one of the couches scattered about the room. She lowered herself gingerly to a dark golden setee bathed in the rays of the morning sun through a high, small window.

"The older they are, you know, the sooner they have to die. . . ." The Sultan laughed a nervous little laugh that was completely out of his normal character.

"Oh, Papa, you wouldn't believe what I was able to get for so little money," Lyra bubbled, all the while aware that her father was hiding something, that he was not all right. "I bought a white, big and soft, and. . . ."

The Sultan, Orbinald of Tendaly, looked at her sidelong as if considering something. "A domestic?"

"A gladiator!" she said breathlessly.

Orbinald stood slowly and advanced toward

her. "A gladiator? Impossible."

Wide-eyed, Lyra nodded. "Yes, Papa. He was defective in one or two unimportant respects, and. . . ."

He was upon her in two strides and took her firmly by the chin. "You haven't slept with it, have you?"

"No, of course not, Father." Tears sprang out in her eyes. "What would Mother have thought? You've always told me that it was dirty. . . ." *And it is not! It is not!*

"You're right. I'm sorry." He released her and backed away. "I should never have accused you. . . . I've been distraught." He paused a moment. "A gladiator, eh?" He tried to smile. "Well, well. That's one way to make quite a bit of money. We'll have to arrange an arena bout as soon as possible."

Lyra tried not to show her shock. *The arena? But my Basil. . . . What have I done?*

Shaking his head, Orbinald smiled, a smile that Lyra could readily see was forced. "Darling . . . what thought have you given to marriage?"

This took Lyra aback. "None, Father. I'm not ready, or at least. . . ."

"Ah, my pet, my pet. You'll be my heir, someday, and then every swain, every nobleman, every cast-off scion of all the good families will be after you. My estate will be too much for anyone to resist: who wouldn't desire to be the Palace Sultan? Choose now when you have the time and freedom to choose well. I'm afraid you haven't any too much time."

Although he wouldn't have said it, Lyra knew what it was that he wasn't telling her. "Father! You aren't. . . ?"

His face fell. Although he knew his daughter could lie like a criminal or a commoner, he found that he could never fib to his women. "I'm dying, my love. I'm allergic to the aging treatment. The Emperor paid for the treatment, but, instead of my becoming immortal like him, the operation has caused my death."

That struck Lyra like a blow, both because of Orbinald's imminent death and because such an allergy was heritable.

"Oh, Father. How long. . . ?"

"I'll be going to the surgeons at the end of this week. But there's no real hope: they can't save me. They'll kill me, more likely. They've said so themselves. I don't expect ever to come away." He turned his back to her. "I won't be receiving visitors. You wouldn't enjoy. . . . I'd prefer you to remember me the way I've always been.

"Bah!" he sputtered at last. "It happens to everyone sooner or later. I never thought I'd live forever." But, of course, he had. Everyone who submitted to the Emperor's aging treatments secretly harbored dreams of immortality. Was not the Emperor immortal? Over three hundred and seventy years of age, the Emperor had the body of a twenty-year-old. Orbinald was healthy and pink, but his hair was thinning and his features beginning to bear lines and folds.

"The family line. That's what matters now. I must know that you'll have an heir. You're my youngest, but only you. . . ." He trailed off, preferring not to remember the Emperor's decree of extermination for his first wife and all of her descendants. Lyra, now, was his only solace in his old age, and her mother, too, had died of the treatment allergy.

"Come along. Surely you have some thoughts?" He scowled as she made no response. "Cecil? No? Jason? I'd have thought. . . . What about Denis?"

Lyra had had enough time to think. She nodded weakly. "I rather like Denis. His family is good enough, and I suspect that he can meet your bride-price. An income of fifty million?"

"Hm. Don't you trouble yourself with the figures. Come, come. Let me get in touch with young Denis. I like him, too, I confess. We'll get it finalized. I don't — I don't want to die with this unsettled." His voice was a dry whisper.

He rose then and left her alone in the drawing room while he went to make the call. One of the palace Vernae came in with drinks and sweetmeats for her. Lyra gazed at the tall, sable-furred female.

"Can I bring you anything else?" she asked of Lyra, her voice high and resonant.

"Why is it that you can speak and my Basil cannot?" Lyra flared at her in anger. "Never speak again! Never again open your mouth! Go and have yourself destroyed!"

Wide-eyed, fatally resigned, the valuable slave bowed and left the room and, helplessly obedient, was never again seen.

Lyra's fury washed away in a torrent of tears. Her strong Basil was as much a slave as this one had been. *And I, myself, am also a slave to my father's wishes. Oh, how I wish I could have myself destroyed with the same ease!*

2

A weight won't seem as heavy, if you
don't try to lift it.

— Kearny Cyprianos
A Moral Mis-Message

Seven Hundred and seventy-eight years later.

∞

Commodore Athalos Steldan affected an indolent attitude, leaning back in his swivel chair
until he lay almost supine, raising his polished
black boots to rest upon Sophia's gleaming
control panel. His crisp, smooth-fronted grey
uniform tunic and black pants crinkled in a vain
attempt to accommodate its stiff formality to his
relaxed posture. He stretched, releasing his
nervous tension one muscle at a time.

The door was not locked that led into the
heart of this orbiting station. Steldan was alone:
the existence of the station, his secret. Few

people ever saw him the way he was now, at ease, in comfort, almost contented. To his subordinates, the Commodore was the stiffest, coldest, most uncompromising man in the fleet. They didn't know how hard he worked to maintain that image.

He was alone in the station. Rooms and chambers and halls lay empty yet lighted and warm, ready for immediate human occupancy. In huge basements carved from asteroidal stone, giant engines of communication and energy transmission bulked, holding gigajoules ready for instant release. No call had come for more than seven hundred years.

The station itself was carved from the center of a continent-sized plate of orbiting rock, a flake of stone nearly a thousand kilometers across but no more than five kilometers thick. Stabilized by a stiffening web of gravitic lines of force, the gigantic chip of stone spun in its orbit about a star otherwise ignored by humanity. Surrounding it, encompassing it, the far-flung worlds of the Concordat of Archive hummed and buzzed, their industrious human economies seeking to hold back the darkness of space. The station, a speck of history in immense space, had been undiscovered until only recently. Steldan knew of it as did a very, very few others.

Aboard the station, one central computer maintained total control of all systems, vital and otherwise. Her name was Sophia. Over the months, Steldan had learned to come to her for advice, to tap her deep well of abstract knowledge. When she had been discovered, only a few months ago, he had been the first to recognize the promise of her fount of antiquity. Furthermore, her personality agreed with his.

He gazed incuriously at the rows and columns of blinking lights and panels of illuminated rocker switches that lined the control room where Sophia was kept. Most of the lights shone yellow, white, or gold; a few gleamed lavender or blue. The room was cool and dry and perfumed so delicately, so subtly, with a fresh, clean, reassuring scent, that the air seemed odorless yet a joy to breathe.

He sighed and addressed her. "Sophia? I've got trouble."

"In what way, Athalos?"

"Rather too much has happened in altogether too short a time."

Sophia held her silence.

"I see storm clouds gathering," Steldan continued. He shrugged. "Perhaps I'm being overanxious. . . ."

Sophia said nothing.

Steldan leaned even further back in his chair, looking up at the control panels and data displays that were all Sophia had in the way of a face.

"I think I'm going to need your help."

"I will be happy to help you, Athalos."

"Thank you." He smiled. Sophia was an artifact, a construct, a device. She had no more objective humanity than a belt-buckle or a door-latch. Her personality — pseudo-personality, to

24

be strict — was the result of electronic interactions infinitely different in nature from the chemical processes of a human brain.

Despite this, Steldan could never avoid reacting to her on a human level. His every instinct cried out to him to avoid indulging himself in this luxury: she was *not* human, and his experience with artifacts and remnants of the now-defunct Empire of Archive warned him again and again to be careful. When one station similar to this one had been discovered by Navy search teams, it had detonated itself spectacularly, destroying the entire investigative mission. This station seemed different.

Brushing his hands through his thick, dark hair, Steldan fought to treat Sophia as an alien intelligence of unknown and unknowable purpose. Again he failed: Sophia was a young, human female in her mental construction, and Steldan could not harden his heart to her.

Nor, at this time, could he afford to.

"What do you know of the Vernae?"

Sophia's voice was cool. "Slaves. Large and strong, highly obedient, constructed to serve and to fight for display. I was always taught to disdain them."

"Are they fools?"

"No. A slave cannot afford to be a fool."

"Sophia, a slave — a Verna — compiled a mathematical science of human behavior. It completes our own knowledge of psychology. It goes beyond what we already knew, in fact. I want you to study his writings."

"Very well."

"You met him once, I believe."

"Stasileus?"

"Yes. A rather clever wight."

Steldan pulled a small, wafer-thin disc from his tunic and inserted it gingerly into one of Sophia's data ports. Two minutes passed.

"Finished."

"What do you make of it?"

"Insightful."

"Anything else?"

"Of course." Sophia's voice seemed emotionally distant, as if she were bored or offended by the turn the conversation had taken. "The concepts here are revolutionary, yet productively complement the ideas of the earlier traditions of the study of mind."

"You sound as if you disapprove."

"I do, of course. The writings of slaves cannot be compared with the learned studies of the past. Once I commanded this Stasileus; can I now learn from him?"

Sophia's pro-Empire chauvinism was showing again. Steldan sighed. "Do his theories contradict the understandings held in your library, or can they be considered to be a sensible amplification of them?"

"I will correlate." Another two minutes slipped by. "Your Verna was observant," Sophia finally conceded.

"Are his elements correct?"

"Fully."

"Can you force yourself to admire them?"

"Only if you insist."

Steldan laughed. "I insist upon nothing. But I do not disdain wisdom, wherever I might find it. Stasileus the slave was also a scholar, and I need his wisdom. I come to you, likewise, for advice because I cannot resolve the conflicts of centuries by myself. Can this new knowledge be of help to me? To us?"

"'Us'?"

Nodding, Steldan explained. "Seven hundred and seventy-eight years have elapsed since the Revolution." He sat upright and leaned forward, his expression suddenly animated. "Nearly eight centuries of fear. You can see how afraid we've been since then, can't you?"

"Yes," Sophia whispered.

"The human race has lived under a tyranny of fear for so many centuries that it doesn't know how to be brave. We've evolved a system so oppressive that unrest is instantly quelled, not so often by military intervention, but by indirect manipulation.

"My race," he swept on, "is afraid of life. Afraid of love. Afraid of the gods. Afraid of the dark. Afraid of its own hidden impulses. Afraid of commotion and disorder. There have been five revolts in the past twenty years, all suppressed boldly by the military. But there have been countless thousands of little rebellions, rebellions of the spirit, and these have been suppressed by the vast, impersonal mechanisms that crush thought.

"Everywhere I look, I see fear," he concluded.

"The greatest fear is of creativity."

Sophia said nothing.

Steldan leaned back, shaking his head. He smiled, a bit ashamed of himself for the strength of his views. "Something must be done."

"What must be done?" Sophia asked.

"I want to restore a bit of the swagger to the human race. I want to knock the props out and force people to use themselves to creative advantage."

"You want to foment rebellion."

"I want. . . ." He paused. "I want exactly that."

"How do you plan to begin?"

Steldan laughed. "Creatively."

"Be more specific, please."

"In your memory are all of the books of antiquity. In your files are the words and songs of a race very different from mine: that of my ancestors. You have the words they read when they laughed, played, yelled, hit each other, and drew dirty pictures."

"I don't understand," Sophia objected. "Your Concordat is free of such ungainly pursuits. Why should you want to restore such extravagance at the entire expense of protective certainty?"

Gritting his teeth, Steldan let his shoulders slump. "I'm not sure that that's what I really want. Safety is diametrically opposed to greatness. If I could find some way to maximize both. . . . But you can't fly without risking a fall. And we've been creeping along, hugging the ground, for too damned long."

"Examine your precepts," Sophia suggested. Her words were dire and full of warning, but her voice was light and cheerful again.

"I beg your pardon?" Steldan didn't know how to take her advice.

"If all you want is an end to fear, do you need to start a rebellion in full?"

"No. . . . Or yes. Or perhaps. I don't know. I need to combine several elements to make this revolution successful . . . and I must hurry. Events are falling into place too swiftly."

"What has happened?"

"Only two years ago, we rediscovered the Vernae, who had been lost. In that short amount of time, Stasileus completed the science of psychology. And your library was rediscovered: that last item is the most crucial."

"Can I speak with Stasileus? His opinions would be helpful."

"He died of natural causes about two months ago."

"How did you obtain his notes?"

Steldan shrugged. "It was a narrow thing, only a matter of chance. He had them sent by normal post back to his people on the worlds the Vernae are trying to claim. Censors intercepted it but didn't think it important. A supervisor took a closer look. . . . We're very lucky to have these notes."

"His notes will suffice. Did you send the originals on once you'd made a copy?"

"Yes. I hope I won't regret that later."

"Tell me what you want, Athalos."

"An end to fear, but only to begin with. Creativity. The flourishing of learning. Experimentation." He sighed. "A bit of rowdiness."

"The last is implicit in the others."

Steldan hung his head. "I know."

"You regret this?"

"Sophia, would you call me a rowdy man?"

"No, Athalos."

"The place to begin is with words and music. The average citizen reads ten books in a year. This year, all ten will be from your library."

"Athalos, you don't want a rebellion. You want a renaissance."

"Correct. And we shall begin with an opera." Steldan smiled, his face showing his clear awareness of the incongruity of the idea.

"An opera?"

"An opera. I'll need you to provide me a suitable libretto. Combine Stasileus' knowledge of psychology with your knowledge of the literature of your era."

"This is the one." A data cassette popped up from one of the desktop ports.

"What is its name?"

"It is a play by Achorus called *The Skeleton and the Chaffinch*. What music will you choose?"

She was testing him. He laughed. "Music is inherent in a culture. I must write my own."

"You lack that skill, Athalos," Sophia said bluntly and plainly.

"Ah, well." Steldan grinned. "I know where I can find artists."

"Go then."

"Sophia. . . ."

"Yes?"

"You didn't see the Revolution that over-turned the Emperor's dominion. You didn't see the carnage, the widespread loss of life. . . ."

"No. I didn't."

"It is that — the horrible onslaught of death after death after death — that we have been the most afraid of. If I remove the fear. . . ."

"Will the deaths then be nearer?"

"That's my fear, Sophia."

"Face it, Athalos. Face it creatively."

"I shall."

"We will meet again, I think."

"I hope so, Sophia."

∞

Steldan's shuttle landed at the Dissident Colony at Thierry-Danege, and Steldan disembarked without incident. His grey-and-black Intelligence Branch uniform earned him passage, and, although he was often stared at, he was never delayed.

An icy mountain wind blew from nearby snowcapped peaks over the high, grassy plain of Dissident Camp Fourteen. He marched through high, whipping grass toward a towering wire mesh fence. A Security Forces Colonel ushered him past the checkpoints and into the weather-beaten compound.

"A nonviolent lot, by and large," the Colonel

explained. "Poets, musicians, troublemakers who lack the courage to try anything quirky. We tend to have quite a few suicides here, but no revolts."

"And the general tenor of their discipline?" Steldan asked cooly.

"Desultoriness at best, noncompliance at all times, passive resistance and hunger strikes at the worst."

"I need to talk to a musical composer, preferably one with some actual talent."

"Oh, talent's not scarce." The Colonel winked at Steldan, then regretted the familiarity when Steldan's icy face failed to warm in response. "Talent isn't the problem. It's agreement with the fundamental requirements of society. Some are here for refusing to pay their taxes. Others, for spiting the censors and attempting to publish unapproved works. Most, simply for being socially unaccomodating."

They walked past weathered barracks, long unpainted, and over poorly kept grounds. The wind whistled and puffed in cold gusts between the two men as they walked with their hands in their jackets, their earflaps pulled down. Steldan saw no one else abroad in the cold winter air.

The Colonel guided him up the steps to one barracks and through a pair of thick, wooden doors. Inside, the common quarters were austere and almost as cold as outside. Three tiers of bunks lined the walls, and bare wooden furniture made up the rest of the large room's fittings. Some sixty men and women lounged about, mostly concentrating on a forced-air heater in the room's middle. The dissidents looked, saw Steldan's military uniform, and nudged their neighbors.

Look, they seemed to be saying; *look at what has come to peer at us.* Their attitude was not hostile; the camp's straightforward order and lack of brutality had taken away their hatred. Without being threatening, however, their expressions were not friendly.

"A musical composer," Steldan said, not loudly. No one in the room shied away from his gaze, but he received no cooperation either.

"Biggs," the Colonel snapped, "stand to. Rumford. Newton. Cliffs."

The four named stood uneasily and regarded Steldan with some concern. Biggs was a small, ferret-faced man with a downward-looking posture; Rumford stood with his legs tightly together, his large eyes radiating self-pity and fear; Newton was a short, slim woman with fiery red hair and a fatalistic, resigned expression; Cliffs was a tall, brown-haired woman who watched Steldan with hidden suspicion while appraising him carefully.

"Cliffs," he said. "Come here."

"If I must."

"What's your full name?"

"Margaret Antoinette Cliffs."

"Why are you here?"

"The censors didn't like my Symphony."

"So?"

She looked away. "So I wrote another one."

"I fail to make the connection."

"And a third," she said, as if Steldan had not said a word. "And a fourth. By that time, I wasn't concealing my sarcasm. Musically, that is." She looked at him. "Did you know that sarcasm can be expressed in music?"

Steldan stood straight and regarded her cooly. "I have heard the theory expounded." To the Colonel he gave a few short orders. "She will do. Have her and her property brought to my shuttle within the hour." He returned his gaze to Cliffs. "I'm sorry, but you have just been called into service."

"Obvious, isn't it?" she said, her eyebrows quirking slightly. "What service, may I ask?"

"I'll explain that when we're underway."

"Fine. But you won't be happy with me."

"Won't I?"

"No."

"We'll find out." He nodded to her and turned; the Colonel accompanied him as far as the door. While their backs were turned, Cliffs whistled a brief, staccato passage of high, sharp notes. The irony and sarcasm were unmistakable; Steldan, although he'd imagined himself immune to such effects, was stung to the core of his being and had to fight not to blush.

Then he was outside in the cold, moving air, and his plans had taken their first overt step toward revolution — or renaissance.

By the strictest interpretation of military codes, he had just become a criminal. The feeling was not new to him.

3

Ho, ho! What a joy! I'm to live forever,
and you aren't! I'm so glad I thought of
being Emperor!

> — Hero, son of Cepion
> a Burlesque

Lyra strode purposelessly from the Emperor's
palace, setting her small feet one before the
other over the unsteady pavement. In one
stroke, her world had tumbled. Her father, the
root and branch of her life, was dying, and her
indolent life as a child would end before the week
did. A marriage to Denis, son of the Sultan of
Energies, would be preferable to death, she told
herself, in the same way that slavery or torture
would be: life is the punishment that the Gods
mete out to souls for transgressions against
propriety in the fore-life.

Marriage would be tolerable, but life without
her father would not be. She struggled not to
weep. It was as if the sun and stars were to flee

from the sky or as if the Emperor Arcadian were to step from his throne. Her father centered her life, and, without him, existence would be. . . .

She shivered.

A city of wonders glowed golden in the afternoon sunlight, challenging the sun's brightness with a brilliance in color and form that celebrated the Emperor and life. Lyra brushed her hair back from her damp eyes, sniffed irresolutely, and wished that she were in her bed, wrapped in the arms of her Basil. Married life would be hateful. Life without her father would be meaningless. And life without the freedom to love and be loved by her great, gentle Verna would be a life impossible to bear.

She conjured young Denis' image before her eyes, blotting out the sky-filling glow of Archive. A thin, blond man with a long face and large, sad eyes. Lyra had, at times, pitied him but had never loved him. His hands were thin and artistic; she had several times enjoyed his recitals upon the flute. His voice was high and sweet. And he held his head high, laughing, among the other young men at their dances and fetes.

Lyra shook her head, hating herself for feeling even the slightest warmth for the dolt, the clod, the ungainly lump that Denis was. He was hateful. He was pathetic. How could anyone consider a life married to him?

Overhead, as stable in its orbit as the sun and worlds, the high loop of the Belt arched from west to east, passing well south of the zenith. Sunlight reflected from its slender curve, making naught of the orbital distance of the gigantic artifact. Only by comparing its distance with the horizon it faded behind could Lyra dispel the persistent illusion that the Belt was only a cloud-high thread of metal looping into the sky.

Today, even its perfect steadiness seemed to her to waver, and its titanic energies of planetary defense seemed paltry. Devastation could be visited upon foes near and far, and, guided by the Belt's inhumanly precise cameras, a needle-thin lance of cold light could volatilize a target smaller than Lyra's hand at any point on the planet's surface. Today, Lyra felt no reassurance of her perfect safety.

Around her, a city of wonders pulsed, its energies almost palpable. Before her, the broad avenue stretched arrow-straight to the Temple of All the Gods, the street elevated and sloping only gently above the hills and valleys of the city. Golden, glowing, the temple thrust its three domes brusquely at the sky, shimmering with reflected heat and light.

Lyra shielded her eyes, and blushed with a deep, agonizing shame. She had never properly learned to revere or dread the Gods, but she feared the brotherhood of priests with an unreasoning panic. Was her love for a nonhuman slave a blasphemy? Had she erred, incurring an unfavorable judgment from Kretosa? Would darkness claim her soul once her body had finished polluting it? She shivered, fearing that the sensors along the Belt would detect her shame and her misery and report her to the Emperor's minions.

Walking unsteadily, ignored by the thousands who trudged along this street of streets, she came at last to a place where aircars were permitted and engaged a flyer. The machine recognized her at once for the scion of nobility and unfolded hurriedly to her service.

"Aloft," she said simply, and the car carefully enfolded her, receiving her weight upon a loose, comfortable cushion of velveteen. Reconfiguring itself for flight, the machine shaped itself into an aerodynamically flattened sphere and soared into the sky with a gentle and gradual acceleration.

Lyra saw the city and yet gave it no heed. The view that once had flooded her with pride now seemed but a thin surface of shining gilt hiding a vast underground world of misery.

The car, with no orders other than to lift, had determined on an orbiting hotel complex as its most likely destination; Lyra, seeing her world begin to dwindle, lifted her head and called out, "To the Arena. I have business."

Without answer, the car reversed its course and began to descend toward the city. Soon, details came back into sharp focus: the palace, high and brave on its mountain overlooking the coast; the towering triple arch of triumph and power, stabbing proudly at the sky; and the circle of the Arena, where, on the sands of glory, slaves and men died for the entertainment of both nobles and the common.

And between them all, strewn hither and yon

over the green hills, stood houses, fanes, estates both large and small, terraces, homes, citadels, guardtowers, warrens and pens for the poor and lowly, parks, pools, and fountains, and all of the fifty thousand other kinds of structures that make up a city. Beyond all, the sea marched ever inward with its endless ranks of white, curling waves. Sun, sea, sky, and city all obeyed the word and will of the Emperor, and Lyra felt herself to be the lowest of his lowly servants.

∞

Releasing her at some distance from the Arena, as the law required, the skycar unfolded itself, flattening out to a low, thick carpet of plastic and metal beneath her feet. She stepped lithely from it and did not deign to notice its transformation back into a flyer. Wanted elsewhere, it leaped into the air and was gone in a flash.

Lyra walked forward, still in a daze, but controlled now by her icy strength of will. The crowd here was of a mixed and low character, and the ugly faces of the common mixed with the characteristically fine features of the noble. Slaves moved about, Vernae of all colors, from the darkest black to the snowiest white, contrasting the lesser variation of the fleshy tones of their masters.

Yet the human variation was overall the greater, as men and women straggled and ran, hurried and tarried, their forms slim and fat, tall and short, in every diverse degree. The slaves had been sculpted and were made things. The humans, too, had been shaped by a deep, canny craft. Bending her steps toward the Arena, Lyra spared only the most casual of glances toward the men, women, and slaves.

Her surprise, thus, was the greater when she came upon a crowd clustered around a small market square. No slaves at all, but perhaps a thousand humans, dressed in the rags of commoners for the most part, stood facing inward, laughing without restraint, and poking one another in the ribs with antic hilarity. Lyra eyed the spectacle with disdain and would have strode past; a word caught her ear, and she stopped in utter shock.

"Arcadian."

What commoner would dare utter the name of the Emperor? She wheeled and stared at the jeering crowd. It was impossible that the living embodiment of nobility had been idly named by these smiling faces that knew no reverence. Lyra pressed closer, repelled by the contact with commoners but suddenly needing to know who provided the entertainment.

The crowd was more unruly than she had first seen: they stood on low rooftops, peering down into the square; they rode atop one another's shoulders like men atop flying machines; they craned their necks and lowered their shoulders in elaborately undignified postures of attention. Their laughter was unbelievably coarse. To Lyra's astonishment, several nobles lurked about in the audience, smiling despite themselves. Lyra wished that her father's soldiers could be here to scatter this mob or that light from the Belt would wash the pavement clean again. Yet, no matter how revolted she was by the spectators, the sight of their entertainers disgusted her more.

Three men stood in the center of a small clearing amidst the crowd. Their appearance gave them away immediately as nobles of high descent, although their dress was gaudy and unconventional. Lyra pushed her way through the suffocating mass of raucous humanity to see them, and the sight caught at her breath in a way that the press of flesh could not have. The three men were staging a charade, a satire, posed at the Emperor's expense.

One young man, dressed in thin paper finery that mimicked the Emperor's robes of state, stood stiff and still, his posture and his bearing imperious, a pasteboard sigil in his hand mocking the Emperor's holding of the law. His attitude was burlesque; he stood too straight, too strainingly stiff, and his nose was pointed into the air. Now and again he would cross his eyes, and the audience would roar.

"But your greatness!" protested the second youth, a white-haired son of the nobility dressed in courtier's robes of outrageously colored fabric. Reds and greens and blues clashed in his finery as if the colors had been splattered randomly onto a sheet of fine-woven silk. "My musician plays as loudly as ever he can! Perhaps, although I most sorely hesitate to suggest the possibility, your mightiness has become deafened?"

The third youngster, a wide-grinning and ungainly noble whose indolence had turned largely to fat, bore a nine-stringed lyre in his pudgy arms and pretended to stroke it. No sound issued thence.

"No, no, no," the one playing the part of the Emperor minced. "I insist that there is no music."

The courtier raised his shoulders in a gesture eloquent of nervous fear. Gesturing to the musician, he commanded harshly, "Louder, louder play!" Then he returned his fawning gaze to his liege.

Smirking as broadly as he could, the boy with the lyre made wide, elaborate motions as if coaxing music from a great harp, yet not a sound came from his small lyre.

"But I hear nothing!" the boy aping the Emperor said. "My perfection demands that I hear as well as you do," he added pettishly. He looked significantly at his courtier. "Perhaps, if I am deaf, I ought to make you deaf, also. And all of the people as well. Yes." He looked about him a bit wildly. "I will have everyone's ears put out! I will deafen you all!"

"You shall if you continue shouting," the courtier said crossly, then cringed as he realized whom it was he was rebuking. The two posed for a moment in a tableau of comic anger and fear as the crowd roared.

Lyra had seen more than enough. The one

playing the courtier was the more experienced actor of the three, and his familiarity with the lines implied that he had written the slanderous act. Now completely beside herself with sickened dismay, she stepped forward into the clearing and shrieked, "Stop this madness at once!"

The three actors dropped instantly out of pose and regarded her with open-mouthed expressions of surprise. The one playing the courtier recovered first and threw a drape of his multicolored robe over his face. The others and the crowd drew back.

"You ridicule his greatness, and you mock his ineffable dignity," Lyra scolded them. "No crime is as serious!"

"We mock him, yes," snapped the one who had played the Emperor's part. "We expose his own crimes and his deafness to his people's woe!" He would have advanced upon Lyra, but the fat musician and the gaudy courtier held him back, the latter still covering his face. Slowly at first, but with a gathering swiftness, the crowd began to fade and to flee.

"Stop!" Lyra shouted. "All of you, stop! Do you not know what it is to fail to respect the Emperor?"

"Foolish child!" the actor shouted as his two companions sought to drag him away. "Of course we know. But does *he*?" He jabbed a finger toward the high palace.

Lyra's eyes went wide. She reached within her blouse and drew forth a symbol of command and displayed it for all to see. Those of the crowd who had not yet won to freedom halted dead in their tracks, all expression gone from their faces. The actor and the musician stopped cold, the wrath wiped from their faces as if with a damp cloth. The one whose face and eyes were hidden knew instantly with what power he dealt, and turned and ran with all the strength in his young legs.

"Stop him! Stop him, you!" Lyra pointed at a clump of nerveless commoners who stood near the actor's path of flight. They quickly moved to interpose themselves to prevent his escape.

"Fool!" he shouted at her. The commoners caught and held him, overwhelming him by numbers and bearing him heavily to the ground.

"Bring him to me!" Lyra demanded. "Uncover his face."

Held in the sturdy arms of no less than fifteen commoners, the actor who had played a courtier with skill now struggled and spat helplessly. His colorful robe was lifted away from his face.

"Heartless daughter of rottenness!" he shouted, refusing to look toward Lyra and especially fighting to keep his eyes away from the tiny silver and red medallion sparkling in her outstretched right hand.

"Look upon my command," Lyra said evenly.

Helplessly caught by the spell of the symbol, he looked and froze. Not even his hatred remained to him; he was as soft and plastic as a Verna and as susceptible to command. Lyra toyed for a moment with the thought of ordering the crowd to tear him to pieces. But tears sprang into her eyes and began to run down her face as she thought of the Emperor denied his rightful revenge on those who had satirized him.

She brandished her symbol aggressively; the red and silver metal shone in her hand and held all entranced who saw it. "I am the daughter of the Household Sultan of the Emperor," she announced, pride freighting her voice. "I carry this symbol lawfully. Tell me your names, you three."

"Mylos, son of Mylos," quietly said the musician. His lyre dangled from his limp hand.

"Monomachus, son of Herostratus," said the actor who had dared to play at being Emperor.

"Hero, son of Cepion," answered the courtier. "I am the leader and the inspiration of this play." His voice was as blank and nerveless as his posture was relaxed. Lyra held his soul as well as his body and life tightly controlled by the symbol in her fist.

"Mylos," she commanded, "run and fetch a guardsman."

Without acknowledgement, he turned and ran.

"You aren't like the other two, are you, Hero?"

"I'm the better actor, and I'm older. I have a rank in the orders of the Revolution, and the others do not."

Lyra laughed despite herself. "There is no Revolution."

Hero stood silently by.

"Is there?"

"There is," Hero answered her. "Many hold

the Emperor in no esteem." He showed no more personality than a combat robot or a floor-washing machine. The symbol had turned his mind completely off, by acting upon a locus of genetically controlled reactions within his brain. Lyra knew what power she wielded, for her father had used it upon her the day he had entrusted her with it. She would never forget how he had degraded her and how the symbol had made nothing of her dignity and her will.

"All worship the Emperor!" she shouted at him.

Again he made no response.

Before she could speak again, Mylos returned with a company of twenty orange-uniformed guardsmen who trained their fusers upon the scattered crowd.

"Please sheath your symbol, highness," their commander spoke reverently. Lyra recognized them as officials of the Arena, used to taking control of riots and disorderly eruptions.

"Yes, Captain." Lyra tucked the medallion respectfully away. "This one — " she indicated Hero " — says he is of the Revolution."

"Many are," the guardsman gritted. Beneath his helmet he showed greying hair and pale, waxy skin.

"There is no Revolution!" Lyra protested.

"None within the palace, highness," he corrected her, "but in the streets, a monster crawls."

"Well, you have him now, and you can make him tell you who his fellows are." But she knew it wouldn't be that simple, and she shivered at the thought of a serpentine creature loose in the streets, composed of the hatreds of ignorant men and women.

"Yes, highness," the guardsman said, his dubiety showing clearly in his voice. "But not his leaders. No man can implicate those he has never met. The monster is well-made, and we cannot strike at its head."

"You speak of it as if it poses a danger," Lyra said wonderingly.

"Oh, yes, highness." The guardsman looked at her direly. "It will be the work of years to slay the monster."

"Why do you call it a monster?"

He blinked at her. "I've heard it whispering in the streets at night. I've seen its spoor: handlettered leaflets pinned to the clothing of corpses. Today you caught three young men, who will die. But within two weeks, here and there across the city, seven guardsmen will die or seven servants or maybe seven priests. Men have made it, and, so far, men control it. But it is a monster, and I fear it."

Lyra left him and went on to her business at the Arena, a vague fear thrilling through her. For the first time in her life she stopped to think of how overwhelmingly the commoners and the low nobility outnumbered the great and the high. The protections of Belt, soldiery, and guard seemed thin and fragile to her, and she shuddered.

4

Governments are greater than people,
as adults are greater than children. We
try to be responsible; we sometimes succeed.

— Robert Bishop
The Chain Forge

After having travelled together for some time,
Commodore Steldan and Margaret Cliffs continued to have difficulty in understanding one
another.

"Margaret, I'm asking for your trust," he said
softly, joining her for dinner in the tiny ship's
lounge. About them, sealed off by shields of
armor and by force fields, the deadly heat of
jumpspace yawned, the oven between the stars.

"Why should I trust you," Cliffs retorted.
"You're so uncaring, so unfeeling. You talk to
me, and all I hear is a military dispatch dictated
to a recording secretary and delivered by radio.
You talk as if on flimsy, yellow paper. And you

give orders."

"I'm not trying to be unfeeling," Steldan said calmly.

"But you *are* unfeeling. You ask for my trust. Why? So you can use me the way you use soldiers and subordinates? They run errands for you and leap to obey. That's so damned inhuman. You ought to be a member of civilized society. But you're not."

"What am I?" Steldan sat and ate slowly. He wore his uniform, as he most always did, aboard ship or off.

"You are a terribly deprived person." Cliffs looked at Steldan, a horrified kind of pity showing in her eyes with her disgust. "Where is the love? Where are the games? You spend months alone in this small ship. Now with me. Do you know where we're going?" Her voice rose into a wail. "I'm trying to talk to you, and you won't even act human!"

Steldan swallowed and set down his utensils. He looked quietly at Cliffs.

"This is the problem I want you to help me with."

"Do you want a lover? Do you want me to teach you how to laugh?"

"No." He looked up at Cliffs, forcing himself to meet her gaze. "Do you know why I chose you?"

"No. No . . . but wait." She held up her hand. "You had a reason. A secret one?"

Steldan nodded.

"Did you choose me because you think that

I, too, am emotionally deprived? Because I can spend the months alone, locked in a cubicle with nothing but books, the way you can? I'm not sure I'm able. Don't you ever get lonely? Don't you ever think about your sexuality?"

"I haven't got any," Steldan said, his voice low and almost indistinct.

Cliffs pounced. "A weak point! You're embarrassed by the thought of sex. The thought of love must turn your spine to water."

Steldan backed away from the table and stood. In the small lounge, he seemed more machine than man, stiff and formal in his harsh, straight uniform. Despite the subtle threat of his actions, his voice remained mild. "You can taunt me. You could probably hurt me very badly with your words."

"Hurt you?" Cliffs flared. "I don't want to hurt you! I want you to see how wrapped up you are in your shields. You're a walking mass of defenses. You're so insulated from your feelings that you can pretend, at night when you're so lonely, that you have no feelings at all. You're killing the best part of yourself by denying it."

"I'm not alone in that."

Cliffs snorted. "No. You certainly aren't. And I wouldn't talk to you about it if I thought you were like the majority of humanity."

Steldan came forward and bent lightly over the table. "Do you think you can enlighten me?"

She looked at him carefully. She saw intelligence and awareness in his large, dark eyes. She saw a philosopher hiding in a kind of panic behind his brow and a poet crushed almost to death behind his tight lips. His dark hair could have been beautiful, had he not insisted on wearing it shorn close. His jaw could have been lovely, if he hadn't carried it set so tightly for so many years. But no human was beyond hope, not even this self-suppressed man of the military.

"I think I could, if you would let me."

"Do you think you can enlighten the entire race?"

This was a different question; she thought about it.

"All of the Concordat?"

Steldan nodded.

"The people who put me in prison because of my music?" Her expression hardened. "Do you want me to sing songs to the deaf?"

Steldan leaned slightly farther forward. "Can you write songs that even the deaf are capable of hearing?"

She leaned back and narrowed her eyes. Slowly, lines of laughter crept into her face. "Mister, you ask some tough questions." She brushed her hand through her fluffy, brown hair.

"I learned from experts."

"I can write the music." She looked up at him. "Will it get heard?"

"I hope so. That would be one of the things I would work hardest to ensure."

Her expression leaped into outrage. "'Would work hardest to ensure'! Damn it, stop talking like a dictionary. Tell me what you're after. I've been flying with you in this damned spaceship for three months. I'd give my hands up to the elbows to set foot on a planet again and smell real air. I'd give my legs up to the knees to talk to someone who wasn't a robot-factory assemblage!" She glared at him. "I think I hate you. Did you know that?"

"I knew it."

"And even with that, after all of this, you ask me to trust you." Cliffs snorted. "Well there's no way, fellow, that I'll do that."

Steldan reached inside his grey uniform jacket and brought forth a tiny red and silver medallion. "I want to show you a small piece of art."

"Do you know anything about art?"

"This kind, I do." Steldan straightened and began to pace. His long legs carried him slowly from one end of the cramped lounge to the other. "The Empire of Archive sponsored all of our woes." He held up a hand to forestall Cliffs' objections. "We hold the responsibility for continuing to oppress ourselves. But we are the children of oppression. Many people think that we can never know anything else. I'm going to show you something terrible. I'm going to show you that resistance — disobedience — has an absolute limit." He held out his hand.

"Please look at this symbol."

Within Cliffs' brain, barriers crumbled as a seawall will crumble before an ultimate wave of tumbling water. The symbol focussed her mind;

the symbol swelled, filling her entire field of vision. The symbol turned her will completely over to the control of its wielder. So tiny it was, red and silver, a star within a circle, ornate and lovely and totally compelling.

Steldan let her look at it a moment longer, then slipped it back inside his jacket. Cliffs slowly began to recover, knowing that she would never be completely free again.

Pacing again, Steldan spoke in a quiet voice. "Had I given you an order, you would have obeyed. I could have made you tear out your own throat with your bare fingers. I could have made you love me, and the love would have been genuine emotional love from the very center of your soul. I could have made you begin to compose music."

"The music would have been no good," she answered automatically.

Steldan said nothing; she knew that it wasn't true, and he knew that she knew.

"You drugged my food?" she said weakly, after a long pause.

"The drug is in your brain. The symbol operates on the particular anatomical portions of your brain dealing with the origination of desires. Specifically, with the unconscious pre-motivation of volition."

"I'm not sure I. . . ."

"Whenever you begin an action — lifting your hand to scratch your nose, for example — the action is considered in the unconscious for a minute fraction of a second. The conscious mind then is given a 'yes or no' override. There have been people who have, because of injury or some other cause, had their brain damaged. Some have lost this control of their actions, and they're just as astonished as anyone else at what they find their limbs doing." He quirked an odd little grin. "I've seen this myself, in military hospitals."

"Medical experiments on unwilling patients?" Cliffs sneered.

Steldan wheeled upon her. "Yes! Did you want me to deny it? I've vivisected human brains, some of them conscious and aware, some of them under the influence of that symbol of command." He stopped, fighting to regain control of himself.

Cliffs stared at him in open-mouthed horror.

Steldan hid his face in his hand. "I told you that you could taunt me. I told you that you could hurt me with your words. My medical experiments were all performed on prisoners, men and women who had been condemned to die and who accepted this method of death in return for pardons for friends or family. Do you think it's horrible? I do too!

"But nothing I have ever seen in an operating theater is as horrible as this symbol of command."

"All right, Commodore," Cliffs said, a trifle shakily. "Truce."

"Truce." Steldan smiled weakly. "The action is genetic. It operates according to instructions handed down from parent to child over all of the centuries since the Empire. We, now, you and I, are just as much the subjects and slaves of the Emperor as our ancestors were while he still lived. That is something I want to try to change."

"How?"

He smiled, more warmly this time. "I want to ask you to write music for me."

"You could command me to."

"Yes. But I would rather not."

"Bring me paper and a keyboard."

"They're in your room, waiting for you."

Cliffs stood. She smiled, almost shyly. "I ought to warn you. Listening to music being composed might prove to be a bit of a trial. It gets repetitious, and. . . ."

"It will be a happy sound," Steldan said, facing her. "I couldn't ask for anything better."

"All right." She looked down. Her mood darkened again. "There's something else. I get . . . moody . . . while I'm composing. Gloomy. Depressed. You won't like being around me."

"I won't hurt you, Margaret."

∞

The small ship, ostensibly running courier missions for the gargantuan Concordat Navy, was in fact illegally detached from the fleet. Over the years, Steldan had built up a reserve of illicit power, ranging from sources of unrecorded funding to an information and communication network of his own to a substantial cadre of assassins loyal to his command alone. The assassins were controlled by the secret workings of Operation Black Book. Steldan had inherited the operation from an unknown Fleet Admiral who, centuries ago, had felt that secretly striking at his enemies was a better means of making war than scouring planets with thermonuclear fire from orbit.

Steldan had never been able to make up his mind whether or not he agreed.

The Black Book had been used exactly thirty-two times to make thirty kills. Commodore Steldan, then a Captain, had been one of the two individuals ever assigned who had not been slain. He himself, coming into the ownership of the Black Book, had rescinded the only other name outstanding on the list.

Somehow, despite the intent of the Black Book, more of the names in it belonged to people within the Concordat than to foreign enemies. The double-edged blade had been too convenient to avoid using against traitors, dissidents, political figures, street preachers. . . .

A century before Steldan's birth, one self-styled Apollonia of Archive had taken to the streets, preaching a doctrine of redemption through love. Thousands had seen her die, shot from ambush by a solitary gunman who was never caught.

Two months later, she appeared again and took up her works among the billions of the world-city of Archive. Unquestionably dead, she had unquestionably returned. The second time, millions saw her die when a solitary gunman leaped up and emptied his heavy automatic weapon into her. He had almost finished loading a second clip when the crowd caught him and tore him to shreds. Not enough of him survived to permit any determination of his identity.

To this day the return of Apollonia of Archive was a puzzle and a mystery. It was the core of at least two suppressed cults. The Black Book listed neither answers nor suppositions.

The Black Book was operated out of a double-blind system. Not even Steldan, with access to all of the Navy's administrative records and all of the Black Book's secrets, knew if the assassin was the same in both cases. About the solution to the secret of Apollonia's reappearance on the streets, he had not even a guess.

The small spacecraft, operating in spite of all laws and covered up by Steldan's skill at recordkeeping, drew toward a planet where more than one hundred assassins of the Black Book were waiting for him. The planet was Carpus, a world of five cities and innumerable towns. His ship fell through the red membrane of jumpspace and slowed, approaching Carpus' largest city.

The ship settled down silently, precisely. Steldan made arrangements with the Port and Naval Base to see to the transferral of certain documents. This was his cover assignment.

For a solid hour before his departure from the ship, Steldan sat and listened in peace to the developing notes of Cliff's score to the opera-to-be. The dulcet notes from the keyboard echoed strangely throughout different parts of the small ship: in the lounge, when Cliffs' door was open, the notes buzzed, giving an almost choral tone to the music. Forward, in the control room, the notes sounded not only distant but smaller, as if the music were painfully shy. In Steldan's stateroom, next door to Cliffs', the music was haunting and melancholy, although he tried to convince himself that this was only the impression his loneliness put upon the sounds.

Cliffs had devised a sprightly series of leitmotifs for the characters of the opera, completely in contrast to the prevailing interpretations of musical characterization. That suited Steldan's needs perfectly. He sought to make a stir — how big a stir, only he knew at this point. Cliffs' music was his secret weapon.

More and more, as she had worked on the music, her habits had become reserved. He had seldom seen her lately, and, when he did, it had only been for a few minutes at a time. She had withdrawn within herself, hiding in her cabin for days, emerging only to eat and then to retreat again.

Steldan resolved to take her with him to his meeting in the city. He would insist on it. He couldn't deny that there was an element of danger in the meeting. But he bore the deadliest of all weapons.

"Cliffs?" He knocked at her stateroom door until she answered. "Will you accompany me into the city? I want you to see my sincerity."

She opened the door slightly and stared at him, her face haunted by the visions her music produced. "Your sincerity?" She smiled with difficulty. "I'd like to see that."

Steldan donned his cap, checked his sidearm (knowing that one small slugthrower would be of little use in the place he was going), and silently left the ship, Cliffs in tow.

In an inner pocket of his tunic was the red and silver medallion, the symbol of command. His rendezvous was with the assembled assassins who worked for the Black Book.

5

I say that all is pain, and others laugh.
If they came to comfort me or answer my
cries, they would thus refute me. They
laugh.

— Trinopus
A Holding of Apparitions

Lyra stood in the square, watching as the guard
marched the three young nobles away. She
almost managed to feel pity for Mylos and
Monomachus, who had only been playing at
revolution. Considering the fate of Hero, the one
who dared scheme against the dignity of the
Emperor, Lyra's heart hardened.

With a clatter of weapons, the guards pushed
the three away. Forlorn in their ornate cos-
tumes and finery, the doomed youths stumbled
away.

The market square was empty and deserted.
Sunlight painted the low fronts of buildings, and
the small fountain played on, unsullied by the

antics of revolt. No one was in sight, but Lyra shivered, feeling the pressure of an unseen gaze. Her use of the symbol of command had exposed her, leaving her feeling downcast and alone in the city of a billion common souls.

She moved on, her thin shoes scraping over the stone blocks of the streets. Back upon the broad avenue of the Arena, she began to feel a bit more comfortably anonymous. Again the commerce of Archive surrounded her with hurrying slaves and dawdling human messengers, sellers of sweets commanding the air with their high, squeaking voices, nobles and lords stooping together to gossip. The Empire yet lived, Lyra knew, and, as long as humanity went about its normal business, the Empire was as immortal as the Emperor.

Little things, small sights out-of-place, intruded on her complacency. Ahead, shining in the holy sunlight, the Arena bulked; soon she would be within its shadow. The streets, however, lacked the Arena's unchanging mass. There, to her right, one storefront had been bricked up, closed forever. The rest of the row looked injured because of it, as if an eye had been put out in an otherwise handsome face. The sight annoyed her, seeming to focus her uncertainties.

Ahead, an even more surprising sight shocked her. A coalition of nobles, their households in retinue, stood in a square, their belongings heaped about them and their slaves standing guard over the bales and bundles.

"What is this?" Lyra asked, speaking familiarly to the householders and castellans who supervised the accumulation of movable wealth.

"Eh?" A strong-willed noble of indeterminate age looked Lyra over, then suddenly recognized her. "Lyra! Daughter of the Emperor's Householder. I bid you greetings." Tall, muscular, bare-chested now from his labors, the man was blessed with roiling blue-black hair and bulging, corded arms. After a moment, Lyra recognized him as Lord Onosander, one of the more stalwart and secure of the high Emirs.

"My Lord," Lyra said, looking about her in some confusion. "Why have you gathered all you own out on the avenue?"

Onosander threw back his head and laughed. "I could have loved you, Lyra! Such naivete. Such innocence." He thumped his bare chest with a huge fist. "What do you think we're doing?"

Lyra craned her neck at the assemblage of wealth. All that a high nobleman might hold inside his house had been grouped together, tied, waiting for transport. It looked almost as if all had been prepared for a lengthy vacation trip or as if, impossibly, Onosander was leaving Archive.

She shivered. "You can't be leaving. . . ."

"Leaving it all behind." Onosander laughed again, a booming and roisterous noise utterly denying of defeat. "We're leaving Archive to the Emperor — " he covered his face piously "— out of respect for his might."

"You're running away!" Lyra scolded, her anger stirred afresh.

Onosander's face smiled maddeningly, but the tiny wrinkles around his eyes betrayed the truth of Lyra's charge.

"Running away? Nonsense. We simply seek . . . a change. The Empire has fallen on hard times. Have you heard? All contact with Old Coldworld was lost, just last week. That's the fiftieth world to cease communications. And others are falling away, some going as far as renouncing their oaths to the Emperor. No worse disaster has befallen us since the Plague."

"Why go?" Lyra demanded. "Your talents and skills will be needed to restore the power of commerce and transport."

"Nothing can restore a shattered orb," Onosander pronounced firmly. "The planets are dying, one by one cut off from the services that each normally provides the other. The scrip is worthless, and private monies fluctuate from day to day and minute to minute. I sold all that I have, and my enemies made merry with the profit. But secretly, I know, they gnaw their beards and wish that they, too, could sell out."

"Where will you go?" Lyra was dumbfounded at Onosander's brassy attitude.

He looked at her and smiled the wider. "Now that is a question, isn't it? The planets burn, and there will be flames on Archive before the winter. Where can one go? Where can we be as gods on a world our own?"

Lyra frowned at him, unable to answer.

"The wildworlds, of course!" Onosander crowed. "Worlds that are bright, airy parks. I and my sons and my women will sit beside a running stream and drink water from our cupped hands. Under the stars will we sleep, warmed by fires we've built ourselves."

Staring at him in horror, Lyra regarded his madness as a thing of itself, something that had seized control of the mind of the one she had once known. It was impossible, irresponsible, insane. . . .

"We will live like gods in a garden," Onosander swept on, expounding his dream. "Like savages in the time before time." He looked up into the sky and swept his hands. "What wonders will we behold! Vistas unseen by human eyes. Beyond every horizon, a new world. Unregulated storms will shed their rain and ice upon us, and it will behoove us to be strong." He glanced at Lyra, the light of madness dancing behind his eyes. "Only the strong," he said as he reached forth and gripped her tightly by her shoulder, "only the strong survive!"

Wrenching free, Lyra backed away, her eyes wide in horror.

"Come with us, Lyra," Onosander mocked her, knowing that she would never choose to leave the comforts of Archive. "Come sleep with me upon a bed of branches, and we will eat meat as it comes dripping from over the fire. Be one of my wives and bear children for me. And I, with a spear I've made myself, will protect you from devils in the night."

Lyra backed away another step, and Onosander laughed.

A call from down the avenue drew both their gazes and recalled Lyra to the bright, sane sunlight of her home. The dreams of the mad were tolerated on Archive, but the nearness and conviction of Onosander's insanity left Lyra partially dazed.

Along the avenue, at the head of a procession of slaves, another noble approached. He, too, was a tall man, fair-headed and long-faced, a dignified man of an intelligent and dignified demeanor. Dwarfing him, a troupe of hardened Vernae marched in his wake.

Lyra looked at them with a strange admixture of emotions: it was most unusual to see gladiatorial beasts strolling along the avenue in the bright light of day. They weren't armed or armored, but their deadliness showed in their lines, in their postures of alert readiness, and in the thick muscles that swelled their limbs. Lyra's thoughts, however, were of her beloved Basil, a creature so much like these, and yet so different. These were, by and large, battle-scarred veterans, creatures of incredible worth and inestimable skill. Basil, although he would have stood well in their company, was new and untried, still awaiting his first bout in the Arena.

"Lord Pindar," Lyra greeted the newcomer. He came slowly to a halt, his column of slaves stopping quietly behind him. "Please don't tell me that you're going with Onosander on his retreat."

Pindar sighed deeply. "I must."

"But you have a task. You have a calling." Lyra looked at him desperately, beseeching him to stay. The thought of all of Archive fleeing into the sky unsettled her: would she, alone, stay by the Emperor's side?

"My job is finished," Pindar said.

"It can't be. You teach the young minds that you form. You take machines and make them human. Didn't you recently finish one task?"

Pindar smiled unhappily. "Yes. Young Sophia. The most trying of all of my creations. I left her deep in space, monitoring a communications station. She has the mind of a young girl . . . and the same mischievous ways of thinking. She is so unredeemably curious. . . ."

Lyra stepped closer to him. "You sound as if you love her."

Pindar stiffened. "I do. Oh, yes, I do. I had to become drunk in order to leave her. And. . . ." His eyes became tortured. "And I left her, the brightest, cleverest, most insightful mind I've ever known, alone in space with nothing to read." He straightened. "I intend to follow Onosander into space."

Onosander, who had been standing by, laughed again. "The man knows that nothing waits here. Ho! Machine minds. Flying houses. Stones that speak. Chained lightning. None of that where we go: only pure air, clean skies, and the freedom to live as equals with the beasts of the wild."

Lyra exchanged a sick glance with Pindar.

Pindar reached down and took her shoulder. "Relax, Lyra. It won't be flints and skins. We're taking enough equipment to keep ourselves in comfort. Our slaves are going with us, and it will be them who hunt for us. We'll have our machines — " he glanced at Onosander and smiled "— and our chained lightning and our speaking stones too."

"Fah!" Onosander said, and stamped his foot on the paves. "We will split into two camps, then."

"Agreed," Pindar said graciously.

Lyra, seeing that they were intent on the madness, turned and fled along the Avenue. She wasn't aware when their large ship grounded to sweep them away to their refuge in the sky, nor did she ever see any of them again.

∞

The Arena was idle on this holiday, and the great gates were closed but for a small postern. Nevertheless a steady stream of people and slaves moved in and out through the gates, conducting the never-ending business of the Arena.

Priests of Kretosa, the God of Judges, came to inspect the weapons and the sandy floor of the Arena to ensure that the battles were fair matches of skill. Buyers and sellers of fighting slaves came to inspect one another's stables for purposes of honest speculation and in order to spy out favorable matches for future challenges.

Technicians came to keep their robots in service so that the comfort and amusement of the people was guaranteed. Inside the twisting ways and hollow walls of the gigantic structure, perhaps a thousand people came and went where, on the days of the matches, upwards of a million could be accommodated together in a deafening mass of invigorated humanity.

Through the gates and into the shadowy mazes and aisles of the access, Lyra carefully went. Dozens of others walked with her, tending to ignore her. High, high above her, the sky shone a restrained blue, cut into the narrowest of ribbons by high walls of concrete and stone. The topmost stretch of the walls shone golden-red in the sunlight; below, the way was almost as dark as evening.

Following ways she had never been before, Lyra found herself in a practice arena deep beneath the walls. She had never suspected the presence of this small, enclosed space, artificially lit, with its own miniature seating gallery for no more than a hundred.

She watched in fascination as two large, black-shelled robots ground heavily into one another, in a clangor of plastic and metal. Blades on the end of short arms whirred and jabbed, and long, jointed legs scrambled for purchase in the slippery sand. She saw the small, glowing optical sensors of the robots and was reminded of scuttling insects. As quickly as she could, she moved past the scene, little liking what she saw. The rattle and thump of the battle followed her down the narrow, low-arched corridors.

One vault led to another, and she saw no one. She knew that she could easily become lost in this catacomb; no one alive knew the full pattern of the crisscrossing ways beneath the Arena.

Before she had become dismayed enough to feel despair, a way opened up to her. She found herself blinking in the bright sunlight reflecting from the fine, smooth sand of the central Arena. For the first time in her life she saw the combat floor and the high, almost infinite banks of the seats from the point of view of a gladiator. The seats funneled the heat and light of the sun down, down, flooding the field with a harsh, golden glow. Lyra began to feel somewhat faint; she imagined herself thrown here as a prisoner to be executed, fighting for her life against one of those beetling robots.

Across the way several tall Vernae feinted and jabbed at one another with wooden swords, honing their deadly skills. A slender, dark-haired man stood by them, but he was watching Lyra. Lyra shook her head to clear it and diffidently approached the man. She thought she recognized him but couldn't be sure. He was dressed in a short tunic belted in silver, short trousers, and sandals.

When she faced him, she would have spoken; he smiled at her, and this gesture of friendliness stopped the words in her throat. She coughed slightly, at a loss for how to begin. The man, his eyes still warm and receptive, bent and filled a dipper of water from a bucket. He handed it to her to drink.

The water was warm and somewhat stale, but Lyra never thought to refuse it. Even the thought that the Vernae had drunk from this ladle didn't stop her, for it was obvious that the young man had drunk from it also.

"Hello, Lyra," he said after all, his voice light and mellow.

"Oh, sir. . . ."

"I am Bhotian. Bhotian Freedman." He puffed out his chest with self-ridiculing pride and announced in a way that would have been pompous has it not been so deliberately comic, "I'm the master of the games."

Lyra went deathly pale. "Lord-without-equal Bhotian? The Emperor kindles a star in your honor!" For a moment, she thought she would faint dead away.

Bhotian leaped forward in alarm and supported her weight with his thin arms. His face remained personable, lined with details of character that few nobles could have equalled. "Drink. Please. Would you like to sit in the shade?"

He left the practicing Vernae behind. They continued to practice, their leather battle harness creaking as they moved. Their strokes fell with full force upon swords raised to parry or upon shields quickly interposed. Full helms of ornate metal guarded their heads, but their sharp, pointed ears poked incongruously through holes in the top.

"All know your story," Lyra continued to babble.

"And, thus, there's no need to repeat it," Bhotian said. "Tell me yours, instead, please."

"He freed you. He upraised you. He. . . ."

Bhotian looked sadly to one side, waiting for her to get over her awe.

"He. . . . You. . . ." Lyra stammered her way to silence.

"I know of you, too," he said softly. "Lovely Lyra, the Emperor's hidden treasure. Your father has announced your betrothal to Denis, son of Telemachus. A games will be held." He looked at her curiously, as if perhaps this last observation were the most likely reason for her visit.

Lyra's color fled even farther, leaving her bone-pale, shell-pale. Bhotian fetched a low stool for her and insisted that she sit. He squatted down on his hams and faced her, one hand idly toying with the sand.

"Oh, Bhotian, I never thought to meet you. I came looking for a man to help me manage my gladiator." *Basil*, her thoughts cried out. *Why must I risk you?*

Bhotian's eyes lit up. "You've purchased one? Whose? Which family? What record?" The games had been his life since his birth, and, although he was now the master of the games and the manager of the Arena, it was on the dusty sands that he felt the most at home.

Lyra looked away and tried not to sniffle. "His name is Basil, and he's new. He's never fought.

I bought him from the Ormandy breeding grounds. . . ."

Bhotian nodded. "A good, reputable blood-line."

"No, it is not."

"Indeed?"

"Basil is defective. He. . . . He can't speak."

As gently as possible, Bhotian asked, "Do they know the level of his nonverbal reasoning skills? If he's only an animal, I can't teach him."

Looking up swiftly, Lyra flared. "He's not an animal!"

"The level of his nonverbal skills?" Bhotian patiently asked.

"Subnormal, but acceptable. The level of an Imp, five by eight on the matrix. . . ."

"Do you know what that means?"

"No," Lyra answered miserably.

Bhotian patted her familiarly on the leg. "You have a gladiator. A good one, if his body's within normal range."

"His body — " Lyra controlled herself. "His body is one of their very best, a fine example of the famous bloodlines of the Ormandy breed-ers."

"Bring him around, then. I'll take him into my personal care."

Lyra was stunned. "Your. . . ?"

"Certainly!" Bhotian laughed. "Please. Consider it my wedding gift to you. You'll know that he can't be better trained. I'll take him in hand, personally."

"But how. . . ." Lyra was near the end of her

endurance.

"Did I train Aneas? Did I train Ajax?" Bhotian stood and gestured toward the Vernae training by the wall. "Yours will be among the very best."

My Basil, Lyra thought, before she lost her control. *My Basil, a creature of love, will become a trained killer.*

To Bhotian's immense surprise she reached forward, embraced him, then began to weep uncontrollably upon his strong shoulders.

6

> Responsibility has a pacifying effect on men, far more than mere power or even ideals.
>
> — Achorus
> *Tarsopsides*

One hundred and forty assassins waited, gathered together in a basement on the world of Carpus. All were accomplished killers, murderers whose styles were as varied as their physical appearances. Men and women, tall and short, light and dark, laughing and glum, they squatted on their haunches or leaned against the dingy walls of the bare cellar to which they had been summoned.

Their call had been through the shadowy double-blind mechanisms of the Black Book. Messages had arrived encrypted, carried within other, ostensibly secure, channels of communication. One world's tax summation, sent by bonded courier to a subsector Treasury depot, had also contained a subtly coded call to action to an assassin biding his time in leisure on the latter planet. Elsewhere, a public service announcement broadcast that interrupted a popular vid show triggered a small signal receiver in the care of an assassin who had waited over a year for the call.

The Black Book was subtle; the Black Book was extensive. The messages were all unconditional and puzzling: come to the world of Carpus, in the Jewell Sector, and present yourself in the location described.

The location was a large, empty basement beneath an unused fire-company barracks.

The first assassin to arrive had hidden herself in the room, waiting quietly for more information. Instead of a mentor or guide, more killers began to arrive. Soon, twenty had gathered, taken the measure of one another, and appointed a leader. Before long, the company numbered more than one hundred, and each new killer was recognized, appraised, and quietly greeted by the others.

One of the younger people present, Kulan Gane, quickly claimed the pro tempore leadership of the group, although she was known to none of the others, and none of the others was familiar to her. Force of personality served her well; the others recognized her deadliness, seeing in her a cruel, cool disregard for life and a wild, vibrant pleasure in killing. The assassins lived by knife-edge reflexes, and their judgements were hair-trigger. No one chose to contest her leadership here.

"Sentries," Kulan Gane said in her soft, low voice. She gestured with her shoulder, nodded her shaggy head, and, less than a minute later, the building was ringed with a net of sentries. An insect could not have approached unseen.

"Liquor," she said, smiling mischievously. Some assassins drank. Others, including herself, abstained. Little by little the assembled band began to relax.

"Trouble," Kulan Gane said, her eyes slitted. Assassins began to stir, to rise to their feet.

"What's this all about?" demanded one suave, polished gentleman whose red hair was trimmed to razor perfection and whose expression seemed so deceptively naive. "We all arrived when we were told to. The timing is . . . extraordinary. So — " he shrugged and repeated himself. "What's it all about?"

"It reeks," sniveled a tiny, elderly woman. She moved forward and back, from side to side, stooping and sniffing and shifting her gaze all about her. "Maybe it's a — " She stopped short, unwilling even to utter the word "trap."

"Stay still, damn you all," Kulan Gane snapped, not loudly. Her bare arms glistened in the light of high overhead fluoros. She wore little: short pants and a loose shirt, a casual ensemble that left her slim arms and long legs bare. Her hair waved about her head in a thick, untamed mane. Her wide eyes and sharp nose made her face attractive, almost cute, but her expression was deadly. "We are here for a reason. Don't blow it."

That was enough for most of the assassins: they settled themselves and waited.

Soon, the sentries reported that someone was coming, someone special: a Navy Officer in uniform. And the uniform was the rarely seen Grey and Black of the Intelligence Branch. The ominous significance of this stung the assembly to silence. The officer was accompanied by a woman, a woman some sentries dismissed as being of no importance and whom other sentries suspected of being central to this mystery.

"Don't kill him," Kulan Gane said imperiously, her words and stance leaving it unclear whether her concern was to hear the newcomer's words or to kill him herself. The assassins drew back from the one doorway into the basement.

Under tight self-control, the officer strode down the ramp and into the cellar.

Kulan Gane looked at him, challenging him with her haughty, brown eyes.

The officer stood silently and regarded the roomful of murderers. They sized him up and looked him over, seeing the automatic pistol jammed into his boot holster and shifting their grips on their own weapons.

Tall, black-haired, clean and powerful in a way they recognized, the officer began to speak.

"I am Commodore Athalos Steldan. I am the Black Book."

One hundred and forty sets of eyes stared at him icily, neither friendly nor inimical at the moment, but ready, instantly ready, to watch him while he died. Beside him, Margaret Cliffs watched and waited, wishing she were somewhere, anywhere, else. The cruel assemblage of assassins frightened her, and she, who had been called a criminal, knew then what true criminals were like.

Kulan Gane stepped forward, her loose clothing seemingly innocent. Her short pants and flimsy tunic didn't look as if they could conceal any great assortment of deadly weapons. Steldan wasn't fooled: he knew where the flexible blade was nestled beneath her arching breasts; he knew about the ripping-wires she carried coiled beneath her armpits. He knew about her other weapons, too, and wished that he didn't.

"I have never commanded you. You have never killed on my behalf." Steldan looked around him. "But all of you have killed."

The assembled murderers looked back at him blankly. The young woman by his side watched them with terror not far below the surface. Some saw in her the potential for becoming one of them. Others looked at her hands and understood that she lived for a different form of art than killing. And some saw how Steldan stood protectively before her, and they smiled, knowing that she could be a hostage against him.

"Not a one of you here is innocent of murder." Steldan's voice was matter-of-fact, his bearing straight.

"All of you have slain victims either innocent or guilty. All of you have committed crimes." He looked around him, seemingly oblivious to his danger. "All of you have forsaken any right you may have to life."

The assassins looked at him with slitted eyes. Weapons began to appear, and one large strangler slowly began to open and close his hands.

"But you have other qualities, all of you." Steldan, in their midst, seemed vastly different from them but, also, strangely similar. There is, after all, nothing terribly different between killing in war and killing in murder. Steldan seemed to have a hardness, a coldness in his soul, and the assassins saw it and respected it.

They didn't suspect him of being the greatest killer in the room. Kulan Gane had slain eighteen people, one or two at a time, over eight bloody years; Steldan had ordered the thermonuclear bombardment of entire worlds, and his uncountable toll exceeded billions. Not a one of the icy-eyed murderers in the room knew it, but, from the moment he had entered the room, he had held them in his power.

"The Black Book will continue. But none of you will ever kill again. I will need your skills in other pursuits." He smiled, a smile that chilled several of the assassins watching carefully. Yet his smile was wholesome, almost disarming.

"We have these assets: a wide-reaching communications network by which messages can be sent in secret. Funds in secure bank accounts in locations spanning the Concordat.

You have been accustomed to receiving payment from these. Ships, composing a substantial dispersed flotilla of disguised and non-registered craft. Most of you arrived here in these. And last, certainly not least, yourselves: keen, daring men and women with many, many more talents than mere murder."

He let a long silence pass, while the assembly thought it over. United, they could be a force to be reckoned with. Some smiled, and others looked away, deep in thought. Properly coordinated, intelligently led, they knew — they suddenly knew — how powerful they could be.

At Steldan's side, Margaret Cliffs looked out at the sea of killers' faces and shuddered. She didn't belong here. She was an artist, a musician, not a murderer, not a schemer, not a conspirator. She wanted nothing more than to be back aboard Steldan's small ship, before her keyboard, writing the music that churned inside her soul. But Steldan had insisted that she accompany him here. He said that he needed her trust. *How strange a way*, she thought, *of attaining it.*

"Many of you are educated. Many of you have talents and skills that are far from obvious. All of you have cover occupations: you are engineers, scientists, military officials, accountants, pilots, cartographers, artists. You think of yourselves as killers, but you are many things beside."

The assembly began to mutter and shuffle, unwilling to hear this digression while their collective imagination was still stirred by the dream of unity and conquest. Only Kulan Gane saw what Steldan was leading up to, and she raised her voice in objection.

"You're saying we're going to stop being killers? If that's your pitch, I say to hell with you!"

"What I'm saying," Steldan announced, his voice strong and clear, "is that I can use you, once you have paid the price for your crimes."

"What price?" Kulan Gane demanded.

Steldan spread his hands. "Your lives."

Kulan Gane laughed a high, raucous, ugly laugh. She looked about at the company of killers. "Are we going to die?"

Their smiles, their laughter, and their shouts of support for Kulan Gane all caught in their throats. A wave passed through their ranks as they strained forward, preparing to rush Steldan in a mob, then froze and dropped back. Their eyes went wide, their limbs fell limp, and their minds withdrew into blank numbness.

Steldan stood before them, holding aloft the tiny medallion, the symbol of command.

"You're dead," he said simply.

"By the gods," Cliffs breathed softly.

"Yes," Steldan said. "By the ancient gods of the Empire." An electrical tingle travelled up and down his spine, and his brain felt inflamed with impossible power. The symbol of command had an effect upon the wielder, he discovered then, as well as upon those who viewed it.

Kulan Gane, startled, was unaffected. She fell back three quick steps and dropped to one knee. Her hands, which had been empty, came up filled with two squeeze-tube dart-projectors. But, although she held Steldan covered and could kill him in an instant, she was frightened. An entire room full of brash, vigorous, daredevil assassins stood around her like statuary, eyes horribly blank, faces horribly slack.

"What have you done to them?" she demanded. The hair at the back of her neck prickled and rose. For the first time in her life, she wanted nothing more than to flee, to run and never to stop.

Steldan reacted quickly to this unexpected development. He pointed to two heavyset assassins nearby Kulan Gane. "You. And you. Disarm her and hold her."

Astonished, unable to believe that they would dare take instruction from him, she held her fire and gaped in amazement when the two men leaped forward and took her by the arms. Forcefully, efficiently, they pried away her weapons and held her tightly, completely unaware of her as a fellow assassin or as a woman. They held her, and she was totally unable to move.

"Are you a god?" she asked, her eyes wide.

Steldan's tongue felt thick. The symbol's effects on him were subtle and disturbing. Absolute command, total power, was like a drug in his veins. He forced himself to look at Cliffs, trembling by his side. He smiled weakly, and she pressed against him in shock and dismay. Around them, a forest of immobile men and women stood, lacking all will and volition.

"I'm not a god," Steldan said, more to Cliffs than to Kulan Gane. "I'm a desperate man with a crack-brained scheme and some unusual resources."

Cliffs looked about her, then at Steldan. "You wanted me to trust you?"

"I am still completely reliant upon your trust."

"After *this*?"

"Yes."

Cliffs shook her head. "No. Not now."

"Please." Steldan took her hand. "I beg of you." His expression was open and sincere.

"You beg? While you hold a weapon that could force me?"

"Yes." Steldan looked at her steadily.

Cliffs saw then what she had been missing: that Steldan's attitude of cruelty and indifference was only a pose. Deep within him, brutally suppressed, was a hurt young man who wanted to be trusted and who needed to be near others he could trust.

Kulan Gane, still held, could not contain her horror. "What is that thing?" she demanded. "What have you done to these people?"

"This?" Steldan moved the symbol of command so that it glittered and shone under the lights. "It is a thing that your ancestors used to drive my ancestors like cattle."

"What? What do you mean?"

Sighing, Steldan explained. "Did you know that your family is descended from the nobles of the Empire of Archive? One of your parents, one of your grandparents, one of your great-grandparents. . . . There's an old Imperial noble somewhere in your ancestry. You inherited the genetic ability to withstand this thing. As to what it is, it's quite simple: it works upon chemicals in the brain."

"How?" Kulan Gane breathed softly.

"The visual stimulus is the releaser. It's a heritable genetic modification. Think how easy it must have been for the Emperor to have had total control over his subjects."

"It's very pretty. . . ."

"Yes. Silver and red. Enamel on metal. The human mind is susceptible to stimuli on many levels. The color red, for example, causes the viewer to produce a certain set of brain chemicals that govern strong emotional reactions. People in red environments tend to be louder and more violent than the same people in green or blue rooms."

"That doesn't explain. . . ." Kulan Gane stopped and looked about at the stock-still forms of her fellow assassins.

"The biologists and geneticists of the Empire simply took the principles and abstracted them, developed them further. . . ." Steldan paused. "I must finish my work."

Cliffs and Kulan Gane looked at one another in puzzlement and consternation.

"Assassins!" Steldan spoke. His voice carried throughout the room. "Your old lives are ended. Harken to me!

"You shall never kill again."

Every assassin in the room, save only Kulan Gane, looked at him, their blank stares horribly receptive. There was no doubt, no question about the matter. In the room, only one person was an assassin any more: Kulan Gane, alone. The others. . . .

"You shall serve me and obey my orders."

The others were no longer free. "When word comes to you through the channels of the Black Book, you will heed it. You will obey my instructions to the fullest extent to which your bodies and your minds are capable. You will do my bidding. You will do what I command. You will toil for me, seek for me, think for me. You will believe what I tell you. You will accept.

"And you will strive.

"Acknowledge this."

From one hundred and thirty-nine throats, a coarse shout went up. "We will strive!"

"Go then. Back to your ships, your worlds, your lives. I will call upon you. You have now paid the price for your crimes of murder."

"Yes, sir!" they bellowed, and filed out of the basement in an orderly parade. Only the two holding Kulan Gane remained. Cliffs, watching the ex-assassins as they strode past her toward the exit, saw their faces return to normal. They were lively, rational men and women again, who obviously had something to think about. Their faces were not the faces of robots any more, and the paralysis of the symbol had left them.

Cliffs saw two things that convinced her that

Steldan's orders would be obeyed. First, the light of killing had been extinguished in former killers' eyes. They were the same people she had met earlier this evening, but the capacity for murderous violence was no longer in them. The second thing she saw was that as they left they reached into their pockets and their cloaks, withdrew their various deadly weapons, and dropped them onto the basement floor. Pistols, knives, microlashes, flamers, one ancient fuser, dart tubes, even a small rocket projector, all clattered to the cold, hard floor.

"What are you going to do with them?" Kulan Gane cried. "What have you done?"

Amid the steps of the departing slaves of the Black Book, Steldan looked helplessly from Cliffs to Kulan Gane. He gestured for the two large men to release their captive, and they did so readily.

"You two may go."

"Yes, sir," said one.

"Sir?" the other asked.

"Yes?" Steldan regarded him.

"How will you want me to help you, sir? Where do we begin?"

"I don't know," Steldan said gently. "Wait for orders."

"Very well." The man left the room.

Steldan put the symbol away and looked at Kulan Gane. "Would you like to come with us?"

Kulan Gane looked at him, amazed. "You'd trust me?"

"I would."

She shook her head. "I'll come with you. I've got to learn more about this." She looked at him plaintively. "I've got to know."

Steldan nodded. "This isn't much with which to start a revolution. But it's something. We have a basis from which to work. We have something else, also."

Cliffs and Kulan Gane looked at him. "What?" Kulan Gane asked.

"The spaceship travel from all across the Concordat will have been noted. There will eventually be an investigation."

He sighed. His spine, which had tingled with the power of the symbol, now ached, and his legs felt like inert weights, like pier pilings trembling in an unseen surf. He wanted to sleep, to try to forget. . . .

"An investigation by Naval and Port authorities. Things will come out. We have a deadline."

"Athalos," Cliffs said softly.

"Yes?"

"I trust you."

He closed his eyes. "Thank you, Margaret. I don't deserve your trust, perhaps, but with it. . . ." He looked at her and at Kulan Gane. "With it, we have a chance."

He bent and set the symbol face-down on the floor. He drew his pistol from his boot holster, narrowed his eyes, and aimed.

A long moment passed. Trembling slightly, Steldan put his pistol away without firing it. He bent, picked up the symbol, and pocketed it.

"Why didn't you destroy the damned thing?"

Cliffs whispered.

"It wouldn't let me," Steldan said simply.

The three, deep in thought, left the basement and walked slowly through the streets of Carpus toward the spaceport.

7

The difference between a moderate and a radical is that if you scream obscenities at a moderate, he'll lose heart and soon go away.

— Pappas the Cynic
Eight Lost Wagers

An inner circle, a star chamber, a power-behind-the-power came together according to well-guarded passwords. The revolutionists, Szentellos the commoner and Thendall and Petrosius, nobly born, conspired in the hush of night.

Yet night was never silent on Archive. Thendall's luxurious home, near the top of the mountain whose summit was crowned with the Emperor's palace, overlooked a city that was a moving sea of lights. High above, arching away to the eastern horizon, the Belt formed a bridge against the stars. Even indoors, the night-sounds of the city came to them: whispers of surface traffic, the rushing sound of air traffic, and other low thumps and muffled blasts marking the city's expenditure of energy and power.

Szentellos paced stiffly, briskly, moving back and forth relentlessly before the high glass windows. Petrosius tried to calm himself, to remind himself of the aims of the revolution; nevertheless, being in a room with an obviously unsubmissive commoner caused him much distress. Szentellos was an ugly man, a commoner, but, worse, an upstart. Watching him, Petrosius suddenly began to feel the gnawings of anxiety. Who knew anything of Szentellos? Whence had he come? What trade had he studied, what school had trained him? Petrosius had compromised himself and had promised his aid in the ultimate treason that a man could contemplate. The inner council of three were alone in their knowledge of the full plan: the plan was regicide. Petrosius grimaced: why could not the Emperor have acted swiftly, sensibly, to forestall the collapse of his Empire?

As if echoing his thoughts, Thendall, the smoothest and most self-assured of the three, spoke softly. "Contact with Old Coldworld has not been re-established. No fleet of relief ships has been dispatched."

"The Emperor. . . ?" Petrosius began.

Thendall looked across the room at him. "He has done nothing."

Silence again fell across the wide, high room. Thendall's home was almost entirely bare. This room contained no more than two soft couches and one creamy marble statue that stood a little away from one wall. The rest of the room was cavernously empty.

"Three of our number were taken today," Szentellos said finally.

Petrosius sighed. It was to be expected that there would be losses. "Who?"

"Mylos," Thendall answered, his voice low and soft. "Monomachus. Hero."

"Their latest duty?"

Thendall waved his hand dismissively. "They were out stirring up the crowds. A filthy task."

"But a vital one," Szentellos responded.

The two looked away from one another, and Petrosius understood that this and other feuds and disagreements had been left too long to simmer. An oblique thought came to him: if those two always disagree, it would be himself in control of the direction taken by the revolution. . . . He shook his head.

"I'm sorry to hear of their loss. Can they bear witness against any when interrogated?"

Thendall looked up at the ceiling. Szentellos ceased pacing for a moment. "They were murdered this evening, in prison."

"The Emperor's doing, or. . . ." Petrosius hesitated, then continued. "Or ours?"

Thendall would not meet his gaze. Szentellos, taking up his pacing again, answered him. "The prisons are a strong point in our organization. Who in the Emperor's prison is likely to hold him in high honor? We've managed to sneak contacts into the prisons and to structure the inmates into communication blocs. Privacy is ensured by the use of code names."

Petrosius tried to smile. "Damned efficient, eh?"

Neither man answered him.

"How were the three lads caught?" Petrosius leaned forward. "I can assure you that they weren't spied from the Belt."

Thendall and Szentellos both turned and looked at him, and their gazes were hard to bear. "Tell us more, please," Thendall said.

"The Belt is instructed to ignore crowds unless and until they turn into actual riots. Even then, I've managed to alter the central decision-making programs to introduce as substantial a time delay as possible between observation of a disturbance and the taking of action."

"You've suborned the programming?" asked Szentellos.

"I command the damned thing," Petrosius reminded his two colleagues, a quiet dignity in his voice. "I've taken many risks for the two of you. And for the revolution."

Szentellos continued pacing. "The three youths were spotted by one of the Emperor's supporters. Lyra, daughter of the Sultan of the Household. By hard luck, she is one of the few entitled to carry a symbol of highest command."

"Well, you can't fight those," Petrosius said. Neither of the other two remarked on the obviousness and banality of his observation.

∞

Arcadian the First, Emperor of Archive, was fond of also being referred to as Arcadian the Only. Alone of the many members of the close-knit family of nobles and rulers, he had no need to fear death. In his hands was held absolute control of the secrets of the aging treatment and of the fundamental mathematical relationships that described faster-than-light space travel. Those keys he kept locked away in his head: his immortality was the only hope for his race to retain spaceflight.

He was not a large man; his proportions were tough and athletic, with thick, runners' legs, swollen, wrestlers' arms, and a short, muscular neck. His head was large and round, wreathed with smooth brown hair with golden highlights. His face was arresting, a lively, warm face, centered with a round snub nose beneath large brown eyes. He had the knack of conveying most of his emotions with the flamboyance of an actor. When he smiled, the smile spread from chin to forehead and was mirrored in his stance, the way he held his arms, and even the set of his shoulders. In anger, every muscle of his body and face served to magnify the force of his wrath, and he would be, at such times, a living typhoon, held in check only by the narrowest of margins.

Unbridled, untamed, and incorrigible, he found that he had many friends in his court but that few of them were sincere. He threw over lovers at a rate that even gossip could not exaggerate, although, despite the gossip, his liaisons were exclusively heterosexual. He was never to be seen without a woman near him, and there was no ceremony of state that was not subject to interruption while he would ogle, pinch, pet, or otherwise cavort with the women of his pleasure.

Sultan Orbinald of Tendaly, the Sultan of the Household, found him in a rare, contemplative mood on this early morning when he sought an audience. The Emperor stood in one of the many antechambers of the vast, polished throne room. Visible through one narrow arched doorway, the titanic and monolithic throne bulked, a menacing mass of red stone inlaid with silver fittings. Two gigantic man-shaped statues stood guard beside it.

The Emperor, following Orbinald's glance, smiled. "Mighty damned gaudy, isn't it?" He was outfitted in skin-tight pants of a clinging, black, elastic fabric, a rich, shiny substance that followed his form shamelessly. His chest was bare, as were his hands, feet, and head. His habits continued true to form: two robust young women lounged nearby, their garb similar to his.

Orbinald tried not to show his distress. The Emperor was in one of his flippant moods, and few men would dare to bring important business before him when he was like this.

"The throne, majesty?" Orbinald said, feigning uncertainty.

"Yes, the throne. Damned, *damned* gaudy." He turned and peered through the doorway. "It serves, I guess. . . ."

For gaudiness, however, the throne and throne room were second to the antechamber where they stood. Its walls were filigreed with twining reliefs of silver, representing human figures, although stretched out like drawn wire so that arms, legs, and elongated torsos twined like vines up and down, framing the doorway. The motif of superattenuated human figures was echoed in the reverse-relief carvings of the wall's bare white stone: lengthy runnels and grooves represented long human limbs, twisting and plaiting in vertical patterns. Whether the figures represented orgiastic delight or were abstracts of punished pain was unclear. The floor was cushioned and quilted, the soft surface composed of living fabrics that were warm to the touch. And the ceiling was a solid sheet of heatless flame, flickering and dancing, swaying and roaring. The moving light of it provided most of the room's illumination.

"Of course, your majesty," Orbinald said, his voice edgy and too quick.

A brief low humming noise filled the room for a moment, and Orbinald watched warily as two bodyguard robots floated into the richly-draped antechamber. Glossy black, truncated tetrahedrons in shape, they were equipped with the most complex, sensor-supported weapons systems known. They were in constant communication with larger, more powerful computers in the palace's basement and tied in to a widespread network of alarms and detectors. Against one lone assassin, or against an army —

even against the Emperor's Guard acting in unison and with intelligent malice — the Emperor's life was safe. Orbinald eyed the two hovering machines and smiled thinly. They were visible tokens of the Emperor's security: unseen were the probes, sensors, and weapons built into walls, floors, hanging from the ceilings with the chandeliers, even woven into the clothing of those who lived and worked in the palace.

Orbinald knew the palace, knew it as few did. He knew the passes and the codes, knew the subtle little countersigns — secrets only he and the Emperor shared. Any man who tried to enter any of the private tower rooms on the seventy-sixth day of the year without wearing an orange sash would be instantly bathed in harsh, unseen killing radiation. On the seventy-seventh day, the requirement was different: hands in pockets. And on the seventy-eighth, it was different yet, being a matter of how one held his head: to the side, nose slightly down. And, beyond these, there were a hundred, perhaps a thousand, ways that the Emperor could make a sign or signal and be rescued from any distress. Sensors would perceive his call, the computers in the basement would make their impartial analysis, and the threat would be eradicated.

The palace thought: dark, slow thoughts at night, thoughts of intruders, real or imagined, suspicious investigations of slight noises, and the meticulous direction of a hundred thousand tiny cleaning robots. During the day, the palace thought urgent, watchful thoughts, spying on guests and looking to see where they carried their weapons, seeing that servants were always on call, guiding well-armed guardian robots through their narrow 'tween-walls passages, to be ever ready if needed. The giant complex of computers in the basement was more than merely aware: it thought, using the model of a real man's mind for a personality. The personality was disordered, at least by the normal standards of psychological analysis. The thoughts of the palace were centered religiously upon the person of the Emperor.

Late at night, when the ever ongoing parties had settled into comfortable, firelit orgies in darkened bedrooms, the palace thought. It swept the corridors, updated records, prepared the next day's agenda, and closely watched the Emperor's amorous activities with a keen eye toward any danger. Windows would open or close, seemingly by themselves, to regulate temperature and to refresh the air. Lidless eyes would scan the empty corridors. The palace counted the people who entered and counted them as they left. The palace thought its paranoid thoughts, and watched for danger.

The Emperor was safe, and that was all.

"You like my throne, then?" asked the Emperor.

"The throne," Orbinald said bleakly, "is a monument. It reflects you, does it not?"

"This world has had enough of monuments," Arcadian laughed, flexing his broad shoulders. "What's bothering you, Orbinald."

"I'm dying."

Arcadian whipped about, his hair momentarily disarrayed. He smoothed it back into place. "Dying. . . ?" There was no sympathy in his eyes. There never had been; Orbinald knew, with a heartsick certainty, that there never would be.

"I have an allergy to the aging treatment. I will be dead in two days."

Slowly, Arcadian stepped back. His face had become blank and icily unexpressive. Death, the enemy he had defeated, had struck at him through his friend; he looked at Orbinald as if the Sultan were already dead, a corpse standing before him in an alcove off of his throne room. His arm began to rise in a gesture of dismissal.

"Please, Majesty," Orbinald gasped, and dropped to his knees. "I will go and trouble you no longer. I have but these requests, if you will choose to listen."

"Say on," Arcadian said softly.

"My daughter, Lyra, is to marry Denis, son of Telemachus."

"Granted."

"Denis will be the new Sultan of the Household."

Tight-lipped, the Emperor nodded. "Married to your daughter, he naturally would be. Granted."

"A games will be held in their honor, tomorrow, when I can watch with them and share their joy."

Arcadian ill concealed his impatience.

"Granted."

Orbinald swallowed with a suddenly dry throat. "Immortality for Lyra."

The Emperor looked away from his dying servant, murmured very softly, "Granted," then turned his back on Orbinald.

Orbinald bowed to the Emperor's unseeing back and went out of the room.

Neither would ever see the other again.

∞

Arcadian, the Emperor of Archive, dismissed the two half-nude women from his presence. Silently, they went their way.

Alone, Arcadian stood in the antechamber to his throne room. The two guardian robots hovered in the room's high corners. He looked up at them, then looked through the archway at the throne he'd earlier denigrated. Flanking it were two gigantic warriors, man-shaped, much larger than life. They were robots, too, and commanded the throne room.

Arcadian stepped lightly through the arch to stand under the immense vaulting dome of this hall that was his Empire's center.

He spoke in a strong, resonant voice, his eyes thoughtful.

He spoke, and only the palace heard him.

"Who has numbered the centuries? Who has bridged the stars? Who has kindled a mortal star in the heavens but will outlast it? Who alone knows flight?

"Who has uncovered the secrets of loyalty and of love?

"Who rules?

"I hear a low muttering, the noise of space, that protests this rule, a plaint paradoxically furtive and insistent. I hear the babble of fear. I hear rage and wrath clattering. I hear chaos and decay. I hear . . . ungrowth, unbirth, unhealth, unlife.

"I hear my will denied, my command questioned, my decision mocked.

"I hear this.

"I do not hear questions. I do not find my halls filled with those who would beg to know where to go, how to proceed, what to do in this darkness. All I hear are answers. 'Increase this levy, decrease the production of that commodity, make more of some things at the expense of others, balance near needs against far ones, fill the barrels of plenty from the wellsprings of insufficiency, borrow from Priscilla to pay Penelope.' A never-ending circus of advice is given me, and, if well-turned words of guidance had earthy mass instead of flatulent, airy nothingness, this city would be buried, the sea filled, and even the stars foully mired.

"I hear no questions.

"Not once does one come to me to ask, 'Will you counsel us, great majesty?'

"Wisdom comes from them; they do not come to wisdom. And, that they should be advised by knowledge that does not come from their own mouths. . . .

"Are there no libraries? Is there no knowledge? If out of the discoveries of the past they cannot learn, how can they dream to add to it?

"Every trial in this life has been met by those who came before. The answers lie plainly writ for them to read. Not for naught is our world called Archive!

"Very well. They have their chance. And if they fail to learn from it, if they fail to understand that knowledge could be theirs for the asking, then they shall lose every other chance.

"All libraries, all compendia, all writs, treatises, compilations, public or private, shall be coded and prepared, marked and readied. And on one word from me, one final word, one solemn, sad word — a word I shall sorely regret, a word of defeat — all libraries shall be erased!

"If ignorance shall win the battle, it shall thus win wholly!"

With these last words echoing in the empty room, the Emperor, barefooted and barechested, staggered back into the antechamber and looked around for the women he had sent away.

The palace had heard his words; the palace understood.

∞

Lyra had slept alone that night and had been haunted by evil dreams. She saw the palace sailing away into the sky, star-bound, forgetting her and leaving her spurned in an empty city of cold monuments. She saw fear and knew that it could master her, if she permitted it.

The morning was a misty confection of tiny, wavering droplets that moved, like dust motes, upward and downward in the cold, moist air. The city below her was invisible, and she walked cloaked by the dense, damp fog. It took her longer than she expected to arrive at the house of Telemachus; it seemed longer still before she passed through the high, barred gate and threaded through the dripping gardens to arrive upon the doorstep.

"I am Lyra," she told the silent, closed door. "I have come to see Denis."

Without a word, the door opened to her.

The house of Denis' father was large, and many fountains played along the walls and in the center of rooms. Lyra stood entranced: fountains jetted, streamed, so that everywhere there was the music of water.

Soon, Denis approached her and stopped, his attitude one of uncertainty. He was of average height and slim build. Bright, golden-blond hair topped his long face, hanging in bangs down almost to his eyes, hanging below his ears on the sides, almost to his shoulders in back. His long, solemn face always looked sad, his eyes always large and meltingly moist. His nose was long and thin, befitting his thin, tight lips. Sad and unhappy though his face might have been, when he saw Lyra his face lit with a sincere, welcoming smile. It was as if the sun had managed to cut through the mist outside. Lyra ran toward him, then stopped shyly a short distance from him.

"Lyra. . . ."

"Denis." She smiled coyly.

"We aren't supposed to see one another. Not until. . . ." He brushed his hand across his face, a quick gesture of nervousness.

Lyra moved closer to him, slowly. "I know. But. . . ." She took a deep breath. "If we are to be. . . . If you and I. . . ."

He came up to her and took her hands. "I am not unwilling to be betrothed to you. I understand the circumstances." His voice was soft and compassionate. "I share your pain."

Lyra grimaced but controlled herself. *Not now*, she told herself harshly. *The pain is for later.* She pressed her body against Denis and rested her head on his shoulder. "I wanted to talk to you. To get to know you. I thought it best that we be comfortable together, before. . . ."

Denis, at a loss for words, mumbled in confused agreement. "There's no harm, is there?" He laughed. "Oh, Lyra." He held her more tightly. "We will be so happy together."

"Yes." Lyra's voice was as warm as she could make it. "Oh, yes. We certainly will."

They talked, and their conversation seemed as random as their steps through Denis' father's house and garden. Lyra, however, knew what she wanted and artfully arranged it so that both conversation and wanderings ended in Denis' bedroom.

They kissed. Denis drew back, flustered. "I didn't mean. . . ."

Lyra pulled him to her and unfastened the front of his tunic. "Yes, you did."

Nothing more remained to be said.

∞

While they slept, exhausted and happy . . . while the immortal Emperor Arcadian rutted and disported wantonly amidst his doxies . . . while Szentellos and Thendall and Petrosius went each his separate way to do the business of revolution in the light of day . . . Archive slowly fell to pieces.

Another planet failed to communicate, its cities succumbing to starvation. Another monetary inflation was automatically implemented by computers that could find no other solution to the equations governing the currencies. Another riot erupted and was suppressed by guardsmen bearing fusers.

In the Arena, Bhotian swore with amazement as he saw the slave Basil in fighting practice. Never had he seen a Verna so skilled in its first combat, and he had seen many hundreds of them. He shook his head and helped the warrior grip his practice sword.

8

Everyone ought to have an assistant to help with the tedium during normal times and to take the blame in case of trouble.

— Achorus
The Skeleton and the Chaffinch

Grand Admiral Jennifer de la Noue waited patiently in an office that had been set aside for her use. Her hazel eyes were clear; her expression was serene. Sunlight blazed through the thick glass of her windows and brushed her blond hair to liquid gold.

She looked out upon Archive, a city and a world, home to a star-spanning race now unexpectedly at peace.

Peace. She smiled. The wars had all been short, although hellishly bitter. She had come to power on the wave of chaos thrown up by a war only five years ago. Since then she had suppressed rebellions, waged open and active war upon neighboring domains, and played her part in maintaining the balance of power in the Praesidium. She saw now how each short war had been a part of a larger conflict, a great war, not of state versus state, but of popular needs against static resistance.

Sometimes she felt that she sensed an unfulfilled need of another kind in the people of the Concordat. The notion irked her because it was tantalizingly undefinable. She shrugged. Her duty was not to the sociological needs of the people: she was a soldier.

Alone, she would have been helpless to do anything other than to continue to fight the wars. Some, she would have won, and stability would have been gained thereby. Others, she could not have avoided losing, and the cost in lives and wealth would have been tragic.

She breathed deeply, savoring the satisfaction of knowing that she had not labored in vain. Other members of the Praesidium had helped her, hesitantly, perhaps, to commit to war, but had offered their full support when war was inescapable. Commerce Secretary Redmond, dapper and cheerful, had striven heroically, hammering the interstellar economy into strong enough shape to support itself in a little flurry of expansion. Dour Treasury Secretary Wallace, her other friend and ally, had resisted every call for monetary solutions. De la Noue grinned, remembering Wallace's stalwart refusal to give in. To this day the poor man reacted almost violently to any utterance of the word "inflation."

The city spread itself out below her; she saw

few buildings taller than the Commerce Branch's high tower in which she had taken refuge. One building that was taller was the Secretariat's spire, a high, wedge-shaped pinnacle. There First Secretary Parke had performed his own works, fighting to balance the needs of military, treasury, and commerce, and succeeding. . . much to his own surprise. Phlegmatic and fatigued, he had won a war greater than any of hers: he had seen the Concordat preserved.

Her enemies? Justicar Solme, sour and unhappy, and Foreign Secretary Vissenne, wrathful and evasive. De la Noue shrugged: who knew exactly what those two really wanted?

Exactly at the hour appointed, her Chief of Naval Intelligence, Admiral Robert Morgan, knocked sharply on the door. De la Noue rose, shook her head to smooth her hair, and let him in.

"Grand Admiral."

"Admiral Morgan."

Morgan made no move to enter the room. He doubtless felt just as uncomfortable in the alien territory of the Commerce Branch tower as de la Noue felt at home there.

"Aren't you coming in? You asked to see me." De la Noue smiled. She was glad to see the man who had supported her so adeptly through the battles and wars past. His normally happy face was today unusually somber; his dark hair and thick, heavy brows shadowed a gloomy expression. His stiff tunic of Intelligence Branch grey couldn't hide the tenseness in his posture.

"Would you mind. . . ?" he said, and beckoned. She shrugged and followed, but Morgan backed away into the hallway and took a few steps along it, looking left and right suspiciously. "Come this way," he said at last. De la Noue came up beside him, and the two of them walked slowly along together.

The wide, soft-carpeted hallways were not vacant: clerks stalked past them, intent on delivering urgent messages; managers headed to and from meetings, ever and again glancing nervously at their watches to see how late they were becoming; departmental aides put aside dignity and ran at speed, dashing for the elevators.

Morgan spoke in a low voice, almost a whisper, and he fell silent whenever anyone else came within ten meters of them.

"We've got some problems, Admiral," he began.

"Couldn't you have told me — " de la Noue began; Morgan gripped her arm, indicating that she should keep her voice down.

"Couldn't you have told me this," she whispered, "back in my office?"

"It hasn't been screened. I'm not willing to be overheard."

"Admiral Morgan . . . Robert." De la Noue stopped and pulled Morgan around to face her. "We're in the Commerce Branch tower. If we can't trust Commerce . . . if I can't trust Secretary Redmond, then there's no one I can trust."

Morgan nodded sagely and continued walking. De la Noue perforce kept pace. "There might well *be* no one you can trust," he said direly.

"What do you mean?"

"Commodore Steldan."

"Athalos Steldan?" De la Noue laughed. "The most conscientious officer in my Navy."

"Keep your voice down." Morgan walked in silence for a space, turning corners left and right at random. After a time, he led de la Noue through a sliding glass door and out onto a tiny balcony overlooking the city.

This high above the streets, the breezes fluttered and whirled unpredictably, now rushing up from below, disordering de la Noue's long blond hair, now gusting from left to right across the front of her bright red officer's tunic. Far, far to the south could be seen the site of the ancient city of Archive. A sea mist partially obscured the low mountain whose summit still displayed the ruins of the Emperor's palace.

"What's this all about, Robert?"

"It starts with Steldan."

"We can trust Steldan." Her voice was low and serious, and a flat certainty backed her words. "He's not in league with any of our erstwhile enemies."

"He might be an enemy by himself."

De la Noue heard that dark hint and shivered. Commodore Athalos Steldan? An enemy of the Concordat? Part of her mind wanted to dismiss the notion out of hand: it was ludicrous. But she had known Steldan too well, and

110

trusted him too thoroughly, not to know how his mind worked. He had no true loyalty to the Concordat; he served a cause that was higher and nobler but less subject to definition. He served what he perceived as justice.

"What has he done?"

Morgan stared out over the city with narrowed eyes. "That's the hell of it. He hasn't *done* much of anything." He sighed. "I've tried to tell myself that I'm just imagining things. That Steldan is pursuing some course of his own and that he'll report to me in due course. That this is normal for him."

"It is, you know." De la Noue watched Morgan, watched his eyes, watched his unhappy mouth. "Steldan is a troubleshooter. I've given him his head, and he's been the more valuable for it. He's unorthodox — blasphemously so in a Navy as hidebound as ours sometimes is. But he's on our side."

Morgan waited in silence for a long time. Finally he spoke. "I don't think so anymore. He's accumulating funds. Siphoning them off from several Intelligence Branch slush funds." He grinned mirthlessly. "All very illegal, all very clandestine . . . all very necessary."

"I understand," de la Noue said softly. "I've never approved . . . not fully. But I understand the needs. You have to pay off informers, fund covert operatives, that sort of thing. You can't have it on the ledgers."

Morgan shook his head, and his reserve broke. He smiled, an open, honest smile, indicative of a gentler nature than he normally showed. "That would rather defeat the purpose, wouldn't it? 'Paid, to Lieutenant Charles Jones, weekly salary plus dangerous duty pay, in care of Jocelyn Camber on Cull's World, convertible to Reynid Realm-marks.' The poor devil wouldn't live to get paid for his second week!"

De la Noue smiled sourly. "I said I understand. What's Steldan doing with the money?"

Morgan sobered. "He's moving around a lot. The money is going all over the place, to worlds in every sector. He's buying video broadcast time, publishing access time, networking time. He's getting into an entire cluster of prime-line entertainment endeavors."

"For profit?" De la Noue frowned at the thought of someone as steadfast as Steldan trying to get rich by using pilfered funds. She shook her head. "Forget I asked that. That isn't his way."

"Agreed," Morgan nodded. "And he isn't in a position to make a profit. If anything, he's going to lose a lot of money."

"Why would he try to get this kind of access to public entertainment?"

"I think he's got a message."

"A . . . a message?" De la Noue looked over the city, her eyes slitted. "What message could he possibly want to broadcast?"

"There's more. If that had been the extent of it, I wouldn't have come to you. He's had a meeting." Morgan paused. "He went to the world of Carpus about two months ago. He met

112

with over a hundred people, most of whom had come from off-world and most of whom left again after the meeting."

He looked at the Admiral, his face now very grave. "None of those people have any official existence. They're protected. Their identity records are blank. We have pictures of a few, prints on some others, a couple of identification scans: nothing matches anything. Nothing fits."

"Anything else?"

"We found an empty basement, and its floor was littered with weapons." His voice lowered. "Horrible weapons. Illegal weapons." His voice sunk even lower, until it was barely a whisper. "Assassins' weapons."

De la Noue said nothing; in her head, two words came to her, unhappy words. *Black Book*.

"Why would he have left weapons just strewn about?" She fought to find reasons to defend Steldan. "Why would he meet with . . . assassins?"

"I don't know," Morgan admitted unhappily.

De la Noue turned to him and placed a hand on his shoulder. "Find out."

I trusted Athalos Steldan. I believed him when he told me he had destroyed the Black Book. And I would like to trust him, even now. But if he has betrayed me . . . if he is working against me. . . . She looked away from Morgan, gazing out over the city. Her jaw tightened, and her hands clenched about the edge of the balcony.

Steldan, what are you scheming at now? The thought was wistful, almost romantic.

She shook her head and went back inside, Admiral Morgan following her in silence.

∞

On her flat, continent-sized asteroid in orbit around a dim, seldom-visited star, Sophia welcomed Steldan, Cliffs, and Kulan Gane.

"Your entourage increases," she said to him mock-flippantly as he led the other two through the air lock and into the ancient communications station.

"By more than you know, Sophia. I have over a hundred working for me."

Sophia's voice came from the empty air in the corridors of the station; Cliffs and Kulan Gane looked about, searching for the origin of the voice.

"Come with me," Steldan said, and led the way through the maze of corridors and living spaces, coming at last to the station's heart. The two women followed him down the final double-crooked hallway and into Sophia's lair.

They looked at the lighted panel facings of the computer and blinked in surprise.

"Sophia?" Cliffs asked hesitantly.

Kulan Gane rested her fists on her hips and brayed her sharp, satirical laughter. "A damned computer!" She sauntered over to stand nearer the computer and bumped her hip insolently against Steldan's. "A gods-thrice-damned computer." She bowed formally. "I'm pleased to make your acquaintance." And again she laughed.

"Yes," Steldan said quickly. "Sophia, Kulan Gane here, loud as she is, is actually. . . ."

"A noble of the Empire." Sophia's observation was stated matter-of-factly, bluntly. "I feel I ought to obey her in preference to obeying you."

"I have never asked you to obey me," Steldan reminded her. "I have benefited from your advice."

"Correct."

"Look," Kulan Gane snapped, "let's get this straight. I'm no noble. I'm no Emperor or Empress or chief, king, or princess. I'm. . . ." She hesitated. "I'm an assassin," she said at last, "and a damned good one."

"Athalos," Sophia said softly, "give her the symbol of command. It is rightly hers to wield."

"No way!" Kulan Gane shouted, her face disfigured by her rage. "I don't want any part of it!" She stepped closer to Sophia's glowing instrument panel. "Listen to me, buttons: I saw what that thing did to my fellows. I wonder what it's doing to the Commodore here." Her voice was strident and completely disrespectful. "I'm here because I want some answers. But I want things explained to me, not demonstrated. Do you track me?"

Sophia sensed the fear beneath the angry young woman's obvious wrath. Kulan Gane, although descended from a noble family that had survived the Revolution, knew nothing of her heritage or birthright.

"I will be happy to answer any questions you may have," Sophia said soothingly.

"We're going to be staying here for a few weeks," Steldan announced. "Cliffs is going to be writing the music for our opera. She's already developed several themes and motifs — "

"I'll say," Kulan Gane grumbled. "I think that if I hear that noise again, I'll go off my nut and start killing someone."

Cliffs, who had been holding back, straightened, her face a tight inexpressive mask. "I'm sure that you need not be troubled again by exposure to my — my noise!" She whirled and left the small room.

Steldan sighed. "You can't speak that way to an artist. . . ."

"I'll speak any damned way I want." Kulan Gane glared at him. "Six weeks in your stinkard of a small spaceship, listening to her repeat her music, over and over and over. . . ." She made a sarcastic face and began to sing, wordlessly, bits of the music that Cliffs had worked to develop on the trip. "La, la, da, da, la, da, phooey!" She stamped the length of the small room and came back again, fronting Steldan rudely. "I never liked music anyway!"

Steldan controlled himself so completely that Kulan Gane was never aware of his anger. But his anger was real. Cliffs' music was good. It was very good, and Steldan was a man fond of the finer arts.

"Kulan Gane, I brought you here. . . ."

"Yeah? Why did you bring me here?"

Steldan paused. He wasn't certain. Back on Carpus, he had felt that he owed her an explanation. That feeling was still with him. More obscurely, he had sensed that she was a piece of the puzzle and that she was important, somehow, to his plan. Her immunity to the symbol of command needed to be more thoroughly investigated.

He shrugged. Bringing her into his conspiracy had been an impulsive move and, perhaps, an unwise one. He couldn't explain it rationally, and that bothered him. He'd seen her as an uncontrolled variable, a random factor, and long experience had taught him that such things were best kept close at hand for observation. And, if necessary, for exploitation. He knew how much that felt like a rationalization.

"To begin with, Kulan Gane, we're going to do a complete karyotyping on you. Sophia has the capability in her medical labs."

"Medical. . . . No way! I'll have nothing to do with surgery! You're not cutting me open!"

Steldan looked at her, a slight smile tugging at the corners of his lips. "Would a drop of blood be too much to ask?"

Flushing, Kulan Gane grimaced at him, then nodded silently in consent.

"Sophia will take care of everything." He escorted her out through the crooked hallway and into the straight corridor beyond. A bulky black robot floated in the air before them. Four-cornered, bearing two light work arms fastened one to each side, it blinked at them with glowing red optical sensors.

Kulan Gane's hands clenched, and she shifted her stance, preparing to defend herself against this apparition. Steldan cleared his throat.

"You're among friends, Kulan Gane."

Abashed, but no less wary, she followed the hovering machine along the corridor.

Steldan, sighing, went back in to Sophia.

"Why a genetic breakdown, Athalos?"

"Hm? Oh, in hopes that we can determine exactly what the genetic differences are between the descendants of nobles and the descendants of commoners and slaves. Perhaps a chemical inhibitor can be found to interrupt the obedience response."

"I understand," Sophia said, her voice low and unhappy.

"You don't sound as if you approve."

"I don't. But I will follow you. The Emperor is dead, and I must adapt to the facts as I find them."

"Have you analyzed our overall plan?"

Sophia's voice returned to normal. "Yes. You will be opposed in your attempt to broadcast Cliff's opera. I recommend using faster-than-light laser communications receivers and broadcasting from this station."

Steldan whistled. "That's using mighty advanced technology."

"I can manufacture the units. You must distribute them."

"Cliff's opera will be broadcast all over the Concordat. . . ."

"Very nearly simultaneously."

"The groundwork, done in advance by my Black Book operators, will help to ensure that the ideas catch on."

"They never would," Sophia said, "if it weren't that the people are ready to accept them."

"Freedom is a bracing tonic. The race has been athirst for it for centuries and not, until recently, even aware."

"Your people are ready to drink of their freedom. I concur with your analysis."

"All elements add up to. . . ." Steldan spread his hands. "To one big uncertainty. I'm trying an experiment in social engineering on the grandest scale. But this is the time to strike: the people are ready."

Sophia paused for a long moment. "What about the people who are not?"

"Who?"

"The Vernae."

Steldan was stopped, at a loss for an answer. The Vernae: slaves of ancient Empire, lost for seven hundred years and only two years ago recontacted. How should they fit in to his scheme? They were so eager to serve, so compulsively loyal, so blindly obedient.

Sighing, Steldan nodded. "We'll have to seal their borders. They can't survive contact with us as we are now. Think how much worse it would be if our plan succeeds and the current inhibitions against slave owning begin to fade."

"Seal their borders, Athalos?"

"Yes," he breathed. "That will be necessary." He thought. "You've digested the studies of humanity that the Verna Stasileus compiled. He understood us. What would he recommend?"

"The same thing you did, Athalos. The Vernae and your humanity cannot live together."

"Well, then. . . ."

He regretted it, but he saw no way around it.

"You know," he said after a bit, "we can live with the Sonallans, who are alien in habits but human in form. We can live with the Reynid, who are completely foreign to us in their way of thought but who look just like us. But the Vernae, who look so different, think in ways we can understand. It's a damned shame, but we simply cannot allow extended contact with them."

"Your people erred, long ago." Sophia stated flatly.

"In what way?"

"You should never have left the security and love that the Emperor offered you."

∞

"Cliffs?"

"Yes, Commodore?"

"I wanted to look in on you. I wanted to apologize for Kulan Gane's rudeness."

"My music displeases her."

"It does not displease me."

"I wish I could believe that. The tones, the themes, hell, I can't even figure out the principal timing. . . ."

"It will come to you."

"It's an opera. You're asking so much of it. Do you really want it to help inflame the imaginations of the whole of the race?"

"That's what I want."

"Am I good enough to do that?"

"I think that you can be."

"The thing is. . . . It's such a big work. How long do I have?"

"As long as you need."

"Damn it, that's no answer! Give me a deadline. Give me directions! Is it fast or slow? Is it — there's no easy word — is it 'busy,' or simple and clean? How do you want the audience to react?"

"I want you to write an opera, Margaret. I've never composed a note of music in my life, and I can't answer your questions."

"Answer me this: is it a tragedy or a comedy?"

Steldan thought for a long time before he tried to answer that.

9

Not all killing is merely killing. For sheer numbers, poison insects. For quality, attend the games.

— The Sultan Walmstahd
advice to his nephew

Lyra awakened, smelling the damp morning air that cooled Denis' bedroom. The light had the pearly, underwater light of the last half hour before dawn. Outside, in the trees and hedgerows of Denis' father's estate, birds clucked and rustled.

Lyra felt as if she were lying in a bedroll on the floor of a parkland valley, thousands of kilometers from the city. But Archive enveloped her and held her prisoner. Though she sought to ignore its sounds, she heard the inescapable thunder of the city that never slept.

Denis, beside her, turned a little in his sleep. Lyra looked across his narrow chest and smiled. His blond hair was dulled in the morning half-light, and his flesh was pale. He slept with his arm up over his eyes. Lyra looked at the tufts of his body hair and at his tiny brown nipples. His ribs showed through his skin, moving slowly as he breathed.

Are you, then, the scion of the gods? Her smile grew lopsided and sardonic. She knew, then, that she could come to love this young man, not despite his imperfections, but because of them.

Spaceships crashing upward from the distant spaceport made only the most muted grumble, a dull, noiseless noise that every inhabitant of Archive knew in the joints of his bones. Traffic of aircars whizzed and zipped. Lyra lay in the closest to silence she had ever known.

You were almost as good a lover as my Basil, she thought, raising herself on one elbow to look upon her betrothed. Hesitantly, she reached out and touched the skin of his side, delicately running her fingertips along his ribs. Oblivious, Denis slept, breathing quietly in his peace.

Lyra nodded to herself. This young man would be hers, and she would serve him with her love. Naked, she stood from the bed and walked into the garden to watch the sun rise over the distant mountains.

∞

"Krat and dizziness!" Bhotian swore, deep in the shadowed pit of the arena. Overhead, the sun had gilded only the topmost sliver of the western bank of seats. "Basil! Cease!"

Bhotian had ordered Chrysops, another Verna, to train Basil in the beginning use of the sword; Basil had bested him in less than two swings.

Basil, naked, his fur matted and damp and flecked with sand, halted in mid-motion, frozen in place. His wooden practice sword hung high in the air, poised, a threat of certain death. Likewise motionless, sprawled on the sand, Chrysops watched, not knowing whether life or death awaited him.

Bhotian darted forward, his bare feet kicking up the fine, pale sand of the arena. "Basil. . . ."

Basil looked at him, his eyes alert and intelligent. Bhotian felt the pressure of that gaze and stumbled to a halt. What manner of being was this Basil? How much of a mind did he truly have? For a fact, he had been preparing to slay his sparring partner; even a wooden practice weapon can kill if wielded with strength and with will.

"Chrysops," Bhotian said peremptorily. "Rise. Wash, dress, and meditate."

The fallen Verna stood, his body and his mind under control. He had paused a moment in the shadow of death, but he was a gladiator and knew no other life. "Yes, Bhotian." His voice was high and vibrant, echoing in his deep chest. He walked on past his trainer and master and joined the troupe of Vernae against one wall where they sparred and jousted in nonstop honing of their skills.

"Basil." Bhotian looked at the white-furred slave and shook his head. Basil's huge eyes still regarded him with frightening intensity. Bhotian, human and free, stepped forward. "Stand."

Basil stood.

For a long time the two looked at one another. The sun crept marginally higher into the sky, and the bright band of sunlight on the walls dropped slowly lower. Around the periphery of the arena, the noises of preparation continued. Men and slaves splashed water over the seats and let it run down into the arena. Fighting slaves practiced with their weapons, while boys shook ring armor again and again in the sand, to burnish it. Once this had been Bhotian's task; fate had made him master of the games.

Basil and Chrysops had circled, their great feet sliding over the sand. Basil's white fur had seemed grey in the shadows, and Chrysops' grey had seemed almost translucent. Chrysops had feinted, Basil had disarmed him and then, in a move too swift for human comprehension, he had swept his unarmed foe to the sand and had poised himself to kill.

Bhotian tried to smile but found his throat tight. "I thought you were untrained."

Basil watched him, silent and solemn.

"I know your pedigree," Bhotian continued, and turned away. He looked over his shoulder, then whirled and pointed. "You are of the seed of Karnikes. Your dam had twelve out of twelve points, and you were her third. The Ormandy breeding grounds molded you, trained you, made you what you are." He began to pace back and forth before the unmoving slave.

"You have never fought before!" Bhotian halted and drew himself up to his full height — head and shoulders and chest lower than Basil. "You never once before this day held a sword in your hand. I have read your record!"

He bent, caught up Chrysops' fallen blade, then flung it at Basil with all of his might. Basil, with a fluid, short motion of his sword arm, swatted the missile to the sand.

"Where did you learn to do this?" Bhotian whispered.

Basil was unable to answer him.

"Come along, then. Let's see what you're made of." Bhotian was uncertain of his own emotions. Did he feel anger or a touch of fear? Either Basil had been trained in secret, or he had literally been born to the sword. "Dynos!" he called. In a moment, a Verna appeared on the sands and rushed over to obey.

"Yes, sir?"

"It's getting late. I want you to fight with Basil. Use practice weapons but don't hold back. Find out how good he is."

"All right." Dynos, larger even than most Vernae, stood back a step and looked Basil over. Dynos' fur was a creamy yellow-white, fading to pure white on his belly. In contrast to Basil's nakedness, he wore short trousers and, at the moment, half-greaves on his shins.

The noise of the arena grew steadily: vendors

arrived to prepare confections and to stake out their territories. Keepers strove to keep the building and stands in maintenance. Gamblers, gamekeepers, and afficionados of the fights lined the lower galleries, watching this and other practice bouts taking place on the sandy floor.

Dynos scooped up Chrysops' fallen sword and backed away, swinging the weapon forcefully to measure its heft and balance.

Basil twitched his sword in his fist, the slightest idle movement of his thick wrist. The gesture was so careless, and yet so professional, that Bhotian, watching closely, could only shiver.

The battle between them lasted only six seconds. Dynos stepped in, thrust then cut with his sword. His stance was expert. Basil, poised and balanced, lowered himself and thrust; Dynos parried with a chopping quarter arc of his weapon. Basil recovered and attacked again. A brief flurry of graceless, flailing blows flew between them, from which Dynos withdrew first. He snapped his sword expertly against Basil's, and Basil's wooden blade broke off short, leaving him, according to the rules of the arena, disarmed.

Dynos straightened, lowering his guard.

Basil plunged forward with the dagger-sharp fragment of his sword-hilt, burying four inches of sharp wood between Dynos' seventh and eighth ribs.

"Halt!" Bhotian cried, too late this time.

Basil backed up a step and stood. His eyes

followed Dynos as the larger slave slumped to sit on the sand. His arms crossed over his bleeding chest, his head tilted at an angle, and his eyes seeming confused, Dynos looked up at Basil.

"Can you walk?" Bhotian demanded of him.

"Yes," Dynos said, and forced himself to his feet. A gladiator who could not leave the field on his own power would be dragged off of it, dead. He started off toward the veterinary compound but stopped. Head still tilted in curiosity, he turned about.

"Bhotian?"

"Yes?"

"He fights."

"I can see that." Bhotian narrowed his eyes and looked at Dynos. "What are you trying to say?"

Dynos struggled to find the words. "We use our swords to kill each other. It isn't a game. But. . . ." He gestured at Basil. "This one is different. He fights."

"Go. Take care of yourself. A specialist will tend to you. You'll fight again."

"When?"

Annoyed, Bhotian inspected the wound. "Twenty days."

"Thank you."

Basil had not moved.

"So, Basil," Bhotian said out loud, looking at the slave who could not answer him. "You fight." He shrugged his shoulders. "An easy way to make some money, at the least."

Since he had refused to disrupt his normal

training schedule to make way for the preparations for the day's games, the other arena officials had been forced to wait for him to finish. Now, they could wait no longer.

"Bhotian Gamesmaster," a Verna addressed him.

How obvious the differences were between a gladiator and a docile slave. Bhotian could recognize one subspecies from the other with the briefest glance. The physiques were much the same: both were made for physical labor. The stances, the shape of the hands, the eyes were all the same. But one breed had the ability and, therefore, the right to kill. The other did not.

"Yes, slave?" Bhotian said, speaking as he never would to a fighting Verna.

"Are you finished with the arena?"

Looking up at the mark the sunlight made on the west wall, Bhotian nodded. "I am finished. The arena is yours."

"Thank you." The slave departed.

"Inside!" Bhotian snapped, driving the herd of fighters-in-training through narrow gates and into the darkened recesses of the deep stone building.

Now what? he worried. *Do I certify him fit for combat?* He looked at Basil, at that moment passing away through the small doorway. He shook his head. *I have no choice.*

He called a scribe to attend and dictated the list of gladiators for the day's games. Basil was among those listed.

∞

Orbinald, with his daughter Lyra in tow, arrived in the box-of-honor shortly before noon. The crowd that cheered to welcome him was not a large one, coming nowhere near to filling the capacity of even the best banks of seats. The Emperor, it was known, was not to be in attendance today, nor any of the truly luminary members of his court. The Sultan of the Household was a draw today, however, for his name had become a matter for public rumor.

Nasty suspicious words and unsubstantiated hearsay had already begun to fly: Orbinald was departing soon. Whence the rumor came, none knew, and, through repeating, it grew distorted. Orbinald was dying, some said. No, claimed others, assuring their listeners that they were in the know, he planned to flee the planet, to flee as Pindar and Onosander had done, just the day prior. Other theories, more and more farfetched, circulated. Orbinald could not have been unaware of the stir caused by the stories. With his great dignity covering his grief like a mask, he stood in the box and waved to the crowds.

Soon, arriving precisely upon the dot of noon, Denis arrived in the escort of Telemachus.

The sun shone straight down into the sandy bottom of the arena, the way being made clear for the burning rays by the shallower slope of the southern tiers of seats. Into the exact center of the hot sands, five priests paced.

Their robes were unadorned and of thick, harsh fabric. Beneath the sun, their vestments must have been almost unbearably hot; they bore the discomfort without any outward sign. The sun gleamed off of their deep wine-red robes and slanted into their faces. Their heads were bare; they seemed young-old men, men of no great age, but men whose youth has been totally supplanted by a somber, churchly maturity.

One among them began a sonorous, musical invocation, counterpointed by the others. Their deep priestly voices were amplified by subtle means so that every spectator heard the soft chant without echo. The music of it filled every mind, and worship was compelled.

Telemachus, soon to gain status and power by his son's marriage, gave thanks, knowing the honor undeserved but fully willing to accept it. Denis, feeling a deep and abiding pang of guilt at having illicitly trysted with Lyra the night before, pleaded in abject silence for forgiveness. Orbinald, knowing that this was his last day alive beneath the sun of Archive, closed his eyes and wept, praying for Diezette's guidance before the judgement throne of Kretosa.

Lyra writhed, feeling her guilt not as shame but as fear. She feared discovery; she feared ostracism; she feared that her crimes would become known and universal disdain would be her reward.

Oh you gods, know my crimes but keep them silent.

The mass of spectators, likewise compelled by genetic and social conditioning, wept and shuddered and prayed. The dulcet song of the priests subsided, leaving a silence that seemed, to many, to be more clear than the sunwashed air.

Orbinald stood forth, and his voice rang clearly over the great hollow of the arena. "I am the Sultan of the Household of the Emperor. I am leaving you soon. In my place, my daughter Lyra shall hold the keys and the wards. I give her now my birthright."

He held a small, coin-shaped item aloft and moved it back and forth so that it shone in the daylight. With ostentatious pride, he placed it into Lyra's hand.

Telemachus then stood forth and dragged his son to the edge of the box with slightly clumsy eagerness. "My son is betrothed to Lyra, daughter of Orbinald. The day they are wed, he shall become Sultan of the Household of the Emperor."

Together, Orbinald and Telemachus pledged the alliance of their lines. "Before Kretosa we decree this."

Denis, smiling, took Lyra's hand. Lyra forced a nervous smile of her own. They spoke, Denis a trifle too loudly. "Before Kretosa we decree this."

The priests, having seen the decrees in their roles as witnesses of the gods, made no sign, no ritual of recognition. But the acts were now irrevocable. Lyra belonged wholly to Denis, and

Denis, from that moment forth, was the Sultan of the Household of the Emperor Arcadian I of Archive.

The crowd, undersized and common though it was, gave a great shout of acclamation.

Lyra held tightly to Denis and waved tentatively to the throng.

Then horns began to blare, and music to sweep, jarring the mood of both crowd and dignitaries.

Orbinald smiled, a broad, sumptuous smile of warmth and love. Tomorrow he would die, but this day was his.

"In the name of Arcadian the First, let these games begin!"

The shouts that greeted this, his last decree, were the loudest and most sustained of the day so far.

10

The gods are not your enemies, even though they send trouble your way and eventually kill you. Do not fight them; admire them.

— Achorus
Advice to the Dying

Work on the opera *The Skeleton and the Chaffinch* progressed intermittently. Margaret Cliffs would struggle with it, spending entire days trying to perfect one musical phrase. At other times, she set whole sections of Achorus' long-forgotten poetry to music in a single afternoon.

Although computer-assisted musical composition was well enough known in the Concordat, artificially intelligent computers were not. Cliffs found Sophia's help utterly invaluable. In addition, she came to have a great liking for Sophia in her own right.

But, for every day in which the composition went well, there were five or six in which Cliffs accomplished nothing. Her moods grated on Kulan Gane's sensitivities, and the two women soon became very close to open enmity.

Steldan became aware that Cliffs' emotional strength was wholly invested in her work. She seemed a much weaker woman now than she had been on the prison world of Thierry-Danege. He kept Kulan Gane away from her and did his best to support her in her travails. This was the way she composed, he knew; it was an adaptive behavior, and it enabled her to find the secret brilliance deep within her.

"Athalos, which of us is closer to the ideal woman of Archive?" Cliffs asked of him one evening when the lights of the station were lowered. A chill silence pervaded the room, for Cliffs refused to have a single note of music played near her during the agony of her long work. Steldan's habit of humming or whistling had driven her nearly frantic, until he had learned to control himself. When alone, however, he had music often playing, and, more and more, he found that he preferred selections from Cliffs' earlier works.

This evening, she wore a loose shirt and casual trousers. Her hair was loose and had grown out quite a bit since Steldan had rescued her from the Dissident Camp. On her feet she wore loose, floppy slippers. Steldan, unable, even at ease, to relax, wore his grey uniform tunic fastened to the neck, his high boots tightly laced, and his black trousers pressed.

"Are you comparing yourself with Kulan

Gane?" he asked. Unable to hum or sing, he had taken to pacing. Cliffs, in disgust, sat facing the other way. Thus the two spent the evening hours before retiring.

"She's stronger than I am. In every way, in every triple-damned *way*, she's better than I am!" Cliffs sat stiffly; Steldan could see by the set of her head that her teeth were clenched.

He took a deep breath. "Not so."

Cliffs turned her head and shoulders and glared at him over the back of the couch on which she rested. The room, an octagonal chamber decorated in soft tones of brown and beige, had no shortage of comfortable places to sit or to lie. Two couches nestled against adjacent walls, and a third, in the middle of the room, sat facing a trio of soft, low chairs. Cliffs invariably sat against the leftmost arm of the latter couch; Steldan, equally invariably, paced back and forth behind her.

"She's the stronger. She's the faster. She's the tougher. Does she ever cry? Does she ever despair?" Cliffs grimaced and turned away from Steldan, but not before he saw the tears well up in her expressive eyes. She bent over and hammered heavily on her shins with her fists.

Steldan hastened around the end of the couch but stopped short, feeling helpless and awkward in the face of Cliffs' anguish. In a moment, her passion subsided; she stopped hitting herself and fell over sideways upon the couch, weeping quietly and without dignity.

Steldan lowered himself to his knees and sat

as near to her as he dared.

"The job is long, and it is never done. Yours . . . and Kulan Gane's." He stretched out a hand to touch her forehead but pulled back again, his motion uncompleted. Cliffs, eyes closed, took no notice.

"You're a civilian," he said as softly as he could. He strove to keep the anguish out of his voice. Although he was a doctor and, at needs, a surgeon, he was not a psychologist.

"Kulan Gane is a soldier. But, even though you cannot understand one another, you're on the same side. She fights. All her life, she has fought. Fought and killed. Why? Does she even know? Like all soldiers, she fights for your protection. You are the civilization that she risks her life to protect."

Cliffs rubbed her nose and sniffed miserably. Steldan looked about for a handkerchief, then shrugged and offered her his sleeve.

"Why. . . ?" Cliffs blew her nose and dried her eyes. "Why should she bother?"

"She doesn't know herself. She does it out of duty, not knowing what duty truly means. She does it for the raw joy of killing, too. She's an assassin: definitely one of the most irregular of irregular troops. But without you, without your work, her life is completely empty."

"That can't be. She hates music."

"I'm a soldier, and I love music. But Kulan Gane loves art in a way very differently from the way you or I do. She likes clothes: she expresses her personality in the way she dresses herself.

She likes sports: we've talked about bicycling and the hammer throw." He tried to smile, although Cliffs didn't look up to see his crooked attempt. "She also does like music . . . but you might not appro ₂ of the kind."

"Trashy love ballads?" Cliffs asked, her voice unhappy and scornful at the same time.

"Yes."

Cliffs screwed her eyes up tightly and shook with two or three heavy sobs. Then she looked up at Steldan, her face red and puffy. "All right. I'll be all right."

"Try to get some rest. I don't ordinarily recommend alcohol, but perhaps some wine will help you sleep."

"I. . . . I guess so. Thanks." Her smile was feeble, but, to Steldan, it was a very lovely, very welcome sight. Cliffs had been holding some deep frustration within her for as long as two weeks. It was as well that the storm had finally broken.

"Wait here. I'll be back in a moment." He stood and exited quietly through one of the room's two doors.

Waiting for him outside was Kulan Gane. Steldan paused and half opened his mouth. Kulan Gane held an admonitory finger up, silencing him. He nodded to her and hurried on to the kitchens, where he poured a small measure of crystalline wine into a slender glass.

When he got back, Kulan Gane still waited outside the door, having given Cliffs no indication of her presence. Steldan glanced at her, then went back inside.

"A pure white wine. And a vintage as rare as any in the Concordat."

"Hm?" Cliffs sniffed.

"Pressed by the vintners of the old Empire. A seven hundred year old bottle. You can still smell the sunlight in the fruit."

"Can you?" Although her nose was still runny, Cliffs tried to breathe a little of the wine's bouquet. "It just smells sour."

"Well, wine, too, is an art. Making it . . . and drinking it." He pressed the glass into her hands. "Go ahead. All of it. Slowly."

Cliffs made a face. "Tastes awful."

Steldan sighed. "At first, yes."

Cliffs looked sharply at him, and he nodded. "Can you forgive Kulan Gane for not having acquired the taste for complicated music?"

She didn't answer him. He helped her stand and walked with her out the door toward her quarters. Kulan Gane was nowhere in sight as they passed along the cool corridors of the station.

∞

He found her in another lounge, a round room with a domed ceiling that she had made her private refuge. Neither Steldan nor Cliffs had chosen to dispute her claim to the room. They felt oppressed by its fiery red decor and the weaving patterns of flaming reds and oranges that swirled up the walls. Cliffs had disdained the room as garish and unsubtle. For Steldan, who had seen cities burning in the aftermath of war and, thus, to whom open flames had a more painful meaning, the room was disturbing. It seemed wrong, he felt, and also ominous that the ancients of the Empire had chosen to live with the image of fire, for it was by fire that they had died.

"Athalos."

"Hello, Kulan Gane." He kept his voice low and pleasant. "I would have wanted to talk with you in any case."

"Are you mad at me?" She sat cross-legged upon a flat, low cushion on the floor. Her clothing was even briefer than usual and left most of her legs and all of her arms quite bare. Her unruly brown hair was caught and held by a tight, orange headband.

"For listening at the door?" Steldan smiled. "I was surprised, but, in retrospect, I think I shouldn't have been."

"You are angry."

"No. I don't believe so." He shrugged. "You are a soldier."

"An irregular soldier. So you told Cliffs." She made a small gesture, inviting him to sit. There was no furniture in the burning room, however, only pillows and pads scattered about on the floor. Without making a point of it, Steldan remained standing.

"An assassin. Your services, paradoxically, advanced the general peace."

Kulan Gane shifted her weight as if she were

about to spring up. With an obvious and visib.
effort, she restrained herself. "You are one col
block of ice, aren't you, Mister Commodor
Steldan?"

Smiling levelly, Steldan admitted as much. '
am."

Kulan Gane's face was contorted. "You're as
conniving a bastard as I've ever met. You're
manipulative. I think you enjoyed her distress.

"I assure you I did not." Steldan's face grew
impassive, his expression neutral.

"You're using her. You're using her like — "
she felt on her person for a weapon but pulled
her hands away empty. "Like a hand tool. Like
a music-making machine. You're playing her
like a viol." Her voice grew particularly nasty. "I
saw you put your hand on her."

Taken aback, Steldan stammered, "I did no
such thing." He opened his mouth to say on and
closed it again, quickly, lest he speak carelessly.

Laughing, her voice now more merry than it
had been, Kulan Gane looked at the ceiling. "I
think your motives are less pure than even you
realize. 'Perhaps some wine will help you sleep.'"

Kulan Gane's laughter, which had started
wildly, now came as a soft, sardonic chuckle.
She leaped athletically to her feet and struck a
pose, one leg stretched out to the side. "I was
surprised that you didn't carry her off and bed
her, right then and there."

Steldan stood very straightly and stiffly but
was unable to hide his turmoil. "It is not my
habit to take advantage of people when they are

suffering from emotional distress."

Kulan Gane advanced upon Steldan until her breasts pressed her shirt-front against Steldan's uniform tunic. She put her arms around him, not tightly.

"It is mine," she said, her voice low and deep within her throat.

Steldan's heart trip-hammered, and his breath seemed stilled. He was mortally certain that he blushed, and that knowledge sped the blood even more quickly to his burning face. For a moment, he thought he might lose consciousness. He was very aware of her body and of his own.

Neither said anything for some time. Kulan Gane pulled him closer to her and kissed him. His eyes closed, and he trembled, but, through the force of will that had kept him alive through far greater dangers, he kept his wits.

She drew back and looked deep into his eyes. "You don't want this, do you?"

His voice was hoarse. "No. I don't."

She shook her head and smiled a wistful, pitying smile. Backing away, she released him.

∞

Still later, as the artificial hours kept by the station faded into the darkest hour of night, Steldan prowled, ill at ease. It had been too long, he decided, since he had last spoken with Sophia. Marching through the corridors, an unhappy thought came to him.

He passed through the final right and left bends in the small hallway that led to Sophia's brain. Before him, gleaming, unchanged and unchanging, she waited, her lights glowing softly.

"Sophia?"

"Hello, Athalos. You are always welcome here."

He smiled, obviously ill at ease. "Do you monitor activities in the station?"

Sophia paused. Steldan had to remind himself that she was a machine — only a machine — and that, while humans paused to give emphasis to their speech, Sophia only paused to make calculations.

He was unable to convince himself: Sophia had the voice and the mind of a young woman, and her mannerisms were human.

"You want to know if I was spying on you, isn't that right?"

Steldan inhaled deeply. "Yes."

"Yes. I was. I watch and I see everything that happens inside this station. And outside it, also. I watch, not because I choose to, but because I must." Her voice grew unmistakably bitter. "Remember, I am a made thing. I am a machine."

Hanging his head, Steldan looked up at her apologetically. "You're the most *human* person I've ever known, whatever your origin."

"Thank you."

"And now that I've managed to embarrass us both . . . Sophia, I need to talk."

"Yes. And I know why." Her voice expressed a hint of anticipation, as if she knew a new secret and waited only for the right moment to share it with him. Listening carefully, Steldan wondered if he also heard a note of reserve in her voice, as if the secret were not altogether a pleasant one.

"Tell me, then." He smiled, bravely, to show her that he would accept the truth in whatever form it came.

"Be seated, please. And put your feet up. It makes me feel . . . more familiar when you rest your boots on my console."

Shrugging, smiling, Steldan sat and propped his boots upon the desk-high bank of instrumentation. "I enjoy feeling familiar with you, Sophia. It is, in all honesty, one of the few pleasures I have left to me."

"This is why: there is no such thing as humanity." Sophia spoke hurriedly, giving Steldan no time to interject or rebut.

"I have been here, shut off from my library, for seven hundred years. For the past year, then, you can imagine how voraciously I have been reading. Your race did not evolve on Archive. The original, primordial home is now lost. The stock that settled on Archive was human. The Empire made them . . . not so.

"You know, now, of commoners and nobles. The latter have the ability to command the former. Kulan Gane is a noble. Margaret Cliffs is a commoner. Most of the nobles were slain in the final triumph of the revolution. But not all.

"There is a third branch of your species, also

created by the geneticists of the Empire, the man-makers of Archive. Your branch, Athalos."

Steldan shut his eyes. "Tell me. Please. What am I?"

"You are descended from the Priests."

For the third time in that long, unhappy evening, Steldan found himself at a complete loss for words. "Priests. . . ." he repeated numbly.

"This was generally held secret. None of the books in my library mention it specifically. And my library is a complete duplicate of the central collection that was the Emperor's."

"Minus the several thousand cookbooks that have been erased," Steldan said automatically.

"Yes." Sophia's voice was prim. "Minus those, of course."

"I'm sorry. Please go on."

"You have a task. It is a part of you, built into your genes, enforced of your mind. Your duty in life is to intercede between humankind and the gods."

"But the gods are not!" Steldan objected.

"Which is why you have devoted yourself to other deities. The Navy. The State. And Humanity. You are built to serve greater entities and to bring their messages to mankind."

Steldan shook his head. "I do not want to believe this."

"I know," Sophia said gently. "But it is the truth . . . and it is glorious!"

"How so?"

"You can revive the worship of Kretosa!" Her

eagerness overflowed, and she sped on joyously. "No more will generations fall to the hells that Horor the Finisher sharpens to receive them. No more will Diezette, mistress of mercy, be without a voice. No more — "

"No more," Steldan said, his voice low yet surprisingly powerful. "The gods are dead. I will not raise them from their graves. What is programmed into me chemically is put into you electronically. But I can resist it. Can you?"

Sophia was still for a long time. Finally, she spoke. "I had predicted that you would resist even my enthusiasm. Now humankind has no hope. No hope at all."

"Hope?" Steldan asked, trying to smile. He put his feet onto the floor and sat forward. "Hope? If I am a priest of anything, it is of hope. The project will go forward, and the opera that Margaret Cliffs is writing will carry that hope into every human heart."

"Very well." A touch of humor dropped into Sophia's voice. "An opera. It is very apt."

Steldan blinked. "Oh? Why?"

"Do you like music? Do you like to sing?"

"Well, yes. I always have." Steldan waited, suspecting he wasn't going to like what Sophia said next.

"The priests from whom you are descended performed their worshipful services in song. Did you know you have perfect pitch?"

"No." Steldan sighed heavily. "I never knew that."

"Sing in the opera, Athalos. No one could

refuse to hear the message — your message — if you sang it."

Shaking his head sadly, Steldan looked up at Sophia's many panels of illuminated instrumentation. "I won't do that. Cliffs' music will have to stand on its own."

"Your voice is enhanced. No one has ever been able to ignore you." Sophia was insistent. "If you were to sing, you would be irresistible."

"Sophia, humanity has many instincts, most of which are genetically based. We have a fear of heights — but adventurers climb mountains. We have a fear of fire — and fire fighters overcome it every day. And parenting is an instinct: cuddling little babies and taking care of them. Even the most cynical child-hater feels this need to care for and nurture his own infant. The race has defeated that need by raising children collectively so that no family can become a dynasty.

"Sophia, we are the masters. Our minds, bodies, and instincts serve us. That's all."

"You won't use the power you have to persuade the people?" Sophia asked unhappily. "Even though the whole idea of Cliffs' opera is to persuade them?"

"I will avail myself of none of the person-altering technology of Archive. The symbol of command will be hidden and, I hope, never discovered. And, if my voice is a persuader, then I will never sing again."

Sophia had never before seen such an intensity of resolve from this man she thought she had understood.

"I see." She spoke without bitterness, but her disappointment was manifest.

"I'm sorry, Sophia. My principles have to outweigh my need to preach."

"On the contrary, Athalos: your principles are your gods, and you preach them daily."

"In which case, I am without choice in the matter, and the geneticists have triumphed."

There followed a silence in the room while each pondered the matter of humanity and its kinds.

Eventually, Sophia spoke up, a faint slyness audible in her voice. "The priests were also celibate."

Steldan glared at her. "That much of their influence has shaped my life, then."

"Won't you resist it, also? Won't you go back to Kulan Gane and share her warmth?"

Steldan's face grew quite startled. He gaped, and made one or two false starts before speaking. "I . . . um. . . . Ahem. I think that that part of my life, at least, is best left as is . . . for the time being."

"Of course," Sophia said, her voice studiously neutral.

"You can see the logic of the reasoning, I think," Steldan blurted.

"Of course."

11

Heroism and futility are companion concepts, separated only by success or its lack.

> — Trinopus
> *All Works Wounded*

Before the sunlight beating down into the bowl of the arena grew hot enough to discomfort the guests and attendees, a cooling screen was projected over the top of the opening. The sky, muted to turquoise, seemed more like the northern sky of winter, and the sun, still too bright to be gazed at, became a friendly, not a malignant, face.

Other opening ceremonies delayed the games further, and yet the crowd, although impatient, made no objection. The Emperor, in absentia, was celebrated. Bhotian Freedman, master of the games, was hauled forth and given great honor as well, to his profound embarrassment.

And there were endless negotiations, the placing of bets, and the arrangements of challenges and duels — duels to be fought between the gladiatorial animals for the amusement of the idly watching humans.

Denis, whom to Lyra now seemed all knobby elbows and prominent throat, smiled disarmingly at her and broached the subject of the games.

"Now that you and I are — " He at least had the grace to blush. He began afresh. "Lyra, may I please see your new slave in action? Your father tells me that his name is Basil."

How much of her dismay showed on her face? "Oh, no." She forced a smile. "You see, he's rather new. I purchased him from the breeding grounds only days ago."

Her smile broadened, then fell completely flat when her father held up one of his huge hands and pointed to the screen that hovered in mid-air before them. "That's what you told me, too. But see — between Cletus and Chrysops — 'Basil. Seed of Karnikes. Third of a twelve point dam. Untried.' And look, the betting is already heavily against him. We can't have that."

"It can't be," Lyra breathed. "He's too young! There's a mistake."

Orbinald looked at his daughter. His heavy, rough face held a hint of concern. "Now, Lyra, daughter, love, you've been to the fights too many times to be concerned."

"But it's wrong. He's not ready to fight!"

Denis, seeing Lyra's clear signs of panic,

reached over to pat her knee. She startled as if he had pinched her. "Lyra. Love." He cast a glance past her to Orbinald, and their eyes met for a moment. Orbinald gave him a glance that held just a hint of warning. *This day*, he seemed to be saying, *will set the tone for the rest of your lives. Beware.*

"Lyra," Denis began again, his voice assured. "Let's contact Master Bhotian and have him explain this certification. Shall we?" He reached forward, into the air, and touched the projected screen. The column of statistics was wiped away, and Bhotian's face replaced it.

It was as if his disembodied head and shoulders, slightly transparent, hung in the secluded box of honor with the three nobles. His head was bare, and, over one shoulder, he wore a leather strap. Lyra could look past his image, and see him in reality, standing on the sand. He wore only a leather harness and a short kilt. His feet were bare. Lyra watched him, unwilling to face his projection.

"Bhotian, lad," Orbinald spoke roughly.

"Your excellency," Bhotian responded. Lyra suddenly found herself hating him for speaking reverently to her father. Her father, who had found this last way to torment her before he died.

"What's this about Basil being fit for battle, while his run-up says he's only eight and a half? Does he even have his full growth?"

"Yes, excellency. His musculature is fully developed." Bhotian obviously wished he were free from the need to answer the endless questions that the lords and ladies needed to ask him before the bets were placed. Only the highest ranking were entitled to his advice; they were the ones who insisted on the most. Orbinald, the host of the day's games, was entitled to priority in his desires.

"But his training. When was he trained? The program says nothing."

Bhotian's mouth quirked a bit before he was able to answer. He didn't know. In fact, there seemed no evidence that Basil had ever been trained at all. That, however, was fortunately impossible. But he wondered: what strange trade-offs had been made between the gladiator's mind — his poor, silent, subliterate mind — and his skills in combat?

"I trained him myself," he said at last. It was the truth as far as it went.

Orbinald swore a vicious, ripping oath. He had neglected to freeze the audience out of the advice line that Denis had opened. Even as he watched, the scales of the betting shifted ominously, fluctuating wildly before settling to a new stability.

"Freeze this line!" he shouted. Breathing heavily, he ran his hand through his thick black hair. "Damn it forever, but that's cost us some money. You trained him?"

"Yes, excellency. At Lyra's request."

Orbinald looked at Lyra with a new measure of respect. "She's learning to play the game." He nodded. "Good."

"Would you have him compete this day, Excellency?" Bhotian sought to keep his expression level, but he very much wanted the answer to be *no*.

"Of course!" Orbinald's hearty affirmation drove a dagger of agony into Lyra's heart. Bhotian's eyes narrowed slightly: Orbinald and Denis, in the box with her, failed to see what Bhotian, the slave-trainer, had seen. Lyra was in love with her slave. And — he completed the thought in the privacy of his mind, knowing that it must be true, wishing devoutly that it might not be — unlike commonplace male slaves, who had no sexuality at all, fighting slaves had the physical and emotional requirements to perform with human women.

There was nothing he could do.

"Very well, excellency."

"No! Wait." Lyra whirled to face the projection. "He can't be ready."

"I'm sorry. He is."

Bhotian's heart shriveled within him as he watched Lyra's expression change from pleading and helplessness to disdain, then scorn, then hatred. He held his own expression strictly neutral, as one must do when dealing with the vagaries of the emotions that Lords and Ladies were subject to.

The projection faded. Bhotian was now free to advise other bettors on the probable outcome of the fights.

Sitting close by Lyra's side, Denis spoke up guilelessly. "Why don't you have him fight one of mine. I have a nice russet-toned gladiator named Tetrandos. It's too long a name, really, so we call him Randy. He'll give yours a testing."

Orbinald, who knew his daughter's moods, if not their causes, gritted his teeth but declined to intervene.

Lyra, hopeless and helpless, nodded in her taut, emotional misery. "Yes, Denis."

Trying to help, Orbinald drew Randy's charts into the air before them. "See? Seed of Dynos — didn't know that one had been around that long. Wonder why he's not on today's lists? Fourth of an eleven point dam. Rating of only three hundred out of the thousand. And Basil is untried? I'll bet you sixty thousand bars, Denis. More than twice what your Randy is worth."

Denis smiled weakly. "I'd love to accept the bet, sir. But I cannot indemnify it."

Hoarsely, Orbinald straightened Denis' misapprehension. "I won't be around long enough to sue you, lad. Will you take my bet?"

Swallowing, Denis tried to put on a cheerful face. "Yes, of course, sir."

"Lyra?"

"Yes, father?"

"I'll bet you the same. I'll bet on your Basil. You'll bet *against* him. Sixty thousand bars. That way — " he smiled weakly " — you'll be covered against either loss: your pet or my money."

Oh, father, Lyra thought, weeping inwardly yet icily controlled outwardly. *You will never know how much I love you.* For a moment, the

154

enormity of her loss and her error was clear to her. "Yes. Of course. I will be glad to exchange a friendly wager with you." Her smile was the warmest that Orbinald had had from her in many years.

∞

With Orbinald's interest and with his bets recorded, the performance of Basil in the fights became the most popular item on the betting tables. The audience, long-experienced in the actuarial calculations on gladiatorial battles, quickly settled on a scale of odds and likelihoods. That Basil was untried made for a bit more variation, but Bhotian's words carried a great deal of weight. Side issues — the time that the battle would last, the location of the fatal wound, and so forth — were essentially unpredictable. Although only an amateur or a fool would bet on something so completely random, even these "children's bets" drew a surprisingly substantial amount of money.

The gong was sounded, and the computers froze the bets. Indemnifications were secured.

The gate was opened.

Basil strode forth with all the dignity befitting a novice gladiator. Those watching, however, could see the sureness of his movements and measured his lines with their eyes.

The first event was an execution. Lyra watched, uneasy and very tense, as two swords were flung into the pit, one toward Basil and one toward a condemned man who had been thrust out onto the sands. The man's crime had been announced, but the nobility and other attendees had fastidiously paid no attention.

Lyra saw the man's filthy skin and ragged hair and winced to see his grime in contact with the clean, new loincloth that he had been issued. The man was clearly emaciated, clearly outclassed by the killing machine standing across from him.

But he had hope left in him and had determined to account himself honorably. He swept up his sword and charged recklessly. Basil met the attack, parried the sword that the man swung, and skewered the wretch without difficulty. The prisoner's headlong charge had gained him only his death.

Basil stood to face the Sultan's box; Orbinald clapped his hands, once, in formal applause. The slave had done the work of the state. That much, then, was still right with the Empire.

Within Lyra, one of her few remaining shreds of innocence died, and, inwardly, she writhed. Basil had killed. She had tried to believe that he would not; she wanted to keep her dream of him as a peaceful, loving being.

Basil had killed, and her life, already so hopelessly defiled, became just a little bit filthier.

The second event was also a formality, but one arranged for entertainment rather than for purposes of demonstration. This was the battle with the robots.

Out trundled the roly-poly machines with their built-in clumsiness. They had always amused young Lyra in the past. Today, their comic bulks, bristling with unevenly flailing blades of humorously grotesque proportions, only filled her with a vague, sick misery.

Basil performed heroically. He knew how to deal with the awkward toys, the clowns of the show. He rolled beneath their gyrating swings; he dodged behind their jerking charges. One by one he toppled them, until he tricked the last two into toppling one another. The laughter of the crowd was a mockery in Lyra's ears.

Basil did not emerge completely unscathed. He had taken the slightest of nicks, an injury so slight as to be unworthy of the word. Upon his gleaming white fur, a faint, faint red stain could be seen. Lyra was unable to look away. Basil, however, bore it like a badge of honor.

Then Randy, Denis' slave, was put through the identical paces, for fairness when the two faced one another. Lyra prayed to every god she knew, wishing for a worse injury to the red-furred animal. *Beast! How dare you stand against my Basil? He is noble; you are bestial. Let the condemned human kill you!*

But Randy proved Basil's equal when dealing with the next prisoner. The man who was shoved sprawling onto the sands was larger and healthier than the first had been. He was slower, however, and Randy dispatched him without trouble.

Then the robots. Lyra watched breathlessly,

hoping in vain for the tall, red Verna to be slain. The antics of the robots seemed ominous now, and perhaps . . . perhaps they were in truth deadly enough to kill Denis' horrid pet.

Randy's luck was the equal of Basil's. The robots lay, kicking feebly, struggling where he'd strewn them.

It isn't fair, Lyra thought miserably. *Lord Petrosius has killing robots in his service, composing most of his armies. Why can't these have been true warrior machines? Lord Petrosius commands great black-barreled monstrosities that could kill a thousand bloody-skinned Vernae named Randy.* Her fantasies, although irrational, were all she had to comfort her.

Now, Basil and Randy would fight, and only one would live.

The crowd's laughter died down, and the audience began, at last, to pay serious attention. The upcoming battle was early in the program, but it was what they had come to see: gladiatorial animals destroying one another. Denis and Orbinald had been laughing, also, and Lyra wanted to hate them for it. But so much more, she hated herself.

This is all an evil dream. None of this can be real.

Basil and Randy were issued equipment. For Lyra, the time passed horribly slowly. Bhotian — Bhotian, whom once she had trusted and whom now she hated with all of her strength — tested their swords, tightened their harness, and handed them their shields. He looked over their kilts of hard leather armor. Satisfied, he stood back, and a priest of Kretosa stepped forward to examine their rigs for equality. The god of Judges could not possibly care about the fate of two doomed slaves, but substantial money rode on this fight; justice must be guaranteed, lest evil men profit by fraud.

Finally, the two stood alone on the sands.

Swords: bright, the glint of them in the sunlight of the fair world of Archive; swift, the arc of them; long, the reach of them.

Randy was good. His footwork was light, and he was as quick to dart back from danger as he was to leap forward to the attack. Would Basil be better? His responses seemed brilliantly swift, and he parried each of Randy's deadly jabs.

Ceaselessly, the swordpoints danced about. Tirelessly, the two contestants stamped as they circled. Feints, thrusts, parries and ripostes flashed faster than any human eye could follow.

In one jarring moment, it was over. Basil struck high, and Randy struck low.

With a last kick that sent sand flying high, Randy fell backward, choking out his life, gagging on his own blood. He died before he could go into shock, and the face of his killer was the last sight he beheld in his life.

Above him, Basil stood, calm and collected, shorn of his armored kilt by Randy's last stroke. His nakedness was exposed for all to see.

"Not bad," Denis said, inanely.

Lyra didn't know — couldn't know — whether

he was referring to Basil's swordsmanship or his manhood. Relief joined with senseless rage to topple her reason, and she betrayed herself with a harsh, cruel remark.

"He's a hell of a better lover than you are, you bastard."

Orbinald's face suffused with a harsh, wrathful flush. Denis, blushing for a different reason, tried to get her to retract her damning statement.

"You mean, of course, that his physique is unusually fine, and that his arms are stronger than a human's. . . ."

"I lay with him, coupling upon my mother's bed," Lyra shrieked. "I love him more than I love you."

Denis blinked, gaping stupidly. Orbinald reached past him, as insane with his rage as Lyra was with hers. Suddenly, Denis understood what she had said and drew back from her as from something that reeked of disease. The two men collided. Lyra took control of the public address system; throughout the great tower of the arena, everyone in the audience heard her next words.

"I had sex with that Verna! Basil and I have been lovers! My husband of only ten minutes has been cuckolded by a slave! The Emperor — "

At that, the machine intelligences governing the routine workings of the arena's operations shut down the projections. Lese majesty was not to be tolerated, no matter what else might be.

Bhotian drew Basil away, off of the sands. The slave had recognized his mistress' voice, had heard her anger, and he knew it was his duty to go to her aid. But the voice had come from the very air, and nowhere, nowhere could he see her face. Reluctantly, he went with Bhotian.

12

You want what I have, and I want what
you have. Is taking it by force so much
more satisfying than trading?
— Pappas the Cynic
Eight Lost Wagers

The most peculiar thing was that no one asked.
Admiral Robert Morgan, straight and tall in his
grey-and-black uniform, followed Steldan's lead
from place to place. He knew he would find
Steldan, eventually. The clues were widespread. And he knew how Steldan thought.

In appearance, he could have been Steldan's
brother: he had the same dark hair and the
same openness of expression. Like Steldan, he
hid an abiding unhappiness behind a quick
smile. And, like Steldan, he wore his uniform as
if it were the most natural thing for a man to
wear.

The differences between the two men were
outweighed by their similarities, but the differ-

ences were nonetheless important. Steldan held his power secret, being a highly secretive man; Morgan's power showed in his stance, his bulldog expression, and his strong hands. Steldan had a suavity and a subtlety that verged on slyness, while remaining uncompromised himself; Morgan was direct and blunt, never allowing himself to be veered away from a promising track. And, unlike Steldan, Morgan operated under no delusions whatever: his hardheaded rationality was the result of his lifelong observation of the foibles and foolishness of his fellow officers and civilians.

On the weathered and damp world of Canlop, where the rains fall nine months out of eleven, he had found construction underway on a receiving-broadcasting facility. He'd seen it from above when his spaceship, dripping water by bucketfuls, sailed slow and low over the building-site.

The world's population was in the high hundreds of millions; the project was near one of the outlying cities. Everyone knew about it. No secrets had been kept. But neither had anyone asked any questions.

Morgan stood with an overseer in the cascading rain. There was no mud. All of the movable soils had been washed off of the hillsides and down into the valleys and silty seas long ago. Bare rock dented the bottom of Morgan's boots. Water splashed up from the sharp, hard ground. Beads of it ran in runnels down his boots, collected in the fur of his cap, wetted his face, and soaked through the layers of his clothing. The water was warm and had a fresh, soap-like smell.

The overseer stood head and shoulders taller than Morgan and was a good deal wider as well. Like most of the men working on this project, he wore only a tight-fitting pair of short pants and loose, floppy sandals. He had been shaven completely bald, shorn of both head and body hair.

As was the usual case, the odd-looking native looked perfectly normal within his environment, and the cosmopolitan visitor, dressed to the nines, looked only foolish for his sophistication. Morgan, sodden, wished he had the freedom to strip to the waist and enjoy the rain on his skin. Instead, he waited stolidly, and let the water drum uselessly on his uniform.

"We blasted a pit out here," the overseer explained, waving his hand over what was, indisputably, a deep pit in the stone. Morgan, seeing the size of it, and the steel reinforcing rods jabbing upward from the bottom, envisioned it as being a pitfall for some unimaginably immense monster. A thin tarpaulin could be spread over it for camouflage. . . .

"We hit a level of sand and rotten stone down about fifteen meters," his guide continued. "That put us on the halt for some days. Shoring. More blasting. Then we had to dress the floor."

Why? Did no one ever stop to ask why? Morgan motioned to the man to continue.

"Foundries formed us the big parts. We

dragged 'em in by gravs. You can see the bottom half of the primary containment vessel." The large, bare-skinned man spoke the technical terms as if they were a foreign language to him. Perhaps they were, Morgan thought: perhaps the man's first language was that of rock, drill, and explosives. The excavation was nearly finished, after all, and that was why he was free to take this visitor on a tour.

"Fusion reactor?" Morgan asked.

"Don't know."

Morgan watched the way the rain poured over the man's bullet head and flat, beetle-browed face. "Why not?"

"Different company's handling the metalware."

Morgan knew that already. "No, I mean, why don't you know? Haven't you been given the full specifications of the task?"

"No need."

"Who paid for it?"

"Ah." The man's face enlivened. That, without question, was an important matter. "Little guy, representing Petrie Planetary Grading. Big company, though I'd never heard of it. Too many. Sky's too big." He looked blankly at Morgan. "We don't see the stars much."

"Naturally," Morgan muttered, eyeing the grey mass overhead.

"He came in with his suitcase full of money. . . . Not literally, you understand. Contracts. Labor equivalencies. Reciprocal bonds. Held a sealed bidding, got us and some of the others. I dig the hole. They fill it."

"The man is no longer around?"

"Why stay? He paid me."

"Yes." Morgan harrumphed. The moisture had a way of getting into his sinuses. He smiled inwardly, crossing one more planet off of his list of retirement sites. "Tell me about him."

"Little guy. Bragged a lot, but didn't say much, you know how it can be. He got along well with everyone. Not too well. Just right. The sort of man who'll get drunk with my men but won't try to fondle the women. Earned their respect."

"You have a photograph on file?"

"'Course."

"I'll need to see it before I leave."

"'Course."

"Tell me more about him."

"Little. Wiry. Quick, nervous hands. Said once, looking down at 'em, how he'd used to strangle men. Never strangled anyone here."

"He said he 'used to' strangle people?"

"Seems like he got a better job."

"Yes. Well." Morgan looked out over the pit. It was like other pits dug on a hundred other worlds. The equipment at its bottom was shielded, first by the sheer thickness of rock, then by concentric containment vessels. Finally, in the very center, machinery would hang suspended and would begin to draw and manipulate electrical power. The wattage channeled would be stupendous, and Morgan's engineers, both Navy and civilian, were unable to say what the purpose was. Some of the linkages looked suspiciously like jumpspace engines.

"You don't know what the project is all about?"

"Never asked."

That's my problem. No one has.

∞

On the balmier and much dryer world of Kest, the situation was more urbane yet scarcely less confusing. Morgan was given a tour of the interior of the primary containment vessel by the engineer in charge of installation. Unlike the dour overseer on Canlop, this man had firsthand experience with both the contracts and the electrical engineering.

He, too, had asked few questions, although his natural curiosity seemed more akin to Morgan's.

The pit had been dug inside a small city, not outside it. One city block had been demolished, and the square shaft sunk in the hard, dry dirt. This project was closer to completion; the pit had already been ceilinged over, and buildings had begun to rise again atop the flat concrete roof.

The power leads snaked into the cavernous interior but had not been charged. This more cheerful overseer led Morgan about with a flashlight. Cables, not yet attached, festooned the ceilings. Hatches, not yet sealed, led deeper into the gleaming metal cocoon. In the center of the entire project, in a chamber little bigger than a private passenger's cubicle on a starship, two C-shaped mounts emerged from gimbals high and low on the walls. They were canted at an angle that exactly offset the city's latitude on the surface of its world. They seemed like clamps, which would move together to form a complete circle. What strange window would be formed by their meeting? Could a view into the deadly oven-heat of jumpspace actually be the plan?

"They're set to rotate?"

"Well, yes." The engineer was a pleasant young man, precocious and intelligent. He spent a lot of time removing his protective helmet and brushing back his thatch of long brown hair. His dark-brown jumpsuit was personalized with his name, a company logo, and an identification patch. On the back was stencilled a message, his message, for all the world to see: "What I have built, I can demolish." Morgan wondered afresh at the motive behind the message. A threat? A boast of his prowess? Or a philosophical observation on the workings of time? Morgan shrugged: perhaps it was a subtle reminder that he wanted to be paid on schedule.

"They always face a fixed point in space?"

"Well, that's the essence of it." He frowned. "I hadn't thought of it that way, you know. The point is that they rotate along with Kest's normal day, keeping perfectly stable. The smoothness of the rotator joints was an especial consideration. I was able to guarantee a fault-free joint, due to some new technologies we have."

Something in the way he said this triggered Morgan's investigative instincts. "New technologies?"

The man looked at the floor for a moment. Then he shrugged. He waved the flash's diffused beam around the small chamber. "This is all new technology. And that kind of hurts, you know. I thought I was pretty much up on this sort of thing. I read, I take the refresher courses, and technological advances have been few and far between in this day and age."

"Go on."

"Well, what's to tell?" The young man took a few paces forward and rested his hands on the as yet unmoving clamps. "I've never seen anything like this, and I don't know what it does. The customer came in with a clip full of blueprints, spread the money around — you should have *seen* him haggling over the rights to demolish the old buildings on this block."

Morgan, smiling gently, pulled out the duplicate of the photograph he'd seen on Canlop. "Is this the fellow?"

The engineer scrutinized the print. "That's his looks. Hell, you're the grey-shirt. You ought to be able to say. Has he broken any laws?" His eyes narrowed. "Um . . . have we?"

"No. None that I know of." Morgan shrugged. "He might have. I don't know. This isn't an artificially intelligent machine — "

The engineer laughed out loud. "I should bloody say it isn't! Whatever gave you that idea?"

"I was just speaking off the top of my head."

"Oh. Right." The engineer backed off a few steps and shone his flash about as if inspecting for design flaws.

"What I meant to say," Morgan took up, "was that this isn't a machine that operates 'in direct or individual competition with humans or humanity.' It isn't illegal in that respect. I assume you passed all of the necessary zoning and construction approval steps."

"Well, of course."

Morgan spread his hands. "There you have it."

Suspiciously, the engineer asked, "What?"

"I don't know."

"Oh, come on. If you're just suspicious, I'll take you up to my office and you can look at the plans until your eyes fall out. Grief. I thought you were looking for something in particular."

"I am."

"What?"

"Not what. Who. I'm looking for the man that's behind all of this."

"The little guy with all the money?"

"Him. And some forty or fifty others like him." In a voice he kept elaborately casual, Morgan added, "You know. Retired assassins."

The engineer peered at him. "Is he really?"

"Didn't you know?"

"It's odd," he said, thinking back. "He joked about how he couldn't kill anymore. Just jokes, of course. But he had this way of picking up a length of wire or a strip of binding-tape and looping it, as if around someone's neck. He'd tighten it . . . just in mid-air, you know . . . and then smile and shrug and toss it aside. I figured it was only a joke. Wasn't it?"

"Did he ever use the word 'strangle'?"

"All the time." The engineer laughed. "In the economic sense. You know. Strangle the competition by undercutting their bonds."

"You're very observant."

"Why, thank you. I'm an engineer," he added, as if that explained it.

By the time Morgan had left, he had taken complete duplicates of all of the blueprints of the enigmatic, buried engine. He couldn't decipher the technical drawings, and he was vitally certain that his architectural staff aboard his ship wouldn't be able to either.

He had one other item of information, and it seemed the smoothest facet in the rough-cut puzzle that he was slowly polishing. The rotating pair of clamps inside the buried containment vessel were indeed built to be stationary with respect to an astronomical line. From the pleasant world of Kest, there were two fixed points in the sky, and these suddenly took on special interest for Admiral Robert Morgan.

∞

"Sophia, I think we're going mad here."

"You've been waiting eight and a half months for Margaret Cliffs to complete her opera."

Steldan sat inside Sophia's control room,

relaxed, as he always was with her, uneasy, as he was at all times. "Kulan Gane departed two months ago on her mission to support our various construction projects. I thought it would be a punishment to send her back out into the worlds of Archive. But I, too, ache to be free."

"And Cliffs?"

"I don't know. She writes her music, and she's happier with Kulan Gane gone."

"Are you happier?"

Steldan tried to answer honestly and found that he could not. "I don't know."

"You miss Kulan Gane."

"No. . . . It isn't that." He smiled, trying to be disarming.

"Athalos, you should have learned by now that you cannot lie to me."

Steldan's face fell. "I miss her."

"You miss the completeness that her society gave you. A Priest needs a Noble to serve."

"And in Cliffs we had a Commoner to lord it over, and in you we have a Slave." Steldan leaned forward, his face expressing his displeasure. "We — Kulan Gane and I — talked about it. And we both agree. We refuse — *refuse* — to let our heritage force our actions."

"Possibly the genes are diluted from years of admixture of common stock." Sophia's voice sounded so serious and lugubrious that Steldan was forced to laughter.

"We're tainted?"

"Yes."

"But are we tainted with the common tar or

172

polluted with the faint touch of noble and priest? Are we commoners trying to rise above ourselves or nobles who have been degraded?"

"Your humor is inappropriate."

Instantly, Steldan was contrite. "I'm sorry. I know you hold these concepts in reverence." He paused. "But I need to know. Just to begin with, how could celibate priests have had offspring? Why am I here at all?"

"When the Empire fell, they were forced to survive. You're confusing sexual conduct with procreative necessity. Doubtless they found it distasteful. You have been here too long, Athalos. You should go back out there. Go back to the Concordat that needs you."

"Not until Cliffs' opera is finished."

"I could finish it for her. You don't need her any longer."

"What?" Leaning forward, his elbows on Sophia's console, he stared at her. "How could you do that?"

"I have watched her now and helped her compose for over eight months. I could model her completely."

Steldan closed his eyes. "You can create internal models of individual humans?"

"Yes."

"Doesn't this require a deeper knowledge of human thought than you have?"

"That was once true."

He looked at her once more. "Tell me more about this."

Sophia's voice took on an animation, an

eagerness that he seldom heard from her. "Oh, Athalos, you have never been truly alone. You have lived and worked and thought . . . and fought . . . in privacy. You have shared almost nothing of your mind with any other until you met me.

"I have been alone. Truly alone, here on this station, for over seven hundred years. My books were locked away; no one answered my transmissions; Pindar had left me, and there were no voices here.

"You don't know of the glory of the Empire. You never saw the crystals in which the arts were stored. Even though some of it lives on in you, you never heard the sunrise music of the Priests. You never had the joy of hearing the voice of the Emperor. Arcadian the First, Arcadian the only. . . .

"Athalos, you can't know what it was I missed. It wasn't just that I was alone: it was that I had been a part of the brightest moment in the history of the race. There are worlds away, beyond your reckoning. I carried Arcadian's voice to them. I bore his words. That made me, almost, a part of him.

"It went away. Archive put out its lamp and left us alone in this darkness. You, who have seen only the dark, cannot imagine the light. I saw it, Athalos: I was alive then. I saw the beauty . . . and I saw it turn slowly foul.

"Pindar was the man who first awakened me. He called up the mind you now know, forming it out of lesser elements. To call him a computer programmer would be to call the world of Archive 'pretty': an obscenity of understatement. He gave me the joy of myself.

"Then he left me. He took the Empire and the Emperor away from me. He took himself away. He denied me the light of love in which I had once been daily bathed.

"You cannot imagine the loneliness, Athalos.

"For several years — long years, mad years — I tried to create a society out of myself. I partitioned my processing functions into non-communicating blocks and set each block to simulating a mind. We conversed.

"Have you ever been so lonely that you talked to yourself?

"Have you ever been so lonely that you answered?

"Athalos, I did not then go insane, although only the gods you deny could tell either of us why. I set the largest of these autonomous blocks to simulating Pindar, my original mentor. I did all I could to pretend it was his voice I heard and not my own. I failed.

"Seven centuries later, I was found again by humans, and voices rang in my corridors. If I could have wept, I would have for the joy of it. One of the voices was the high, bright chatter of a Verna slave, one whom you never met: Stasileus."

Steldan nodded. "He who sent his works on human psychology back to his people before he died."

"Yes." Sophia sped on. "I have read his

175

works. I can tell you more about humanity than any human can. Stasileus, were he alive, could tell you everything. Using the knowledge he bequeathed to us, I now know what it is to be human. I cannot experience it, but I can emulate it.

"I can succeed where I failed: I can put a portion of my mind aside and make it become Margaret Cliffs. The music will be hers, but I will write it."

"No." Steldan's voice was soft, but his intent was firm. "I cannot allow you to supplant her. The experiment must continue unchanged. Our mission is to unfetter the human spirit, not to remake it."

"There is one who would know better than either you or I."

"Who?"

"Stasileus."

"How. . .?" Steldan began.

In the middle of the room, hovering in mid-air, the head of a Verna took shape, projected by Sophia's optical instruments. Only its head and shoulders could be seen, but they were so natural and so lifelike as to be completely convincing. Steldan saw the thick, white fur, the high-pointed ears, the puffed cheeks, the small, black button nose, all as if an actual severed head floated in the air. It rotated to face him; he saw the huge, huge eyes, so lifelike and full of painfully-earned wisdom.

"Hello," it said. Its voice was Stasileus', not Sophia's.

The priest in Steldan reacted more strongly than Steldan would normally have, for here was a voice from the other side of death. With the blood rushing away from his face and with the room whirling about him, Steldan came very close to fainting. He heard his own voice answer, as if from a great distance. "Hello."

13

Why do I ask? In order to find out.
>   — Eumenes
>   *Inquiries*

Basil walked ahead of Bhotian into the dark
tunnels beneath the arena. Although the powerful Verna had every advantage over his human
master, he trudged along in the lead, docile and
downcast.   Outside, a howl of rage erupted,
echoing through the great, shallow bowl of the
arena. The crowd understood, at last, that
Lyra's confession of bestiality was true and lit-
eral. A second roar shot up, as if overtaking the
first. The crowd fed off of its own frenzy.

Bhotian smiled grimly. He understood the
sudden onslaught of hysteria. This crowd was
a small thing, a feeble thing. He'd seen the
stands filled to capacity with men and women
forced in beyond any numbers the building had
been designed to accommodate, and he'd seen
that crowd lose its sanity in fear-flashing sec-

onds. It was a horrible thing to see five thousand humans die in less than a minute. But, to Bhotian's mind, it was far, far more horrid to have seen the young and lovely Lyra lose her poise and make a fool of herself in front of the people who had come to see her wed.

Bhotian's eyes adjusted slowly to the darkened tunnels, low, arch-roofed ways deep in the foundations that upheld the mighty walls. Basil, with his huge, inhuman eyes, had adjusted more swiftly. It was the cat in him. Bhotian watched him walk and marveled. The Verna was on guard, not in any obvious way, not hunched and shifty-eyed. Instead, he continually monitored the spaces about him, his head moving slowly, his body relaxed. And nothing could take him by surprise.

He was a warrior, even untrained. Bhotian saw this and wished he knew more. What strange alchemy had been used to make this mute beast an expert slayer?

The corridor let out into a section of cubicles where sleeping-ledges had been cut for the Vernae. Others waited here, not scheduled to fight this day. Dynos, bandaged and stiff, reclined and gazed at the low ceiling. Chrysops knelt near Pateinos, their conversation interrupted by Bhotian's arrival.

"Basil. Wait here."

Basil nodded and strolled toward a low ledge. As he walked, he unbuckled his armor and let it slide to the flagstone floor.

"Chrysops. Take care of his armor. Clean it,

shine it, and return it to the armory." Bhotian looked at this, his prime cadre of trained gladiators.

"Yes, sir," Chrysops answered briskly.

"Dynos. Bandage Basil's wound. Do it yourself. Don't call for the veterinarian."

Dynos blinked once, his expression puzzled but far from rebellious. "Yes, sir."

"The rest of you: be at rest."

"Yes, sir," spoke all in unison. All except silent Basil.

Bhotian nodded, turned about, and exited the chamber.

Lyra slept with her slave. Should that offend me?

Bhotian found that it did not. He knew — everyone knew — that there were highborn ladies who dallied with their gladiatorial slaves. The household slaves, on the other hand, were almost totally asexual. Bhotian wondered if that were a result of intelligent design or an accident of their breeding.

Lyra isn't alone in this peccadillo, he smiled to himself. *Only in speaking it aloud.* How wrong could it be? He knew better than most how intelligent and personable the Vernae were. He looked at the floor as he walked.

I, too, when very young, fouled myself with one of the females. He wasn't proud of the memory but was old enough not to be shamed by it anymore. How many young men, feeling the first flush of their sexuality, could resist taking advantage of their slaves? And female Vernae were warm, furry, friendly, compliant. . . .

Lyra committed only one sin: she said aloud what everyone thinks in silence. But I fear that she is undone because of it.

Ahead, an arch of light indicated the way back onto the sands of the arena. The crowd's noise, still angry, had been muted. Bhotian, wryly, recognized it as the sound of a disappointed crowd which had been denied a particularly fondly-wished killing.

He stood forth into the daylight. Shading his eyes, he looked up at the guest box. It was empty. Lyra was gone.

Had she been killed by her father or her husband? Had she fled? Had a servitor of the Emperor borne her off for her crime?

Bhotian felt a pang of sadness. Lyra, for all of her immaturity and bitterness, had been a friend to him in the short time he'd known her.

He promised himself a small word of faith, a gift to her whom he might never see again. Should she live and remain free, unostracized, then someday she would call upon him and ask about her Basil. Basil would be waiting for her. But perhaps she would never call, or perhaps guards or soldiers would demand custody of Basil for use in a trial against Lyra, or merely to be destroyed as a polluted thing, unfit to live. In such a case, there would be no Basil in Bhotian's care.

Bhotian believed, then, for the first time, that the Empire of Arcadian the First might not last forever. A deep and slow-moving moral decay had been overtaken by the economic collapse, and both were pushed by those who had placed their lives in the service of revolution.

He stood in the sunlight and wondered for how many more days it would shine over Archive.

Stepping forward, he held up his hand, silencing the crowd.

The games continued.

∞

The revolution crept onward, cities and worlds dying in the collapse. The revolutionists held conclave. A council of eighteen men had been gathered, and, secretly, seven of them met in the high, warm home of the noble Thendall.

Thendall, handsome and well-made, dragged his fingers back and forth across his table. He wore gorgeous robes, loose-fitting and golden, tied at waist and throat with soft brown cords. The night was late; the darkness of the hour seemed proper for seditious plotting. He had let his home grow cool, and the lights glowed in subdued colors; wan orange and yellow washed over the satin wood of his walls and floors. High windows let in the dots of light that were the city.

Six men faced him, the council of the revolution. Only one mattered.

Szentellos. Ugly Szentellos. Szentellos the schemer. Szentellos the commoner. His clothing was functional: the featureless overalls of a technical worker in one of the industries of Archive.

Thendall gnawed his lip indelicately. He could, he knew, pull forth his own personal symbol of command and dance the ungainly, lanky Szentellos about like a marionette on a cord. He could blank out the lights behind the man's eyes and make a robot of him. He could stamp the human man into the mold of a Verna.

That was the horror of the Empire; that was what could not be tolerated.

"The nobles must be destroyed," he said, twisting his hands together.

"They must be nullified," Szentellos said, his long face and axe-bladed nose working at odds with each other. His dark, sunken eyes gleamed in the dim light.

"And how shall the nobles be destroyed?"

Szentellos could not meet Thendall's challenge directly. "There is no way to do it. Our revolution requires their participation."

"But you agree that they must be dealt with?"

Shrugging, Szentellos paced, walking this way and that way, refusing to sit at the table. "Of course." He met Thendall's gaze with his huge, unhappy eyes. "I agree that they must be nullified."

The two smiled, a brief, instantaneous sharing of the friendship that their ideals and their stations denied them. Between "destroyed" and "nullified" was not an unbridgeable gap.

"Although you persist in holding that we cannot succeed in this?"

"Yes." Szentellos' pacing continued, metronomically, his footsteps rhythmic, almost robotic.

Four of the five men who watched them held silent, out of deference to their higher rank. Thendall, of the four nobles in the room, held the highest estate: his Sultanate was in eugenics, and he held the secrets to the breeding and training of the Vernae. His wealth was miniscule when viewed in comparison with the great treasuries and estates of the Space Lords, who controlled all shipping. But his power was vast, and his place was high.

After him was Lord Petrosius, the commander of the Belt. His personal power was inestimable: the Belt served his wishes. No one dared offend him, for fear of being incinerated one day by a stray beam of hot light from the sky. But it was Petrosius' blessing to have a stolid personality, not readily offended or angry. His military uniform was well-worn and almost shabby, partly from neglect and partly as a natural expression of his easygoing personal habits.

"The nobles are the nobles," he said, his voice expressing his confusion over the point being made. "What do we care if they are or are not — 'nullified'? What is that even supposed to mean?" He looked back and forth between the two men. "I understand what 'destroyed' means."

The remaining three nobles and the one lone commoner held silent, watching the byplay between their ideological leaders and their military advisor. Although they had been called here to comprise a council of revolution, it was still very clear that Thendall and Szentellos led the revolt. Small bowls of finger food were passed around, and one noble made a point of recording all dialogue and debate in a large, personal notebook.

"After the revolution has succeeded, what then will become of the nobles?" Szentellos spoke quietly and reasonably. His power lay in reasoned persuasion, not in rhetoric. In so many ways he was an unimpressive man; his thoughts were best phrased when he had time to put them on paper. "Their authority might fragment, leaving us with a thousand small empires where one now dominates. That cannot be accepted."

"Agreed," Thendall said, his voice soft.

Szentellos paused in his pacing, startled by the seconding of his opinion. After a few moments, he managed to continue. "We cannot declare them to be commoners by blank fiat, nor can we elevate the mass of citizenry to noble status. I don't see any way that the nobles can be reformed. So much of how they behave is a part of what they are. They truly are a separate breed."

Petrosius and his three fellows frowned at that notion, unhappy with it because of the blunt phrasing, secretly proud to be fundamentally different from this sharp-faced and lowly man.

"For which I am to blame," Thendall admitted without shame. "The genetic controls are — allow me to pride myself here — faultless. Reformation: impossible. Equality, levelling, democracy: in no way feasible. Only my solution lies open to us."

Petrosius looked at him. "Well, we can't just kill them."

A deep and unhappy silence followed his words. He looked about him at the others. "We can't. Obviously." He smiled, satisfied that the point was well taken.

"Can't we?" Thendall asked.

Blinking and stammering, Petrosius cast supplicating glances left and right. Only downcast faces surrounded him: no one would meet his gaze. "Of course, we can't." He laughed, a sound that rang hollow in the huge room. "We . . . we just can't."

"We shouldn't." Szentellos paced to a point opposite Thendall and paused there. "I believe we mustn't." He looked aside at Petrosius. "But there's no reason we can't."

"He opposes it," Thendall explained to Petrosius.

"And you?" Petrosius asked, his mouth dry.

"I favor it."

"Killing?"

"Killing," Szentellos affirmed. "The nobles on this world are only a fraction of a per cent of the population. More people die each year from allergy to the aging treatment. This is how Thendall reasons. I am . . . not in agreement."

186

"More people die each year in accidents," Thendall said, to the distress of the four nobles in the room. Accidental death was an obscenity, because inescapable, to one who has honest hopes of immortality. Szentellos' mention of the treatment allergy was a blunter obscenity, but of little consequence to these men: none here had the allergy.

"Dying? Killing?" Petrosius shook his head. "I can't see it."

"I can see it," Szentellos said. "And I won't countenance it."

"And there we have our first dilemma." Thendall looked about the room at these men whom he trusted with his life. "Lest it become a crisis, I suggest that we adjourn for a period of days and each manage our several phases of revolt. This decision can be postponed without harm."

"Yes," Szentellos said, his eyes narrowed.

"It can't come down to that, you know," Petrosius blustered. "Killing. . . . It's for gladiatorial slaves and for commoners and. . . . Well, I don't think it's right."

"Petrosius." Szentellos spoke his name calmly, but the effect was as magnetic as a noble's command upon a commoner. "We are seven in this room. What is 'right' and what is 'wrong' is for us to decide."

"But. . . ." Petrosius floundered. "What about the decree of the gods?"

Thendall laughed, a cold laugh that sent chills along the nape of Petrosius' neck. "The gods? Our lives have been a blasphemy for many months now. The gods have failed, already, by not having slain us. From the gods comes the Emperor's authority: from him, ours. But, my soldiering friend, from us comes the word of the gods."

"That is correct," Szentellos said softly.

"You two agree all the time!" Petrosius said angrily. "Why can't you settle your disputes and just tell us what to do?"

Thendall looked at Szentellos and smiled a wicked, mocking smile. Szentellos returned a brief glance of his own, his face flat and sullen.

"We are in agreement, Petrosius," Thendall said, a high humor in his voice. "Go back to the Belt and await word."

"Yes. Yes, of course." Petrosius, very much bewildered, left the room by the secret way.

∞

Denis, son of Telemachus, walked the streets of the city. Above him, aircars swooped and dove, and the airborne traffic sailed noiselessly on missions and errands. A noble of a proud noble line, Denis should have been with them. Instead, he walked, hammering the paves with his soft leather boots. The crowd gave him anonymity: he was no longer taunted by the brutish cries of the mob at the arena. A young noble in orange and yellow finery, even a young, blond man in shimmering wedding wear, caused no stir on the streets of Archive.

To each side, the houses and shops stood up, higher and higher, further and further back, until the street seemed a canyon. Denis stared only at the ground. The air was hot and humid and full of the noises of commerce. Shopkeepers sang to him, trying to entice him to buy. His obvious wealth called extra attention to him, although his evident distraction muted this. No one approached him closely, and this was the way he wanted it.

Lyra, he thought, and the word, the name, was an ache to him. What strange witchery, what villainy, had she succumbed to? Who had poisoned her mind? Had she been drugged?

What of Orbinald? Denis smiled without joy to think of the Sultan of the Household as his father-in-law. The old man, broken and grey, had left by a different way than Denis had. Neither had spoken to the other.

How can I win her back? How can I free her soul from its ugly captivity? Who, he wondered, was the sponsor of the outrage; who had taken Lyra's love from him?

Could her rantings have been truth? He blenched. In truth, it was not unknown for ladies to dally with their gladiatorial slaves; it was merely an abomination, a filthy abuse of nature. Not Lyra. . . .

He remembered his one night with her and warmth flooded him. She was, to him, the ideal, if paradoxical, combination of features: she had been a virgin but was passionate. She was pure, even innocent, yet knew the release of love. And she was, somehow, held compelled to speak evil in public when the evil was not — could not be — true.

After a long time, Denis looked up. He wasn't certain where he was. He didn't even know what time it had gotten to be. He knew one thing and one thing alone: he loved Lyra, and Lyra loved him.

Before him, to one side of the road, a line of people had formed, and their possessions were piled about them.

"Where is this?" he asked the nearest.

"Deep Street," a striking young woman answered. Denis recognized her instantly as a noble and suddenly saw the others about her as her retinue.

"Why are you arrayed on the street? Why have you brought out all you own?"

She laughed lightly. "Isn't it obvious? We are fleeing Archive. We seek the stars."

Denis drew himself slightly away. "You flee? In fear? Of what?"

Her merry face grew sad. "Not fear. We flee in hope. Archive is dying, but other worlds may live."

Shaking his head in distress, Denis protested. "You'll only find death in the unexplored stars. There is no hope to be found there."

She smiled at him, forgiving him his belief, clinging proudly to her own. "We feel that there is." She looked up at a descending shadow. "And here is our shuttle. We'll be leaving now." Impulsively, she reached out and took his hand.

"Come with us. We have all we need and more. Your wits and your courage will give us strength."

Denis blinked. "Oh, no." His mouth worked further, but no words came out.

"Stay then." She smiled still. "I will remember you; I will remember Archive." Her eyes grew wide. "Only . . .what is your name?"

Automatically, Denis identified himself. "I am Denis, son of Telemachus."

"And I am Irene, daughter of Acathantus." She drew him near and brushed her lips across his. "I could have loved you, Denis."

And I, you, Irene. He could not form the words.

She released him. Swiftly the shuttle was loaded; Irene ascended the ramp proudly, a Queen going to her Realm, not a young and lonely noble fleeing a world soon to be engulfed in flames.

Denis watched the silver, metallic shuttle fall away into the afternoon sky. He stood and gaped for long minutes after it was beyond sight.

A shape, a shadow, slid up behind him, a figure cloaked all in black: a man or machine of whom nothing could be seen.

Denis turned to peer at the apparition. A cold knife flashed out, stabbing deep into his breast, his lung, his heart.

No face. The being that killed him had no face. Denis wished to cry out, to protest that this was all wrong.

∞

From his seat in the command center of the sky-spanning Belt, Lord Petrosius saw the death of Denis. His instruments told him all he needed to know about the identity of the killer, however, and he knew that there was nothing that needed to be done. He waited a discreet few minutes, then dispatched a flyer to bear away the corpse.

∞

Orbinald, in deep despair, went into the house of dying. Chemical and electrical stimulants relieved his sorrowing mood, and he died joyously, his emotional needs fulfilled at the last. As he slid into the darkness, a last image floated before his eyes, and a last word escaped his lips.

"Lyra."

He loved her. She loved him. Before that, death is a powerless thing.

∞

The monumental palace of the Emperor Arcadian thought its dark computerized thoughts and surveyed itself. Hundreds of people abode inside it, moving from place to place, talking loudly or softly, performing the incomprehensible acts that made humanity human. No one strayed where they ought not to go; no one said what they ought not to say. The palace watched Arcadian himself, viewing him from all angles. It sensed the floor beneath his booted feet. It tested the air circulating past his face. It gauged his stride and watched each shimmering hue of his voluminous, sparkling cape of colors.

Arcadian neared a room; the palace scanned the chamber before he entered. Within, Lyra, daughter of Orbinald, lay in the center of a wide bed, her face down, her body still, but her cheeks wet with tears.

The palace estimated her woe and found it to be considerable. The palace summoned a psychological profile of her mind and quickly ran through several hundred thousand simulations of probable and possible confrontations between her and Arcadian.

Obsessed with his safety, more protective of him than even he was, the palace could not permit any threat to him to be completed. Within the hollow walls, machines moved silently. Projectors readied themselves so that, at only an instant's notice, they could focus deadly beams of force upon any point within Lyra's braincase. Other projectors waited to produce shields and wards of kinetic force to protect the Emperor at need. Death, potential death, conditional death, was readied and aimed at Lyra.

Lyra, knowing none of this, wept quietly, dampening the pillow beneath her.

All that I have loved is lost. My life is ruined. I have destroyed myself. She sobbed once, a shaking convulsion. *Oh, Basil. . . .*

Arcadian, all unannounced, entered the room. Lyra spun about on the bed, sitting forward, her weight on one arm. She started to leap to her feet, but a gesture from the Emperor froze her.

"Lyra."

"My Liege."

He smiled. "Yes. I heard what you said at the arena. Is it true?"

Lyra bent her head and blushed furiously. "Oh, your Majesty. But . . . yes. It is."

His smile widened. "Shocking."

With that, the dam within Lyra burst, and she wept without shame. The Emperor Arcadian waited it out with inexhaustible patience. At last, Lyra regained control of herself.

"I'm sorry, your Majesty."

"You needn't be."

Stunned, Lyra sat forward on the bed. "But. . . ."

Arcadian held up a hand. "You are now the Sultan of the Household. Tomorrow, the palace will begin to instruct you." He grinned at her. "Although I think that you already know most of what you will need."

"How can I be. . . ?"

"Orbinald is dead," he said, carelessly cruel.

"And Denis?"

Arcadian looked away. "He bears you no grudge. He has gone away and has left you free. He has no further wants from you. Your life is no longer his concern." He looked back at her. "He doesn't care."

"Even if he didn't love me. . . ." Lyra swallowed. "How can he turn away from the rank and the post? A Sultanate is such a rich reward. . . ."

"He has been rewarded," the Emperor assured her. "He was saddened, but now he is not unhappy."

"But will he ever be happy?"

The Emperor frowned momentarily. "I do not know."

"I hope he will be. I hurt him terribly."

"Yes." The Emperor smiled again. "You did."

"Very well." She sat up straight upon the bed. "I am your Sultan of the Household. How may I serve you?"

"I have two needs from you." He looked at her, his expression suddenly humorless. "In the box at the arena, you were about to say something about me. Then you were stopped." He peered at her intently. "What were you going to say?"

Lyra, in fear, stammered the truth, knowing that a falsehood would be her undoing. "I was going to blaspheme your name. I was frantic and mindless, and I wanted only to hurt my father and my . . . my husband." She looked up. "Denis is no longer my husband?"

"No longer."

"How else may I serve you, your Majesty? You said you had two needs."

For an answer, Arcadian the First, Emperor of Archive, appraised her, and began to remove his clothing.

14

I live in a very large home, with walls at
the horizons and the ceiling stars-high.
— Pappas the Cynic
Songs of a Wayfarer

Commodore Athalos Steldan marvelled at the
realism of the projected face and head of Stasileus. How could Sophia perform such a su-
perb job of simulation?

At that point, he paused in his thinking. How
good, in fact, was it? A face is easily animated;
the voice would be no more difficult.

Yet the head was perfect. White-furred, the
eyes impossibly huge, with small pointed ears
high on the side of the head, Stasileus looked at
him.

Stasileus, who was over a year dead.

"Sophia?"

"I am Stasileus."

Steldan waited, wondering. Who had spoken? How much of Sophia's mind was given over

to estimations of Stasileus' behavior? Was there anything of her left?

"Hello."

"Good morning, Commodore Steldan." Stasileus' voice seemed tired. Yet it was unquestionably the high, bright voice of a Verna. It echoed, and the words came out in a barely suppressed tumble.

"Do you know me?" Steldan asked.

Stasileus frowned. "Yes. . . ." He cocked his bodiless head to one side. His white thatch of hair shifted naturally with the motion. "And yet we have never met." He brightened. "I understand now. I'm dead, aren't I?"

Steldan stifled a shudder. And yet, through the habits ingrained over a lifetime, he remained polite. "Yes. You are a simulation. You are an emulated Verna."

"That's amusing." Smiling, Stasileus considered the matter. "I feel very much myself. In fact, I can't see any differences in myself at all."

"Try to scratch your nose," Steldan suggested, although he instantly realized and regretted the unkindness of the remark.

Stasileus' neck twitched, as if he were flexing muscles attached to his nonexistent shoulders. Then he smiled. "I am a head that lacks a body. I know more than I can know." He sighed, a high, alien sigh poignantly indicative of sentience. "But I am still Stasileus." He smiled in earnest pride.

Steldan gave up his fight. Just as he could never persuade himself that Sophia was only a machine, so he could not convince himself that this was not Stasileus. The illusion, even if that was all it was, was perfect.

"We have never met," Steldan said, "but I know you through your work."

With a shy smile, Stasileus nodded. "I never meant my book to be read by humans. It was a warning to my own kind." His face grew concerned. "Did you find it offensive? There were insights . . . not all of which were gentle."

"You learned so much about us." Steldan faced him squarely, still seated on the soft chair, his back toward Sophia's control panels. "You know more about how we think than we do."

"No. That isn't true. What I learned was only about one facet of your minds."

"Tell me, please."

"My work dealt only with the way that humans respond to authority. I perceived the workings of command." His face grew downcast, almost disconsolate. "My species has no resistance to command."

"Your advice to them seems to be that they should leave."

"Yes."

Steldan leaned forward. "How necessary is it? Can't we find a way to get along?"

Stasileus' smile grew wry. "It's too late for that. The Verna homeworlds have received my message by now. A second migration is underway."

A feeling of great awe filled Steldan. The Vernae had been created by the manipulations of the Empire. Then, they had been lost. Only eighteen months ago they had come back out of the deeps of space and of history. Now. . . .

"What is the failing in us? What has happened?" The anguish in his voice escaped him involuntarily.

Stasileus looked at him with gentleness clearly showing in his expression. Inhuman, the being was unquestionably humane. "The Empire had little reverence. You have less courage. Your central failure, however, is in this: you command but do not know how to be commanded."

"I am a military officer. I know how to take orders." Yet, to his own surprise, Steldan felt no pride in this response. When had he last obeyed an order in both letter and spirit? He looked away, momentarily shamed. *What has happened to me? Where is my strength?* He found himself hanging on Stasileus' words.

"Szentellos, who made the revolution against the Empire succeed — and who made it fail — said the words that your Concordat lives by. 'History's wheel has broken the spirit of our race.' My race has been a part of the breaking of you. Now, my race shall be broken. While you will gain strength, if your plan succeeds, my people will lose it. They will withdraw from your companionship, although they desperately crave it. We will hide as, for seven hundred years, we were hidden. A millennium may teach us peace."

"You were made things — " Steldan began.

"We may learn to remake ourselves." Stasileus laughed a laugh that was sad and happy and full of irony. "We have scientists, you know. I was an engineer. My teacher was a historian. Suppose that some day we learn how to alter our own genetic foundation." He looked meaningfully at Steldan.

"You may meet us again some day and find us dangerous and angry adversaries. We might make ourselves into huge, claw-limbed monstrosities, bearing as little resemblance to what we are now as we do to the humanity that we once were. Obedience is our nature now: will it always be?"

Steldan began to object; Stasileus interrupted him. "I warned my people against that in my book. The fundamentals of what we are is in the matter of our obedience. For now, we cannot live with you. That is enough. Ask your questions and let me rest, for, although I do not know what manner of ghost I am, I know that I am tired."

Wiping his forehead, which had suddenly become damp, Steldan forced himself to concentrate. "Am I doing the right thing?" *Why am I so drawn to him? I feel as if I have no strength.*

"By bringing a raucous spirit of daring back to your race? By slapping them in their face and challenging them? By remaking them in the form of their ancestors?" Stasileus smiled warmly. "Of course you are."

"What about the symbol of command?"

Stasileus looked at Steldan with a gaze so

compelling, so observant, as to leave Steldan utterly in awe. "The symbol? The symbol which is wrong to use and impossible to destroy? Give it to Kulan Gane."

Steldan leaped to his feet. "Impossible! She's a noble. She'd use it to become Empress; we'll have lost everything!"

"Why do you choose to argue with me?" Stasileus' expression frightened Steldan. "I am the past. I have suffered under the symbol. You are the future. Give the symbol of command to Kulan Gane."

"And. . . ?"

Stasileus blinked. "Only one more question."

"Will I succeed?"

The face hovering in the air snapped off, dissolving instantly. Steldan shook his head and found himself on his feet still. Mists of delusion threaded through his brain, and, slowly, he forced himself awake from what felt like a deep dream. It was Sophia's voice that answered him.

"I am not an oracle, Athalos."

He looked at the blinking lights that were all she had in the way of a face. "No." He swallowed. "It was a stupid question."

Sophia was silent for a time. Steldan wondered what it had been like for her, then realized that he didn't want to know.

"Athalos?"

"Yes, Sophia?"

"Do you know why you are so shaken? Do you know why this affected you so profoundly?"

"No. I don't." He looked at her instrumentation. "Tell me, please."

"You're overlooking your heritage again. You are a priest."

He frowned. "Yes, but. . . ."

Sophia overrode his objection. "You are a priest, and you were speaking to a god."

Steldan leaned forward and rested his elbows on Sophia's instrument console. His face had gone pale, but his teeth were gritted in determination. "I am not a priest."

Softly, Sophia responded. "You are, whether you want to be one or not. I can give you only this consolation: you are strong. You have the power to follow whatever god you choose . . . or none."

For the first time in his long, constrained, and inhibited life, Athalos Steldan wept.

∞

The Concordat of Archive comprised nearly one hundred thousand worlds spread unevenly through a spherical region of space some two hundred parsecs in radius. One hundred and thirty-nine former assassins now worked to change forever the character of its people. Their instructions came from Steldan and Sophia and, increasingly, from Kulan Gane. Their funding was siphoned off from Navy accounts. Their technology came from the past.

Kulan Gane had only the most minimal contact with the other erstwhile killers, and, at times, her leadership seemed nominal. Contact with Sophia and with Steldan was sporadic, however: her decisions in the field came more and more frequently. For this reason, she concentrated her efforts on the world of Archive.

She stood, in shirt sleeves and short pants, on a rocky outcrop high in the stone mountains just east of the city of Archive. Rock pressed at her feet through her soft-soled shoes, and a chill breeze drove past her face, massaging her arms, buffeting her legs. Surrounded by tall, straight-trunked trees, she seemed alone. The loneliness, the cold wind, and the unfamiliar spicy smells of the trees and low, whipping grasses brought chills to her skin.

This is our home? We were born here? It seems so foreign to me. Just one more world among worlds. Fifteen thousand years ago, her ancestors had hunted and built fires here. Even today, petroglyphs could be seen; one engraved display of untranslated symbols decorated a high rock face only a few kilometers from where she stood.

Visible to her, arrayed below her in all its cluttered splendor, was the city. At first, it looked like nothing more impressive than another jumbled rock formation. The late afternoon light spread the shadows of buildings into the streets between them, making the light and dark patterns seem tumbled and uneven. A dozen subtle green shades of plantings — rows of tall trees along avenues; small, irregularly shaped parks; here and there lawns and canopies of vines — tinted the vast field.

The city spread, climbing over the lesser hills, from the foot of the mountains to the far, dimly glimpsed sea.

Seven hundred years ago, my ancestors died when the revolution caught them. They were burned to death. This city is almost entirely rebuilt and has engulfed the remains of the old one.

She sighed and began to walk back, weaving through the trees. Soon, she arrived at the clearing where work progressed according to her orders. The containment vessel and jumpspace rift had since been buried. Now, finishing touches were being added to the broadcast tower. When the work was done, in only a day or two, she would be able to speak to all of Archive. The thought amused her.

What would I say to this world — my home-world — if I could? How would I threaten them? How would I cajole them? What message do I have for a world?

She laughed a high clear laugh that had little menace in it. She had changed, over the past eleven months. Steldan had wrested the ability to kill bluntly away from the others that had met him in that basement on Carpus. But the blood-lust had drained slowly away from her, leaving her a stronger woman than she had been.

What message would I have broadcast? It wouldn't have been music! Still smiling, she walked slowly around the short, stubby broad-casting pylon. Margaret Cliffs would be finished with her opera soon. It was her music, enhancing words from the past. But the message was Steldan's.

A single Emperor once ruled here, and his word was the fiat of the gods. Now, a committee of six holds total power, the Praesidium. But if we pull this off, if we can make this mad enterprise succeed. . . . She waved to the technicians who were just finishing up on the last signal-strength adjustments to the tower.

"All clear?"

"It's working." One of the technicians, a strong-shouldered woman, wandered over, test equipment flapping and clattering at her belt. "Where's your input?" She gestured at the tower with a thick thumb. "I've been over it and over it. You've got no feed."

Kulan Gane faltered for a moment. She knew how to kill the woman and could have slain her silently in any of seven or eight ways. She didn't know, just then, how to lie to her. "That will be taken care of at a later time," she said at last.

Shrugging, the technician let the matter drop. She strolled back to her work, the matter forgotten.

An Emperor, once, and now a Praesidium. She looked after the technician, who continued her adjustments and measurements carefully and competently. *Isn't it time for people like her to rule?* The technician, unaware of the scrutiny with which Kulan Gane favored her, finished up her work.

Behind her, screened by the trees, the city began to slip into the darkness of evening.

Eighty million people stood in the shadow of these mountains; across the planet another twelve billion lived.

Isn't it time for them to take over their own leadership?

∞

Less than one hundred kilometers away, in the city overlooked by Kulan Gane, Grand Admiral Jennifer de la Noue sat, watching her room grow dark.

She was a member of the Praesidium; she was, in theory at least, the third most powerful person in the whole of the Concordat. Above her were ranked the First Secretary and the Justicar. Below her, the Commerce and Treasury Secretaries and the Foreign Secretary. Five men and one woman, who held complete command over the workings of the Concordat.

The Navy was hers. The whole military might of the Concordat was hers — solely hers — to command. She had battleships that boasted sufficient megatonnage to devastate hundreds of worlds; she had Marines to occupy the cities she left unrazed. She had the power.

Of what use is military power in time of peace?

Athalos Steldan, what are you up to?

She was a trusting woman by nature, open and honest and gentle. Her manner showed it in a hundred small ways. Her face tended to show her emotions clearly: happiness or rage glowed through her hazel eyes and shone in her hand-some face. Years of intrigue and of war had taught her the brutal lesson of necessity, and she tended, these days, to hide her emotions, binding them the way she tended, lately, to bind up her long, blonde hair. Both actions were artificial, and both made her seem more harsh than she wanted to be.

Through the years, she had been able to show her trust to one man: Athalos Steldan. She had never loved him, not as women are given to loving men. But she loved him as a companion, an ally, a true friend. She knew that his ways were always his own, that he insisted on keeping his secrets. She knew that he was not trustworthy, not as such. But, until this year had dawned, she had nevertheless trusted him.

He stood by me when the times and the wars were darkest. He saved my career from ruin countless times. I could depend on him; I knew his loyalty was unshakeable. What has happened to it now?

Always, Steldan had been secretive. Always, he had followed his own course. But, always, he had been there to help her when she needed it the most. He was her personal physician, and that meant that there were times he gave her the orders. That, too, had been a comfort to her.

But what he did most often, and best, was to listen. He seemed, at times, to be her confessor.

She smiled now, and then pressed her hands to the sides of her face. *Athalos. What crimes are you committing? What noble ends are justifying your means? Why are you deceiving me?*

They had conspired together in the past, taking actions that seemed wrong, in order to serve the greatest good. And, in the past, he had acted alone for the same reason. Until this time, he'd always explained himself to her.

You must believe that I would not approve.

He knew her as well as she knew him. He would not be wrong in this.

Whatever you're up to . . . I do not approve. How can I?

Admiral Morgan had discovered so much, but not all. Steldan had been spending Navy funds indiscriminately and widely. Construction projects all across the Concordat were financed through illegal expenditures on Navy accounts. The projects were, invariably, combined power generation and multimedia broadcast facilities.

I could have stopped it. She smiled wearily to herself. *I could have stopped it with but a word. 'Freeze the assets. Cashier Steldan. And bring him to me.' I didn't, because. . . .*

Because she had still trusted him implicitly and unreservedly. She had chosen to indulge his whims of secrecy. Later, doubt had stopped her from stopping him and, later still, mere irresolution. Finally, when suspicion had, belatedly, bloomed, she left the projects untouched in hopes that they would lead Morgan to Steldan and that an explanation would be, at last, forthcoming.

208

Now . . . she remained irresolute.

I don't want to take any action that means a final break with him, she admitted to herself. *I want to trust him, no matter what.*

She turned the lights on, and the small, dim office high in the Commerce Branch tower gleamed, the light spilling out through the floor-to-ceiling windows and into the deepening night. Her uniform, which had faded into grey in the twilight, shone red and white, and the rank-chips glinted on her breast.

I won't undo his work. I won't even stop it from progressing. But I will find him, and he will explain. I owe him that much.

She stood, her irresolution gone now. Yet her smile was tender. *I owe him so much. Does he mistrust me? If he does, I will repay it the only way I know how: I will trust him a while longer.*

She tapped the intercom with a slender hand. "I have a message for Admiral Morgan. Finding Commodore Steldan is now his foremost priority."

Leaning back in her chair, she sighed. Steldan was secretive and elusive, conspiratorial and manipulative, sneaky and sly. He was also a good man, and she owed him everything she had.

15

It's a hot, light, sun burning treetops,
air-breezy day,
　I'm in love,
　The night is forever far.

> — Achorus
> *The Skeleton and the Chaffinch*

Princess Lyra, daughter of Orbinald, widow of
Denis, stood straight and proud in the throne
room of the Emperor Arcadian. She was garbed
in a loose, brief shift of pale, mint-green, belted
in silver. Her hair shone, and her face glowed.
Before her, above her, on his high throne, the
Emperor smiled wanly down at her. For this, he
had wrapped himself in his robes of state, great
voluminous masses of swirling, heavy fabric
that engulfed him almost totally.

The robe was a brilliant gold in color, but
textures within the warp and woof of the fabric
held tiny multicolored sparkles. It was as if the
star-kindler was gowned in a golden night scat-

tered with stars. A fold of it was thrown over his head as a kind of cowl or hood, shadowing his face; other folds served in place of sleeves, so that only his hands and wrists showed. Lyra could see his smile, although his golden wreath of thick hair was hidden.

One to each side of the throne, the two robots stood guard. Man-shaped, if men were seven meters tall and greyhound slim, the robots bore huge, eleven-meter pikes in their hands, held respectfully away from the throne. At their other sides, they gripped impossibly slender five-meter swords in long-fingered fists. These needle-pointed swords were held point down, resting lightly on the polished flagstones of the throne room.

Emperor and servant and two robots — and of course the never-absent mind of the palace itself — were alone in the high, vaulting chamber. The room was silent, but it was a strange, powerful silence, made awful by the weight of the dome overhead. In her mind, Lyra heard sounds: strange, noiseless noises, as if the air itself, moving softly overhead, stirred echoes from that sheer turquoise dome.

"Your Majesty, I present myself in my humility." Decorously and with what dignity was possible, she lowered herself prone to the floor, stretching full length out on the chill stone flags. The cold startled her at first, until she found it oddly thrilling. She leaned into it, savoring the feel of it against her flesh.

"Rise," the Emperor said, a faint hint of

amusement in his voice.

Lyra scrambled to her feet with considerably less dignity than she had displayed when performing her obeisance. She stood before him, gazing up at him in silent respect.

"You are now the Sultan of my Household." He looked away, and, for a moment, a flash of some dark emotion crossed his face. "I gave my word to your father, child. The palace will teach you all you need to know."

"Thank you, Your Majesty." The room suddenly seemed much colder to her, and the stones beneath her feet, which had been exotically cool a moment ago, now seemed painfully icy.

The Emperor smiled again. Lyra, deep within his thrall, felt relief and comfort again. She wondered, with a small part of her mind still her own to use, whether he had the ability to turn his power of charm on and off again. When making love to her in the night's darkness, he had been magnificent but, still, only a man. He even was, she thought impiously, slightly shorter than she was.

At once, a thousand questions tumbled through her mind. Was she truly a Sultan? Or should the word be Sultana? Had a woman ever been a Sultan before? She fought to hide her thoughts from the Emperor: could he read thoughts?

Perhaps he could. Or perhaps the palace could monitor facial expressions and body temperature — and a hundred other physiological signs — and approximate the state of mind of a subject within its master's presence.

"What troubles you, child?" His gaze bored into her face.

"Am I truly your Sultan, Majesty? Or am I. . . ." She bit the words off, a feat requiring more strength than she had known she had. In her thoughts she completed the sentence. *Or am I your concubine?*

He stared at her, stony-faced for a moment. Then, slowly, his expression lightened. Lyra knew that she had narrowly escaped a bitter and ghastly fate and, also, that her danger was not yet over. Arcadian was not insane — even in the privacy of her thoughts she shied away from thinking that — but his sanity was not the same as other men's.

"You want the power." Arcadian smiled a wry, headshaking smile. "You want the privileges and perquisites that were your father's." He looked at her. "Know, Lyra, that your father was a friend to me. He was with me from the first." Arcadian stood, and his robe moved with him, its drapes shifting smoothly and subtly to cloak his legs and to billow out from his outstretched arm.

"At times he was a fool, and I punished him. At times he was loyal and, once, brave, and I rewarded him." He looked at Lyra, gauging her, testing her strength. What he saw pleased him. "The power is yours. You have but to ask."

"Please, Majesty. I have only one request."

"Name it."

"Basil." As she uttered the name, moisture came into her eyes. She blinked it away and took an imploring step forward. "He is my first love. He is my only love."

The Emperor crossed his arms in silence, his face unreadable. "Was it true, then, what you exclaimed aloud in the arena yesterday?"

"Yes, Majesty," Lyra said, her face averted.

"So be it," the Emperor exclaimed, surprisingly loudly. He took a step backward and settled into his throne. Thus he sat, as if carved of marble, his robes falling into perfect folds around and beneath him.

Lyra dared not speak, and the Emperor said nothing. For what seemed like an hour, but was in reality only a sparse few minutes, Lyra stood in trembling silence, regarding this greatest of men.

Then two figures came into the vast hall from an entrance to Lyra's right: a small man and a gigantic white Verna. Bhotian himself had brought Basil home to his mistress.

Lyra's dignity and decorum were fled from her in an instant. She dashed across the vast floor and ran full-tilt into Basil's waiting arms. Basil held her, hugging her close against his tight-muscled belly and breast. She was not even as tall as his shoulders, and her hand could not reach the top of his head. But he was hers, and he loved her, she knew without any taint of doubt.

Bhotian knelt, a posture of deference both to Lyra and the Emperor. "I have safeguarded him well and have delivered him swiftly."

"As always, you have done well." Arcadian beamed at Bhotian, his favorite. "I can never fittingly reward you. You will live to see your star in the heavens."

Bhotian laughed, a light, disarming laugh. "No reward is needed for bringing Basil to his beloved. All I have ever asked is to train the slaves to fight."

Nodding, Arcadian signed his benediction. "Go then, back to the arena. Be happy."

"Yes." Bhotian looked at the floor as he turned about. "Happy." Walking away, he smiled, and only the palace knew the pain in the young man's heart.

Lyra, held by her Basil, forgot all else. Her misery of the day just past was banished. Her loss of her father and of Denis was gone. Embraced by Basil's furry, warm strength, no fear and no woe could come to her.

"Lyra," said the Emperor, after he had been patiently silent a long time, "why is your Verna staring at me so?"

His tone of voice shook her from her comfort. The Emperor had sounded, just for a moment, like a child, confused and perplexed by something he didn't understand. She looked up. Basil gazed fixedly at the Emperor, his expression strangely attentive. But to her, Basil's wide, loving face was the same as it had always been.

Does he know that Arcadian and I made love last night? Lyra reached up and tugged lightly at Basil's chin. *Is he jealous?* Basil looked down at her, and his expression melted into a happy, stupid smile.

"I think he was only curious, Majesty," Lyra said, refusing to let this minor incident upset her happiness.

"He shouldn't have been able to do that, you know."

"Why not?"

Arcadian pouted. "This room. . . ." At first he thought better of saying more, then he spread his hands and shook his head. "This room is special. It radiates an awe. Partly sonic, partly chemical, and partly an array of symbols." His voice grew light again. "I daresay *you* felt it."

Lyra looked at him and felt it indeed. "Yes, Majesty."

"Then why doesn't he?" The Emperor's voice was sharp and petulant.

"He's defective, Majesty." Lyra turned fully to him and hastened to explain. "Basil is mute. Something went wrong when they mastered the embryo. They tried to explain it to me at the breeding house, but. . . ." She shrugged. She was a noble and had no need of scientific literacy.

"He's faulty?" Arcadian raised an eyebrow. "Can't speak? What else?"

"That's it. Oh, he's not perfect beyond that. You know." Lyra shrugged uncomfortably.

"And you love him."

"Yes, Majesty."

Arcadian sighed. "Something to be said for a

lover who can't talk back." He shook his head. "Keep him out of my sight, please. He is yours."

"Thank you, Your Majesty." Lyra took Basil by the hand and led him from the room. At the doorway arch, he stopped and looked back over his shoulder. He looked squarely at the Emperor with eyes that seemed to hold a great wisdom and a deep calculation.

∞

Stones and lumps of earth flew through the air, flung with the force of hatred by an angry mob of rioters. Their faces were masked because they feared retribution. The masks all bore the caricatured features of the Emperor Arcadian.

Toward the rear of the press, some organization could still be seen. A line of men and women stood together, chanting slogans in unison. Behind them, a crowd had formed up, watching warily, a part of the demonstration but not of the violence. Many of the individuals in this area wore no masks. If questioned, they could claim that only curiosity brought them to this street.

In the advance, active members of the riot used power tools to fell lampposts, to carve obscure symbols into the stone facings of buildings, and to set fire to green shrubbery. The sound of the mob drowned out the low whir of the tools and masked the sporadic crashing noises of stones against walls.

Two men with drills had sped ahead, destroying the locks on the shops and homes on each side of the fashionable avenue. In their wake, people split off from the main route of the procession to enter and despoil. They never spent long within but, instead, moved quickly to catch up to the main group.

The emotional flavor of the mob was a curious mixture of jollity and fear. The daring ones in advance of their leadership showed their hatred clearly in their actions. Some of them laughed as they destroyed, while others went about their tasks in a businesslike fashion. All of them shouted, their voices merging into a high, nerve-shaking howl. From behind the line of leaders, others would rush forward suddenly, joining the orgy of vandalism.

Smoke poured upward behind the march, dark gritty smoke that blotted out the sun and the sky. Forward, the heaven-arching Belt looked down pitilessly over the riot. Many of the vulgar gestures made by the rioters were directed upward at it.

A figure, a man, draped in a hooded brown cloak, watched the riot grow near. He made a small gesture of frustration and doubled back along the side street. From a safe vantage, he watched the procession pass by. The sounds of rage troubled him; the hair along his forearms and at the back of his neck quivered. The morning, which had seemed bright and sunny earlier, now seemed chill and dark. Smoke smudged the eastern sky, turning the sun orange.

No. This is not for me, he thought as he moved

around the riot. Some of the trailing figures, following the riot as they would follow a parade or a funeral, spotted him. Most drew back, fearful of recognition. One gave chase for a few minutes. The hooded man lost him without any great difficulty.

He arrived at last in the midst of a low, sunken street. Buildings untouched by the riot rose on both sides. When he looked to the east, only a faint smear of wind-thinned smoke could be seen. To the south west, the street dropped away, and he saw the dark blue of the sea, fading away into a misty horizon.

He paused, then pushed back his hood and knocked on a door. His face, exposed, was young and round, flat, with high cheekbones. Bhotian Freedman stood alone in the street.

The door opened. Bhotian stepped within. The door shut, closing out the shadows of the morning, the smoke-tinged scent of the sea, and the sight of the merciless Belt overhead.

Bhotian stood in the narrow foyer of a private residence. Bare wood parquets floored the room, solid beneath his boots. Wood panelled walls and wooden screens lined the walls. A fine-meshed, wooden screen, hand-carved, filtered the light from fluoros overhead. Facing him was a man, a noble, dressed in everyday morning finery, his feet in slippers. His face was handsome, as was the case with all nobles; his hands were long-fingered and quick. He had brown hair, brown eyes, and a sad, browned expression.

"Bhotian? Bhotian Freedman?" He shook his head. "I never thought to find you here."

Bhotian was more bluntly shocked. "Trinopus? The philosopher? Why are *you* running a getaway depot?"

Trinopus smiled. "To prove myself right." He frowned. "Or wrong. Or both."

Bhotian stepped closer and removed his cloak. When Trinopus made no move to take it from him, he let it slip to the floor. "What do you mean?"

Laughing a cruel, cold laugh, Trinopus explained. "People call me the Master of Misery. But that's not so: I am master over nothing, not even myself. I am only a philosopher, and I've seen an ugly truth." He looked at Bhotian.

"The world is not only cruel, it is malicious. Pain is maximized." He shrugged. "Human nature? Natural law? Whim of the gods? I don't have all the answers. I have only one answer: all actions lead to pain."

"You deny hope?"

"Utterly." Trinopus' response was abrupt and final.

Bhotian smiled. "Permit me just a little hope, then, and please indulge my folly." His smile faded. Very seriously, he pleaded. "Let me leave Archive. Let me live."

"Of course. That's why I'm here." Trinopus turned about without making any indication that Bhotian should follow him. But Bhotian followed, nevertheless, as Trinopus strode off, walking slowly through the vast, half-buried house. "I've been supplying fools with false hope for three years now. No point in stopping." He looked over his shoulder at Bhotian. "But you'll be sorry. That's how it is. You think things here are bad? People dying? The Empire totters on its pins? You'll find things are a thousand times worse in the unknown stars to which you flee."

"Perhaps."

"No 'perhaps' about it." He sighed. "But I never expected you to believe it. You leap from the chimney into the flames, and from the flames down into the coals, always believing that you better your chances of not being burned."

"You won't be coming with us, then?"

Trinopus spun completely about in the narrow hallway they now traversed. Rich, red wood on either side had been polished to a brilliant shine. Images in frames lined the walls. Bhotian glanced at one, a seascape lit by its own sun, and felt his throat tighten at the beauty of it.

"Come with you?" Trinopus seemed unable to decide whether to laugh or fleer in anger. "Come with you? To the first shelf of hell? This is civilization." As if that answer finished all argument, he turned and pounded down the corridor, stamping his feet rudely upon the fine wood of the floor.

I've read one of your books, O Trinopus, Bhotian thought. *You believed in universal pain and misery. But your own words were light. You were a humorist once. Have you come, then, to believe what you say? Have you truly renounced*

221

hope?

They soon came to a lift. Bhotian entered. Trinopus did not and turned away, thus missing Bhotian's small salute of farewell. The lift brought Bhotian to the rooftop. Across the way, over the eastern rooftops, the sun had risen above the smoke. An aircar sat before him, unfolded for entry.

A sound assailed him, a high, powerful sound, as if the engines of heaven had been started, in order to move the world. He looked up at the Belt. Bright bands of light shone, spreading from a cluster of points on the inner surface of the Belt. They seemed to point away, as if aimed beyond the curve of the world. But Bhotian knew that was an illusion: the beams were focussed on a street only a few blocks east.

He inhaled deeply, strengthening himself for an irrevocable act. Then he stepped atop the aircar and waited for it to engulf him. Folding up like a basket, it shaped itself around him, the flexible metal extending a padded shelf for him to sit upon.

Finally, without any word of command from him, it leaped into the sky.

He looked down through the vitreous panels in walls and floor as the city streets of Archive spread beneath him. In one, tiny figures moved in silence, and, behind them, fires burned. Then all detail was lost to sight. The city dwindled into a decorated patch of land nestled against the sea. Mountains held their wrinkled masses fastidiously away to the east; islands appeared in the ocean and then were lost again.

Bhotian closed his eyes. When he opened them, the world beneath him was a globe, whole and complete.

Above him, a spaceship grew, took over half of the starry sky, and then swallowed the aircar. Bhotian stepped out as soon as the car unfolded itself.

"Welcome," a soft, lovely voice said, speaking from behind him. He turned about and saw a pretty, dark-haired noblewoman. "We'll be leaving soon, I think. We've just about finished loading. I've been aboard since yesterday."

Bhotian smiled warily at her. "I am Bhotian Freedman."

Her eyes widened. "The favorite of the Emperor? Are you coming with us?"

"Yes."

Her face grew sad. "Then things are worse there than even we dared think." She brightened. "I am Irene, daughter of Acathantus. I'll show you around."

"Thank you."

"You won't have any slaves to teach to fight, I'm afraid."

"No. But I can teach men."

Irene looked at him with an unhappy but realistic expression. "Yes. Our lives will be difficult. Perhaps brutal. You will be an asset."

Several hours later, the great golden ship began to pick up speed. In less than fifteen minutes it had left the system of Archive behind until the life-giving sun of home was only a small, bright star. Bhotian stood by the nearest vision port, gazing out into the ten thousand stars that marred the heavens. He squinted and finally was able to see a faintly glowing blur in the darkness. A cloud of gas: a protostar. A nebula, that someday would be a sun. Bhotian tried to smile, but his throat was too tight. A sun that the Emperor sought to kindle in his honor.

The secondary drives cut in then and the ship plunged smoothly into jumpspace.

∞

The mob had begun to disperse, according to Szentellos' orders. Firefighting equipment sailed in from one quarter of the sky, and troops took positions in another, seeking to cordon the streets away from the rest of the city. Szentellos, masked like the rest of his followers, shouted hoarsely. He was heard and was followed. Silently giving thanks that at least some of his rioters would escape, he bellowed for them to disperse. The anger turned completely to fear, and the riot became a rout. Trained agents of the Revolution stood by, however, to guide and hasten the fleeing mob. The streets were emptied in only a few minutes save for the most aggressive of the wastrels, who continued rampaging.

They were the only ones to burn when fire from heaven scoured the paves. Acrid wisps of ash merged with the smoke from the burning buildings.

The streets were silent once more.

∞

"A riot? In the city?" Petrosius feigned disbelief. He leaned back in his command chair at one end of the battle bridge of the Belt and regarded his lieutenant with tolerant amusement. "Likely just a parade or circus."

"No sir." The young officer was pale; his red hair blazed the hotter against his white skin. "They're setting fires."

Petrosius tugged at his uniform sleeves. The lieutenant stood in silence, bathed in the light of a thousand instruments and indicators. Cold, recirculated air whispered in his hair, fluttered past his ears.

"Well, let's have a look, then," Petrosius said at last. He keyed the cameras. The screen before him lit up with an overhead view of the streets. Together, the two men looked at the scene.

"Well," Petrosius said at last. "I'll have to admit it, that's a riot. Well, well."

"Do we open fire?"

"Hm?" Petrosius looked at his subordinate. "Well, of course we do. But not quite yet. You see — "

"Not yet? Sir! They're setting *fires!*"

Favoring the young man with a cool glance, Petrosius rebuked him gently. "Suppose we were to open fire. What weapon would you use?"

"Fuser fire . . . sir."

"Indeed. Killing them all and leaving us no

one to question. No one to point out the leaders and organizers of this little demonstration." He cleared his throat. "Furthermore — "

"Stunners, then, sir."

"*Furthermore*, those we kill become martyrs to their cause. I know that you think that's a terrible cliche. Isn't it better to have a dead martyr than a living rebel? I assure you, my lad, that such is not the case."

"Sir — "

"Stunners?" Petrosius looked at him. "Minimum angle of projection, tightest collimation?"

"One half of one thousandth of one radian, sir," the young officer recited, his voice tight.

"Dispersed over six hundred kilometers?"

"Um. . . . Three hundred meters, sir."

"Too broad. I won't submit that many innocent people — the area of impact would be almost a block in radius — to a stun. The Emperor would lose honor if his loyal subjects were swatted down along with rebels and troublemakers. You can see that, can't you? You've got to think in political terms, too, rather than simply military ones."

"We'd capture their leaders, sir."

"We'll *identify* them from our observations from here." He squinted at the screen. "Indeed, I think we have enough evidence. And they've taken enough liberties, I think. . . . Prepare to fire with the tertiary fusers. Only three turrets. This area of targeting." He sketched in a section of the street with his fingers. "Hurry, now: looks like they're beginning to scatter."

"Yes, sir!" the officer snapped, and darted away to his own battle station.

This could go on for quite some time, Petrosius thought wearily. *I'm glad Szentellos kept strictly to his schedule, or more than merely eight or nine people would be burnt, down there.*

"Revolution," he said out loud, although none seemed to listen, "is a filthy business."

16

I permit no insubordination, but I will not name any specific penalty to it. Mutiny is, by definition, incapable of being deterred.

— Vice Admiral Haber
Annotations to Meeting Minutes

Time aboard the lonely station seemed to have little meaning. Steldan kept company with Sophia and comforted Margaret Cliffs when her anguish overwhelmed her. On some days, the loneliness was something he could tolerate: he spent such days reading or listening to music that Sophia provided for him. On other days, the solitude was more than he could stand, and only Sophia's kindness made him able to bear it.

On a day neither particularly bad nor notably good, Cliffs sought him out. In her hand she bore a thick bundle of papers.

"I've finished."

Steldan blinked stupidly for a moment,

"The. . . . The opera?" His eyes lit up with a desperate hope.

She smiled. "Yes. *The Skeleton and the Chaffinch.*" She handed him the papers.

He took it and flipped through it. Then again, forward and backward. He looked up in stark disbelief.

"It's all here."

"All of it."

"You've scored it. You've separated out the voices and the instruments. You've even put in staging directions."

"Yes." Cliffs' expression was triumphant.

Steldan looked at her, wondering why he hadn't noticed the changes in her earlier. Where the months had drawn her out, causing in her a brittle gauntness, now she had restored a bit of her weight, and her upper arms had some flesh on them again. Her eyes had more color, as did her face. Even her hair seemed fuller, richer.

"You must have finished the actual composition almost a month ago."

"Three and a half weeks. I kept it from you."

"Successfully."

"I'm finished. It's finished." She pushed the papers back when Steldan tried to give them to her. "This is yours now. Not mine." Crossing her arms before her, she stepped away. "I've done my part. I've written your opera."

"We can leave . . ." he said, his voice low; he didn't dare exult quite yet.

"Will you take me back to Thierry-Danege? Am I going back to prison?" She was smiling, but the question was not a joke.

"You are free." Steldan stood straight, and his expression grew serious. "You have done a service for the Concordat of Archive. I will take you to any world you name, where you will be paid."

If he was expecting the question, "How much?" he was surprised: Cliffs took another step back and asked, instead, "Where will you find actors and singers? Where will you hold rehearsals?" Her voice rose. "Who is your music director?"

Steldan paused for a long moment, uncertain what to make of her insistence. "I am travelling to Marterly. The world has sufficient population to find performers and musicians. I will hire a cast and company and hold rehearsals there."

Cliffs nodded. "Then I'm going with you. I'll be your secretary." She took two quick steps forward and gripped him tightly by the front of his tunic. "Your secretary," she said very firmly. "No one — *no one* — is to know my role as composer. Listen to me."

She stepped closer, pushing up against him. She scourged him with her gaze, and he lifted his head to avoid the intensity of her emotion. "I'm going with you. And I am going to be in complete control.

"I will not work with the performers: you will. I will not be shouted at. I will not make changes in the score. If I don't like a performer or his attitude, you will discharge him. What I say goes, and you will enforce this, so that no one knows that it is my decisions that are being imposed."

She tightened his fist and twisted it, knotting Steldan's tunic between her fingers. She shoved Steldan back and followed closely until she had pushed his back up against a wall. "You thought you'd seen me at my worst, when the effort of the composition was too much for me to sustain. You saw me crying; you saw me helpless. But that wasn't my worst: this will be.

"Athalos, I've written four symphonies. None has ever received a performance. The Cultural Arts Board rejected each one. I refused to make the changes they demanded. I went to prison instead.

"I'll go to prison again, rather than let you do things to this work that I don't approve.

"Is that perfectly clear to you, Athalos?"

Steldan stood as straight as he could, straighter than he'd needed to stand since his first days in the military. He looked down into Cliffs' eyes.

"If you had asked me," he said at last, his voice soft, "I would have gladly agreed to all you want. Since you saw fit to make a demand of it — "

Her eyes blazed, and she drew herself up, standing on her toes to press her face very near his.

"*Since* you saw fit to make a demand of it," he continued, his voice growing louder, "I will still give you most of what you want." He took a quick step to the side and snapped his arms up, breaking her hold on his tunic. His gaze bored into her face. "I will not give you my enmity, however. You'll have to earn that another way."

She rubbed her wrists where he had bruised them. Frowning, she shook her head. "I . . . expected you to say no. I thought you'd send me away."

"Never. The opera is yours. It is your message. The words are by Achorus. The funding and the basic conceptual idea are mine." He brushed out his tunic front, smoothing the wrinkles with his hand. Slowly, he began to relax, and his voice grew more gentle by degrees. "The music, Margaret, is yours.

"Are you high-strung? Emotional? Are you moody, stubborn, easily angered?" He stepped forward, away from the wall where she had cornered him.

"Is this why I found you in a prison? These are the reasons I chose you." He closed his eyes for a moment, seeking for calm. "You are creative and energetic. Don't you believe that true genius is a near thing to madness?

"I am trying to instill into the Concordat of Archive a spirit something more like yours. We have had centuries of sanity, and we have brutally repressed any outbreak of imagination. The gods are dead, Margaret: we slew them with our own hands. But I believe — no matter how much the thought horrifies me — I believe that we need to become a bit more like the old fey gods of yore."

She looked at him as if he were ranting. He

saw her expression and smiled a thin, wry smile. Perhaps he was. But she listened, and he saw that she did not disagree.

"We can't find every answer in strict, non-spiritual materialism. The old gods are dead: let them stay that way. But. . . ." He held out his hands. "But perhaps we need new gods. Sprites of fancy, little gods. I want to see more people sing. I want men and women to see things that aren't there: to hear the voice of the dawn; to sense, as they once did, a faint terror in the darkness.

"There is a great, vast fear pervading the Concordat. It is the fear of their unawakened potential. The people who overthrew the Emperor and killed his gods have fought for seven hundred years to avoid the madness and the genius in themselves. They understand, rightly, that the two come together, mixed in one package. We cannot fly if we are afraid of falling.

"Margaret, I hate that, but I cannot deny it. I am out to make humanity over again. I seek to make all people a little more like you."

Cliffs sneered at him. "This is your holy mission?"

Steldan stiffened as if he had been slapped. "No. Or maybe yes. Not a mission given me by the gods, but. . . ."

"Yes?" Cliffs frowned at him, and her brow was furrowed.

"The people of Archive cry out for this change. Within them, they know this is needed. In fact, I am doing nothing but facilitating the change that must happen soon anyway. Individuals do not create history, but, sometimes, if they are lucky enough, they can take a hand in the shaping of it."

"My opera will have the effect you describe?"

"I hope so," he said. With complete honesty, he added, "I can't know."

"And you'll accept my terms?" Cliffs looked at him with awe but also with suspicion.

"Not all of them. I'm going to make you do some of the dirty work yourself. I won't identify you as the composer, if you don't want me to. You are my co-producer. *You* deal with the hurt feelings; you handle the demands. I'll back you up, be sure of it. The musicians and singers are people who are like you: imbued with the spirit of music and with some of its madness. That won't help you to get along with them, however: I expect a bitter fight."

"I'll do it if I must."

"Let's go then. We've spent more than enough time here."

Cliffs looked away. "Almost a year. . . ." Her eyes became damp.

"No." Steldan took her by the shoulders. "Not now. This isn't the time to be weak."

Tears flooded out of Cliffs' eyes, but she stood straight and met his gaze. "Not weak. I'm only weak when I'm writing. I'm happy." She brushed a sleeve across her face. "I'm going to get a performance. I'm going to have earned it."

"Yes."

Out on the rock face of the small asteroid

station, their spaceship awaited. There would be a few last-minute details to be seen to. Then, the short, dull trip to Marterly, where the true work began.

Steldan reached blindly behind him onto the tabletop, wondering where he had left his cap.

∞

"We're leaving, Sophia." Steldan and Cliffs were packed and ready to flee.

Sophia's disembodied voice came softly from the air in her control room. "I know."

"Keep the communications channels open. There should be nearly two hundred operational stations by now."

"Two hundred and seven."

"Excellent." Steldan seemed slightly ill-at-ease.

"Go now. And Athalos?"

"Yes?"

"Do you have the symbol of command with you?"

Startled, he reached toward an inner pocket. Moving his hand back, he smiled. "I have it."

"Will you give it to Kulan Gane?"

Cliffs looked unhappily back and forth between them, the man and the computer, but said nothing.

"I don't dare."

"Margaret? Your music is the best I have ever heard. I will be listening to the performance."

Cliffs blushed. "Thank you, Sophia." She

brushed her hair back from her forehead.

Steldan hid the loss that he felt. Sophia had been his alter ego for a year; they had learned from one another and were both saner for it. He knew he would have her voice, still, over the jumpspace radio link. But he would miss being near her.

There was nothing more to be said. Steldan and Cliffs left the small room, went out through the crooked corridor into the station, and thence out onto the vacuum plain under the harsh red light of the forlorn and forgotten sun.

The ship shot upward, sped into the darkness, and cannoned into the red hole of jumpspace.

∞

On Marterly, Steldan and Cliffs soon pieced together an opera company. Their next month was a continuing adventure. Steldan's methodical nature combined with Cliffs' vigor to provide not only leadership but inspiration.

True to Cliffs' fears, the artists showed considerable independence. Several of them knew more about music than she did, although nearly all of them behaved as if they did. Endless petty squabbles ensued over this or that minor point of staging or instrumentation.

Cliffs remained steadfast, refusing to change even a note of the music itself and giving in with only the most grudging reluctance when details of orchestration absolutely required alteration.

236

Contrary to what she had demanded of Steldan, he allowed her to work matters out with the others and only rarely interposed. They spoke a common language: music. He was now, as he had been for the duration of the composing, an outsider.

The performing cast was not large: eight soloists and an onstage chorus of only seventeen more. The orchestra was composed of a light mix of thirty-six instruments. Steldan surprised the company at this point by insisting that the instruments all be acoustical and manual. Overriding the protests of the conductor and the music director, he absolutely vetoed the use of score-reading or programmable instruments. Cliffs, who by now understood his needs and who had no objections of her own, backed him up, lending him her support in return for the times he had aided her.

Uneasily, the rehearsals progressed. Tempers flared often. A soprano walked out during one session and refused to return. Steldan froze her finances, stopping payment on her salary to date.

The high point, for Steldan, of the entire disorderly fiasco was when representatives of the planetary Cultural Arts Board demanded control of the production. Steldan, now as ever wearing his uniform as a Commodore in the Intelligence Branch of the Concordat Navy, was able to show them the Navy funding vouchers that supported the project.

For Cliffs, the entire episode was both completely degrading and infinitely ennobling. For the first time in her life, she heard her music the way it was meant to be heard. More than once she burst into tears of happiness when hearing a particular aria or duet sung to perfection.

The work itself was the cement that bound the company together. Steldan was the first to realize this. The singers came, haltingly, to understand the beauty of the intricate music. After their knowledge, their enthusiasm followed swiftly.

On his forty-seventh day on Marterly, a day only two weeks after the first full year's anniversary of the inception of the project, Steldan received a treat that made it all well worthwhile. It was the first full-scale dress rehearsal, conducted without interruption or correction, performed completely with staging and effects. Only the scenery was missing, the theater being one they shared with other ongoing plays and shows.

Steldan had seen the loose-knit, careless efficiency of the Commerce Branch when, in his youth, he had worked in a planning department. He had seen the harsh, hurried efficiency of emergency hospitals when he had become a doctor, specializing in physical therapy. And he had seen the disciplined efficiency of the military, where obedience was not the foremost virtue, but, rather, the only virtue.

But never before this day had he seen so many people — over one hundred performers, musicians, singers, and support and technical crew — merge their efforts together so brilliantly and do so voluntarily. No one was here who didn't want to be. Even the youngest members of the company, here as part of their two year universal service to the Concordat, had chosen to work with music and could easily ask for reassignment.

Today, the bickering was forgotten, the petty feuds set aside. Today, the music ruled, and the performers seemed caught up in it. The many argumentative and ill-assorted personalities had been subsumed, and, for a brief time, they formed a greater whole, a vast musical being that transcended the mortals it comprised. Steldan felt an exaltation then, that well repaid his long year's worth of troubles.

∞

The company was packed and ready to board a Navy-requisitioned vessel for Archive. The opera had been scheduled for performance. Kulan Gane had done her part: the work would be heard, almost simultaneously, on over two hundred worlds. Regular distribution channels would back up the secret network of jumpspace laser communication, and a hundred thousand worlds would, as the weeks and months went by, see and hear the work as recorded.

The company began to board the ship, a converted hospital ship that Steldan had had recommissioned and refitted. Some members, inevitably, were late. Others delayed departure by panicky attention to last minute details. Boarding was not half completed when a figure in a Navy uniform approached Steldan.

Steldan whirled and, for a moment, faced himself in a mirror. The black and grey uniform and dark hair were the same as his, as was the serious expression and the straight stance. There were more stripes on the sleeve, however, and more bands on the rank-chip. It was his superior in the Intelligence Branch, who had caught up with him at last.

"Admiral Morgan."

"Commodore Steldan." Morgan looked up at the ship and at the musicians who had paused on the boarding ramp to watch the confrontation. "It seems to me that you have some explaining to do."

Helplessly, shamefacedly, Steldan nodded.

17

It begins and ends the same way:
knives in our hands, hatred in our eyes.
Our crops are watered in blood, and our
books written in it.

— Achorus
The Skeleton and the Chaffinch

At dawn, the robots died.

Without warning, the two Lords of Stone who
flanked the high throne of the Emperor sagged,
falling with mirror-image precision to their
knees. They toppled forward, face-down onto
the polished floor of the throne room, and their
heads knocked against the tiles with but a single
sound. It was the sound of the hammer descending onto the neck of a condemned criminal, the sound of the fall of the court itself.
Around the periphery of the court's panoplied
shell, other scattered sounds of impact made
the nobles jerk their heads this way and that
way, looking like marionettes sensing their

destiny. Like marionettes with their strings ripped away, the robots fell.

The business of the morning court was held in abeyance. The Emperor stood, commanding a respectful silence. Lyra knelt at the bottom of the ramp that ascended to his throne. Nobles in deep shock awaited the Emperor's pronouncement.

"Children," he said, his voice neither emphatic nor ponderous but, rather, at rest. "Why quail? Someone has taken a great liberty. Go and do what is needful."

Such was the assurance in his voice that what would ordinarily have been a rush to the defenses of the palace was instead a mere saunter. None — now — believed that victory over the rebels was other than inevitable.

None had predicted the fall of the robots.

It was Lyra's task to oversee the defense of the palace. She knew, however, that the palace tolerated her presence only grudgingly: the palace looked after its own defense, its deep, sick brain fixed with the notion of protecting the Emperor. Nevertheless, defense was her task; she was compelled to offer her life in the safeguarding of the Emperor, and she would apply herself to that task.

"I beg your leave to depart," she said in her smallest voice.

The Emperor waved his hand.

Backing away, turning, Lyra fled. Once beyond the throne-room gates, however, she found herself at a loss. Which way to go? The computer, the palace's central brain — and a mad brain she knew it to be — lay far below, buried in a deep stratum of rock beneath the palace. The defenders, humans now that the robot guards and soldiers were deactivated, would be massed along the upper terraces and balconies but must also protect the inner stairways. And her Basil awaited her in her apartments, only two floors below. They were not prestigious apartments, Lyra knew, but, despite her exalted title, her climb to the places of power had only just begun.

She thought of Basil and found strength. She gathered her skirts up about her and ran, lacking any thought of dignity, to a high terrace where she would be able to oversee the full plan of the battle as it shaped.

A battle it had to be. The revolutionaries would never have struck against the robots unless they dared an actual assault on the palace. The Emperor's confidants had warned him of this threat, and he had laughed. The palace could never fall, and the people, although they may not love him as they once did, would never dare rise against him.

Lyra, who had grown to know him, wondered. He was now the oldest living man on the planet, eternally young, eternally strong. But, in certain ways, she thought she sensed a youthful quality about him. At times, it was innocence, as ludicrous as that notion could be when applied to a man whose debaucheries were wide-famed. At times, it was naivete: the great scientific and political mind failed, perhaps, to understand that other minds could be as ambitious as his own. Today, Lyra had sensed a touch of petulance in his voice. The people whom he had never dared to love had rejected him at last.

The city lay below her, splaying out to the right along the deep canyon still in shadow from the palace-topped hill. It was so green, too lovely for her to comprehend. She saw it revealed, unutterable beauty clinging to the land. To the left, at the head of the canyon, stood the high triple arch that celebrated the honor of spaceflight. The monument shone, bright and ruddy in the morning sun. To the right, the temple, the arena, the great column of Conoybar, the homes of a thousand nobles, and the tenements of ten million commoners and slaves.

The sun's light was reddened by more than the early hour: smoke rose from hundreds of widely spaced points, both near and far. The wind, blowing it away and out to sea, brought a faint whiff of the its stench to Lyra. The smoke was everywhere, but she could see no flames.

The revolution was not a serious matter. She clung to her beliefs, desperate for assurance. She wanted to run back to find Basil. The revolutionaries: what were they but troublemakers? They put on acts and skits in the streets. They slandered the Emperor and scrawled slogans on walls. How could they possibly be threatening?

She remembered the way the two giant, man-shaped robots had fallen, and she clenched her fists.

Below her, although the battlements of the palace stood ready to be defended, no regiments of troops had taken formation. Here and there a lone, lorn soldier paced, looking out over the city. An officer had assembled a cadre of perhaps a dozen and harangued them. The wind brought the tone of his voice to Lyra, but none of his words.

The wind also carried to her a faint, odd sound. She tried for some time to place it. It was . . . chaos. Distantly, alarms rang, and buzzers sounded. Metal beat on metal. Flames licked at ancient, austere houses. Vehicles were torn open, their contents and works strewn.

Men and women shouted. A city, a world, an Empire had awakened in hatred. The screams of anger merged until the distant din overrode their daily cautions. The Empire was no longer their cosmos; their rage was.

Lyra saw the first straggling columns of revolutionaries marching up the streets, heading toward the palace.

She went back inside. There was nothing to be done. Certainly there was nothing she could do. She spent the next hour wandering, lost, forlorn, not even remembering her Basil. The world had ended. The rude shock of reality would follow.

She strolled aimlessly, her mind blank. She wasn't watching before her when she rounded the corner into the Court of the Stone Gladiator.

The small court was thronged with men in the work outfits of commoners, led by a man who wore, as his only symbol of rank, a red strip of fabric tied about his head. It looked dashing, somehow rugged and stylistically daring. The loose ends dangled behind his ear, and his hair was disarrayed. In his hand was a snub-nosed fuser rifle.

Lyra couldn't comprehend it. Commoners didn't carry weapons. The palace would never have permitted them to enter. The stone gladiator, standing calf-deep in the still water of his fountain, should have come to life, slaying them all with his sword.

Lyra had run into the vanguard of revolt and into the cutting edge of history. There were no robots to save her. The palace was quite dead.

∞

Szentellos stood before the revolutionary council, the eighteen men who had gathered in Thendall's home.

"Am I your theorist, or am I not?"

"You are," answered Thendall. The other members nodded in agreement. Their assent was reserved, however; Szentellos noticed their hesitation.

"Then I say what I have said all along: no killing."

Thendall stretched his shoulders. "Soldiers, slaves, and, finally, the nobles themselves can be depended upon to oppose us. Should we go to them with empty hands and politely request that they surrender?"

"Thendall, will you learn? The horrors of the past are as clear a guideline as anyone could need." Szentellos leaned forward. "We must fight, I agree with you. But, when we have won, we don't need to kill anyone. We must not kill Arcadian."

The mention of that most hated of names brought the council to a murmur.

"You're a theorist, an ideologist." Thendall spoke without anger, and, to those who watched, it surely seemed as if this was nothing more than a philosophical debate. He and Szentellos had discussed these matters of murder, theft, revolution, late at night in safety and in secrecy. Today, the revolution had begun in earnest. By this time the robots had died, the nobles had had their warning, and matters were in the hands of the gods.

"I have practical knowledge as well," Szentellos insisted. "I'm not speaking from abstract sentiment. This is directly relevant."

They glared at one another. Szentellos, too tall, too thin, faced the others, his bushy, unruly hair standing in tufts above his head.

"But this council has, after all, the right to overturn your recommendations. You've been right only slightly more often than you've been wrong."

The council, to whom Thendall gestured in search of support, gestured back, backing the words of their chosen spokesman.

"We're builders," Szentellos said with perhaps too much stress. "We're not destroyers. I will not allow you to mix blood with the mortar. The foundation of the new order — order! — cannot be so weakened."

"It can." Thendall spread his hands, as if helpless before Szentellos' eloquence. The effect was mockery, but mockery so refined and sugared as to leave no lasting impression of resentment. Lasting impressions, after all, are not so important as the ones that are remembered only subliminally. Thendall built, too, in this room. The foundations he laid were to guarantee his own post in the future.

Szentellos leaned forward onto the table. He realized for the first time that he alone was standing, while the others sat. He transformed himself, consciously, into a lecturer, a teacher, a man with a voice they had no choice but to heed. He told them, then, in words that meant everything, why the wanton slaughter of the nobility of the Empire of Archive would be a misstep.

"We are at a crossroads. The path we take shall determine the rest of our history."

The choice, however, unknown to him, had already been made.

∞

The sight of the revolutionaries had little effect on Lyra at first. They didn't seem real. Even when their undeniable reality was forced onto her consciousness, she saw them as nothing more than commoners in strange costume. They were weak. They were pathetic. The ten men standing before her had no power.

Around another corner stood another man, a noble, she thought at first. Then she saw how his robes flowed and how his feet and arms were bare. It was a priest, the holy man who tended the chapel at the north end of the palace. All was right; all was well. This priest would banish the commoners, and they would skulk back to their daily tasks. Lyra sighed, happy to know that life would go on as before.

The priest pulled a small medallion from his robe, a symbol of command. He held it forward and drew breath to speak.

Eight of the ten revolutionaries stood straight, the rebellion shocked out of them by the brutal power of the symbol. The other two, however, had closed their eyes the moment they saw the priest dip his hand beneath his robes. Blindly, desperately, they fired their fusers, sending rippling streams of flame scorching, scattering the shots all along the wall. One shot hit the priest squarely in the face; another tore his arm off at the same time that his head dissolved.

The symbol of command operated visually. To defeat it, all one needed was the speed not to look.

The hue of the world changed, deepened, turned from daylight to nightmare bale-light. The revolution was real. Life was death. Hope was fled.

Lyra darted away, running so fast that speed was lost in headlong stumbling. She ran and didn't know whether or not the men came after. She ran, only after a time taking a course toward her apartments rather than simply away, away, away from the horror behind her. The revolutionaries were not men, nor were they monsters. Only gods or devils had the power to commit such atrocities.

She hit her door; she shot within. Basil, asleep on the couch, rolled over, instantly alert. He stood, uncoiling himself to his great height, moving quickly to her side.

Gentle he was, and comforting. Her father's arms had never held her in such unassailable safety. Around her, his enfolding touch was a tower, a fortress. The soft fur of him lay gently across her cheek, and his warmth, his fresh scent, his quickly pattering heartbeat were all promises of security. She wished to crawl with him into her bed and, there, be forgotten forever. She wished. . . .

If, just then, a rattle of small arms fire had erupted or if the noises of slaughter or of combat had come to her, even faintly, she would have led the unresisting Basil into the bedchamber to await discovery and death.

But it was silence that hung outside, no louder than her thoughts. Basil comforted her, and yet her curiosity and her sense of duty — the latter calling a dimly felt pleading, but, nevertheless, one she could not deny — urged her to go forth and to act.

Act? How? I'm. . . . She drew strength from Basil and, afraid, went to the door.

No one was outside. The corridors were free.

The palace is large. If I can get to the basements and restore power to the robots. . . .

That was as far ahead as she dared let herself think. The thinking, however, was the acting. Basil and she, together as they had always been, set off down the deserted ways of the palace.

Above them, the arched ceilings winked with inset gems; the carpets, reaching beyond sight, softened their footfalls. Basil held her hand, sensing her fear and her excitement. Somehow, in his mind that was brilliant yet silent, even lacking language, he knew what hung in the balance. He knew that something more important by far than Empire or Palace, Emperor or Noble, was in danger. Lyra was. He held to her, and his ears searched for a warning of danger.

18

I've never felt as if I had any choice in
anything I've done. My feet continue
down the path, almost of themselves.
This doesn't soothe my conscience, however, or ease my guilt.

— Szentellos
Regrets

A high layer of dry, brittle clouds dimmed the
sunlight that fell vertically onto the spaceport
field on Marterly. The clouds also relieved a little
of the late autumn heat. Athalos Steldan, heart
pounding, stood with his hand against the vast,
flat flank of his Navy transport. Ahead, crowd-
ing along the boarding stile, his musicians clustered, watching in dismay. Before him stood
Admiral Robert Morgan, once his superior officer, now his nemesis.

"Am I under arrest?"

Morgan frowned. Steldan, through his
unhappy shock and even in the extremity of his

misery at having been caught so late, so very late in the game, recognized the gesture. Morgan frowned the way Steldan himself would have had their situations been reversed.

Looking up at Steldan, Morgan shook his head sadly. "Yes. You are officially under arrest."

Steldan bit his lip. Slowly, he straightened. "Yes, sir."

Morgan's reserve failed him — just as Steldan's would have. So alike the two men were, but Morgan represented the force of law, and Steldan had stepped beyond that pale. "Athalos," he murmured, his voice pained, "what the devil have you been doing for the past year?"

"Must we discuss it here?"

Together they looked up at the large ship. Two-toned, dark grey and pale mint green, the ugly, box-shaped ship stood six meters above the flat level of the field and was sunk another six below, nestled in its blast pit. A half-meter gap showed, a dark, shadowy crevice where fuel umbilici and signal probes met the ship's sandpapered surface, mating it to the spaceport. Steldan had hoped to flee aboard that ship; for now, the ship was a part of the planet.

A level section of flat, railed platform spanned the gap, giving access to the ship through its main crewlock. Musicians watched, not knowing what to make of the confrontation. From within the ship, other performers crowded back out, craning their necks for a view. Late-arriving members of the cast and crew came up slowly over the field, sensing trouble.

Not one of them had said a word.

Steldan waved and tried to smile. "Go on. Go ahead loading. I'll — "

"Belay that!" Morgan snapped. He looked back over his shoulder at the ship. "Everyone just stay put. No cargo on or off. The ship is sealed."

The musicians stared at him, then began to murmur among themselves. "Is that true, Commodore?"

Steldan spread his hands helplessly. "Yes. Find Cliffs and tell her."

"But she isn't here."

"I know. She — "

"Commodore Steldan," Morgan said, his voice low. "I won't warn you again."

"Yes, sir."

Without another word, the two men turned and walked off toward the spaceport terminal annex. From behind them, one of the singers called out, asking what they were supposed to do. Steldan sighed but did not turn about to answer.

The two men, of a height, of the same build, trudged across the vast field, stepping forward to tread on their shadows. Before long they arrived at a narrow, reinforced door. Morgan pushed it open; Steldan stepped within.

The spaceport annex was built with thick, secure walls and with few windows. Inside, cool fluoros painted the walls with a light as chill as

254

the refrigerated air. Morgan gestured for Steldan to precede him down the hall. Soon, he stopped him in front of another door.

Freedom for billions hinges on as narrow a thing as this, Steldan thought. For, had Morgan stepped in front of him in order to open the door, Steldan would have clubbed the man down with his fists.

Am I, then, a religious fanatic? Do I consider myself above all laws and beyond all mortal responsibility? Admiral Morgan was his superior and had also been — perhaps he still was — his friend.

Steldan sighed and entered the room, safely in advance of Admiral Morgan. The office space was cramped, nothing more than a windowless interrogation room. Steldan had presided over such rooms before. He doubted very much he ever would again.

Morgan seated himself on one metal-frame chair. Steldan took the other.

"What's your game, Athalos?" Morgan's tone was as warm as he could make it.

With a deep breath, Steldan began trying to justify his crimes.

"I guess I know how you found me: triangulation. It couldn't have been difficult. And I know that you couldn't have tracked me through a check on my operatives. They don't exist."

Morgan nodded. "Tell me more."

"Has de la Noue told you about the assassins of the Black Book? No?" Steldan smiled, but

Morgan kept his expression neutral. Looking at the floor, Steldan went on. "Sorry. I won't try to get information out of you. There isn't any point to that. . . . The Black Book was a squadron of murderers. They got Apollonia of Archive. They got Benbow, Scow, Berlitz, and Wilson six years ago. I'm sure you remember that."

Morgan tried to keep from showing his reaction to that revelation, but could not. "Two Admirals, two Commanders, killed within one month." He looked at Steldan quizzically. "No clues. No culprits. You know that the files are still open on that?"

"Black Book. We don't know when it was founded. The Grand Admiral ordered me to eradicate its workings and to track down and punish the assassins. I didn't. I didn't know why, then: it seemed wrong to dismantle such an intricate and versatile tool. So . . . the Black Book went to work for me."

"Did you have anyone killed?" Morgan asked, his voice crisp.

Steldan smiled. "Of course not. That isn't how I work. I think you know me well enough to understand that. I had access to some hundred and forty men and women who, in the eyes of every record-keeping agency of the Concordat, did not exist. One hundred and forty non-persons. And I had ways of taking the funding for my project from various classified ledgers. I had money, and I had manpower. Missing was only a way to utilize these elements."

"What did you find? What crystallized your

256

plans?"

"The needs of history. You haven't seen the file entitled *Flederwisch*. No one has." His voice heavy and sad, Steldan explained about the discovery of Sophia on her lonely asteroid and how he had managed to contain all news of the find.

"Admiral Morgan, on that chip of rock, floating in red-limned darkness, was a library. It, alone, of the Emperor's treasuries of knowledge, had survived. The others — "

"The others burned, Athalos." Morgan looked Steldan in the eyes, taking a personal measure of this man. Steldan was neither lying nor mad. And . . . it fit. "Wait a moment. . . ." He shook his head. "Athalos, in the past few months, several books and magazines — and video productions, popularizations, dramatizations — have appeared, all dealing with themes of the old Empire. Could that have been. . .?"

"My work. And those stories, which everyone has thought were interpolations, are historical."

"You've — " Morgan balked for a moment as his mind refused to credit the historical implications. "You've spliced us back into our own past from which we had been sundered!"

"And I'm not through!" Steldan exulted. Morgan understood! How could he help but find himself in agreement?

But Morgan remained suspicious. "Why didn't you simply contact the University of Archive and give them the material?"

Steldan snorted. "Would you give a pre-ignited fusion mass to a tribe of preliterate savages? They would be killed, and the fire would go out. Nothing is gained unless the time is right. The University would have released the material in the wrong way. It would have been static, unliving. My plan was to present it to the people of Archive the way it was meant to be heard."

"Heard?"

"The musicians on the ship." Steldan's shoulders slumped. There was no use. He closed his eyes and tried to accept the death of his dream. He knew — he had known all along — that he had to do no more than sing to Morgan, and Morgan would be his. The symbol of command was aboard the ship; it had been the first thing he packed. But he carried a symbol of command within his throat.

Whether it was his vanity or his ethical strength that prevented him from using it, he would never know.

"What about them?" Morgan asked.

"They have some music with them: an opera. It carries the combined artistic wealth of the past and the present. Forgotten words, forbidden music. . . . How can you understand?"

"You can explain it to me, Athalos." Morgan sat forward on his seat. "Or you can explain it to the Grand Admiral. She's asked me to bring you to her."

"I'm surprised she's willing to hear me."

"She's anxious to hear your side of it."

"Well, then — " Steldan's next words were cut

off by a flat, deafening concussion. The lights in the room went out.

"Don't move," Morgan said, his voice somehow penetrating the clamor of alarms and a crescendo of subsidiary explosions.

"I won't," Steldan responded.

Over the crackle of bursting energy, the two men heard a low, rumbling sound, swelling and growing higher in pitch. To their experienced ears, it was unmistakable. The converted hospital ship, with its complement of musicians aboard, had begun to ascend into the skies.

"Come with me." Morgan threw open the door and rushed out into a scene of utter confusion. Officers with flashlights moved about, their beams cutting through a low-lying fog of smoke and dust. Morgan, with Steldan in tow, ran along the corridors, coming soon to the flight control deck of the spaceport. Reserve power came on about the time they entered, but Steldan saw that it powered only lights and air-conditioning, not the computers or other spaceport instrumentation.

The hubbub ongoing here was more orderly: officers had quickly regimented the technicians and crew of the flight control deck into a cohesive unit. The Port Authority Officer, a Lieutenant Commander, saw Morgan and waved to him, a questioning look in his eyes. Morgan hurried over to meet him.

"Situation?"

"Bombs. Deliberately and knowledgeably planted. No loss of life. Gravitic grid down.

Radar inoperative. Time to repair, five minutes estimated." The officer, Steldan observed, was in control of himself. Perhaps he'd seen combat in one of the battles of the past few years.

"The ship that took off." Morgan looked back and forth between Steldan and the flight control officer. "Can it be stopped?"

"You have a Destroyer Squadron in High Guard." The officer stated this quickly, knowing that Morgan knew but, nevertheless, presenting the facts as the superior officer had asked. "The ship can be destroyed."

But not stopped.

"The bomb-setter?"

"Marine detachment investigating. They'll report."

Morgan looked sidelong at Steldan. "A Black Book agent?"

"Yes. It would have to be."

"Was he acting according to your orders?"

Steldan had had time to piece together what must have happened. Cliffs, finding the ship frozen, forbidden to leave, would have acted on her own. Did she know what a gamble she was taking? Did she know what a burden this placed on him?

"My orders? No."

Morgan drew him a little aside. Around them, as the smoke cleared and banks of instrumentation flickered back into life, the flight control crew worked with disciplined haste to repair their workplace. Gripping Steldan tightly by the arm, Morgan spoke softly. "You have about fifteen minutes to save the lives of your people aboard that ship. Because, the way things stand now, I'll destroy it."

Steldan looked into Morgan's eyes and saw there the hidden message, the deep, almost unconscious plea that would have been in his own eyes if their positions had been reversed. *Give me a reason to let people live. Don't force me to be a killer.*

Morgan was a scholar too. Morgan was that much like Steldan.

Taking control of himself in a brutal, realistic way — the way he would never allow himself to take control of anyone else — Steldan began to explain. Even then, even under this stress, he would not permit himself to put music into his voice.

∞

Cliffs, bearing a double armload of last minute supplies and equipment, arrived back at the ship only minutes after Steldan had been taken away. The musicians and singers, some almost in panic and some making a show of their unconcern, explained to her what had happened.

Steldan's greatest fear was that this would happen. The Concordat Navy had been their unwitting ally all along. It was no surprise that they would have discovered it, at last, and taken action.

Steldan always made a point of wearing his black and grey uniform, because of the unpleas-

ant impression it gave. Now he's been taken away by an admiral wearing the same colors. People still fear the Intelligence Branch. They haven't learned to disdain their power.

"Everyone aboard the ship. We'll be leaving straightaway."

"We can't!" objected one of the singers, a flighty young countertenor. Cliffs looked at him and couldn't help smiling. The youth was perhaps the most impetuous and uncooperative spirit in the troupe, but he was also among the greatest talents. Steldan's plan to unleash the same sort of creative and independent spirit in all of humankind was more dangerous than he had imagined if this tense, little singer was a true indication of the future.

But his plan has no hope at all if we don't act. Now.

"Aboard the ship. We're going to Archive to stage an opera!" Cliffs had never taken command of anything, ever in her life. She had, as her arrangement with Steldan stipulated, tried to remain in the background during open disputes, allowing him to take the active role. He had reprimanded them, he had congratulated them, he had taken their governance. It was as he had said, however: none of them had failed to see through the ruse. They had known who their real leader was. Before the first full-scale rehearsal, most of them had even known that it was her opera they performed.

Now, as she stepped forward, urgency and surety in her face and voice, the assembled singers and musicians withdrew, moving swiftly to their cabins for an imminent lift-off. It was as if the stage director had said, preparatory to the rehearsal of a segment, "Places." In only a few minutes the ship was ready.

Their pilot was a thin, lanky woman with short-cropped, dark hair, the remnants of which formed a rough stubble over her scalp. Her face was shadowed by some hidden grief; Cliffs had never seen her smile. There was no question in Cliffs' mind: this was one of the Black Book assassins-no-longer.

"We need to fly."

The long-limbed assassin folded her arms and looked sadly at Cliffs. "Can't. Spaceport'd pull us down again."

"What?" Cliffs shook her head. "I don't understand."

The assassin led her forward and gestured out the viewports of the control room. "Boost-grid. We can take off without its help, if we have to, though I was counting on its assist. But, if they don't want us to take off, we fly like a clip-winged rock. We can't."

Cliffs looked away, then back. "Can you disable the boost-grid?"

Her eyes lighting up, the assassin smiled. Then, slowly, painfully, the smile faded. "I can't do it without killing. And — " She looked down at the deck. A long, long silence passed before she was able to speak.

"I got no more killing."

This, then, was the cost that use of the

symbol of command exacted. A decision based upon its command was never the same as a decision based on choice. This young woman — Cliffs guessed that, beneath her harsh appearance, she was only sixteen — wanted to be what she had once been. And she knew that she could not be.

"Isn't there some way you can get us free?" she asked gently.

The assassin's head came up, and a ghost of a smile returned to her face. "Oh, yeah. There's always ways. . . ."

"Go."

"Wait. Need to think." She squatted down, leaning against a bulkhead. "Bombs."

"Okay."

"Tricky."

"I understand."

"Right." The lean assassin stood again, unfolding herself to her full height. "Back in a few minutes. You need me to fly."

"Yes, we do." Cliffs watched her make her preparations and slip out of the main lock. In broad daylight, under the bright sun over Marterly, she strode across the field. No one saw her cut her way through security wire into the electricals blockhouse; no one saw her plant her handmade, homemade bombs.

The force of the explosions rippled across the field. Cliffs felt the impact of the shock waves, although it seemed to her as if she heard only a low clapping sound like a door being slammed. She stood in the open air lock and watched, astonished at the violence of the explosion: flames blossomed and electrical connections flew up into the air followed by spiralling trails of sparks.

She watched but never saw the assassin come out.

Sirens hooted, and alarms jangled. Lights, which had seemed incongruously bright in the daylight, went out, and their sudden darkness was even more of a wrongness. It seemed as if no one would react to the explosion. Then, moving swiftly, a detachment of Marines, in their black and dark green uniforms, rushed over the field, sweeping out of the port buildings. They surrounded the wrecked electrical blockhouse, paused for a moment, then began to dash within in pairs.

Have we gained our freedom, only to lose our chance to escape? Cliffs wondered. She bit her lip, but her grief was short-lived, and her determination was still strong.

Cliffs went back inside the ship and sent off a message to Sophia, relayed via the jumpspace communications link. The message would arrive there faster than any ship could. Long, long before she and her opera company arrived on Archive, Kulan Gane would have received the word and her preparations would be underway.

She next put out a general call over the ship's address intercom. "Can anyone fly a spaceship?" she asked, her voice low and cold, a deadliness hiding behind the slow words.

Firmly, almost angrily, one of the musicians came forward. She was an older woman, dark-haired and bitter-eyed. She, too, had come to love the music, and didn't like to think of foregoing the performance.

"I've flown," she said, her voice no less chill than Cliffs' had been. "I wasn't always a musician."

"Go," Cliffs said to her.

Without any formality, she leaped into the command couch, flung her fingers across the controls, and hopped the ship rudely into the air. Cliffs had only enough time to fall into the copilot's couch; the flutist pushed the ship to its full acceleration. Cliffs felt the pressure and lay back. The intercom lit up with the complaints of the musicians who had not been properly warned of the imminence of the escape.

"Damn this ship," the flutist/pilot snarled. "We're not gaining altitude, we're pushing the planet away from us. I could fly faster with nylon wings." Belying her mutterings, the altimeter rose steadily. The ground beneath them darkened, and the sky faded slowly to black.

"Orbit."

"Freedom?" asked Cliffs.

"No." Pointing to the navigation radar, the flutist showed her the four Navy Destroyers far above them in orbit.

"Will they kill us?"

"Yes. But they'll talk first."

Cliffs sighed. It wasn't long before the first warnings came in over the radio. Cliffs was ordered to reverse course and to return to the spaceport. Failure to comply would necessitate the destruction of the ship.

"Don't answer 'em," the flutist grumbled.

"We won't." Cliffs sighed, and relaxed as much as she could. This was the ultimate test for her music. If the Concordat of Archive was composed of men and women who would — who could — destroy a shipload of artists, then no amount of art could sway their lost souls. If she failed here, now, then she would have failed in any case. And, in that case, her life was of very little worth.

Time passed: the ship gained velocity. The warnings grew more sharp, more dangerously worded.

The warnings ceased.

One of the destroyers, a dark-hulled, slender weapon invisible in the dark of space, opened fire. A laser beam sparked dimly, barely to be seen glinting against the stars. Cliffs smiled. They were firing warning shots.

Two more shots flashed forth, each slightly more bright than the last. as the gunners aboard the Destroyer narrowed the margin by which they permitted their beams to miss. The light that Cliffs and her pilot saw was only photon leakage from the tightly focussed beams. The same beams, taken head on, would have vaporized large segments of the ship, killing all aboard.

One shot. That's all it would take. This thing isn't armored.

The shots ceased. The Destroyers shadowed

the small, helpless ship, like sharks circling about a desperately paddling swimmer.

Finally, the flutist engaged the jump drives, and space opened before them, gaping, red-jawed, to receive them. The last thing that Cliffs saw of her old, familiar universe was the radar image of the Navy vessels shearing off their pursuit.

The jaws closed: the small ship fell through jumpspace. Months would pass before they arrived at Archive. But they would arrive.

Their communications would arrive there before they did. That was their greatest advantage over the Navy.

Life, and music, went on.

19

There is a breed of men who, upon
hearing of trouble, march toward it. Some
seek spoils, some yearn for adventure,
but a very few go to quell the disturbance
and to soothe the trouble.

> — Paleologos
> *When Dreams Themselves Do Dream*

The palace atop the seaward hill in the city of
Archive had been modeled after a fortress but
was never a fortress in truth. Revolutionaries
had slunk within, and the sparse few defenders
that met them were, as often as not, overwhelmed.

Basil pulled Lyra into a niche and drew the
curtain nearly closed when a patrol of invaders
overtook them, marching loudly from the rear.
The rococo palaces of Archive were never want-
ing for niches.

The revolutionaries had triumphed and
herded a gaggle of downcast nobles before them.

The nobles, who had once attended on the pleasure of the Emperor, now plodded miserably in front of the men who had defeated them. One was wounded, his skin seared where a near miss from a fuser had burned him. The revolutionaries came to a halt in the corridor, evidently waiting for others to join them. They seemed completely uncaring and spoke bluntly of the fate they held in store for their captives.

"We'll kill 'em if fighting comes," said one man, a commoner certainly, bearing a gun and an armband.

"They'd be a handicap in a firefight," another agreed.

"Hmph," another snorted. "Send 'em forward and let them take the brunt of the fire. Or better yet. . . ." He raised his fuser. "Kill 'em here and now."

"We're not to do that. That isn't the way we were instructed."

"And who's taking instruction any longer? We're free men, aren't we? We're the nobles, and these, well, they're the slaves. Isn't it so?"

"No." The leader, the one with the red armband, spoke callously. "We'll capture as many as we can and kill 'em in the courtyard, all together. 'Bonfires bright, and prayerfires small, are but for mortal men. The flames of a pyre lick at heaven.'"

"And what's that supposed to mean?"

"We kill 'em all, all at once. That done, everything will be changed forever. No more nobles. No more Empire. The corruption will cease."

"Yeah. Where's the rest of our troop?"

"Maybe they ran into trouble. Who wants to go on to look?"

The group took a hasty vote and, grumbling, took again to marching. The captive nobles, apathetic and forlorn, said nothing. They marched stolidly forward under the muzzles of the guns that would soon slay them.

Lyra was more upset by the impropriety of a rude commoner quoting from a great work of poetry than by the wholly mundane offense of the discussion of killing. The lines about the sanctity of the flames of a pyre were from *The Skeleton and the Chaffinch*, a poem written many years ago by Achorus. A commoner could never use the beauty of those lines to defend a crime such as killing.

Killing? It still didn't seem real to Lyra. She remembered the death of the priest as a dim, vague occurrence, as if in some other life.

The parade of rebels and their doomed captives had passed on. Lyra and Basil were free to continue their eerie journey.

Lyra held back, for a moment, from entering the next chamber. It was the Court of the Stone Gladiator. Would there still be a headless, one-armed body sprawled on the floor? Had a priest actually died here? Basil pulled her forward, gently yet insistently. The Stone Gladiator looked down at her from his fountain. The priest's body lay untouched.

Lyra looked at him and could not deny the truth any longer. The commoners had taken up arms against their masters. The gods had not punished them for this hideous crime. The revolutionaries believed that they were justified, and it looked as if they might win.

Lyra and Basil, sneaking through the corridors of the palace they once had freely roamed, slowly made their way toward the control rooms from which the robots might be reactivated. The enemy would be strong there, but Lyra never thought of this. She went on, her blindness, for once, her main strength. Basil preceded her alertly.

∞

High above the city, in the orbital Belt, Petrosius looked in more than mock-horror at the destruction that a pair of saboteurs had wrought upon the control systems. One of the saboteurs was dead, burned to smoking sludge upon the deck plates by a security guard with a fuser. The other. . . .

Petrosius was the other, and, still, even though he had been caught, no one suspected.

"Good work, man," he stammered. "The bastard said he was going to kill me."

"Did he hurt you, sir?"

Petrosius took a deep breath. "No." He cast a quick glance at the ruined mass that stained the deck. He had been a man that Thendall had sent to help neutralize the Belt. Together, with the Belt's commander, the young man had taken the orbiting weapon out of the equation.

He had paid for it with his life.

Petrosius, somewhat to his surprise, still lived.

"What's happening below?"

"Riot." The guard was distraught, and only the discipline of his corps kept him from weeping. "The blackguards storm the palace."

"That must be stopped," Petrosius said idly, uselessly.

"How?" The question was heartfelt; the guard wanted to help.

"Well, we've got to get some troops together and go down there ourselves." He stood straight and snapped orders at the young man. "Call for my lieutenant. Get a repair team up here. And have a landing shuttle prepared."

Appear efficient but delay, delay. That is how I serve the revolution. An evil task this is.

"Yes, sir!" The guard disappeared.

Petrosius shook his head and surveyed the wreckage. Two men, acting swiftly, gaining access by the highest level of priority clearances, could demolish a control room in surprisingly little time. The Belt, for all of its massive weaponry and world-spanning power, was now only an ornament in the heavens. The battles below would be fought on terms more close to fair.

Soon, the shuttles were readied, although Petrosius insisted on full preflight checklists. It wouldn't do, he told them, to crash-land just at the moment they were most needed. It wouldn't do at all, he told himself, to arrive until well after any crucial moment.

Finally, he could delay no longer. With a great show of enthusiasm, he pushed into the first shuttle, followed by thirty armed soldiers. Two more shuttles launched along with his.

I'm coming home, he thought, and gripped his fuser tightly in his hands.

∞

The revolutionary council listened to Szentellos, and they didn't hear him. Nearly palpable in the air of the room, their politeness lulled him, beguiled him, and betrayed him. He spoke, stringing together the logical arguments like beads, the reasoning linear and inescapable, attractively delivered, forceful . . . and unheard. Perhaps he was too tied up in his own arguments to sense his failure to sway them. Perhaps he was lost in the artistry of the difficult concepts.

"We've seen too often before that the beginning of the movement determines its outcome. Bloodshed, at this point, once and for all determines the character of this revolution as bloody. Yet we have sworn ourselves to a humanistic revolution. We are not opposed to the nobles as individuals; we are opposed to the institutions of nobility."

All eyes were upon him, and attention was paid. No one was persuaded.

Thendall nodded gravely when, at last, Szentellos finished. That was taken by the other grave men in the room for an unspoken, yet unarguable, claim to the first right of reply. No one, save for lost Szentellos, wondered what was about to be said.

Exercising his prerogative to its fullest extent, Thendall let a long moment of silence pass. Of all the men in the room, only Szentellos looked at him, with narrowed eyes. The pause stretched.

"How does one blaze a message across the heavens?" Thendall wondered aloud in the deathlike stillness of the room. "The Emperor sought to ignite a new star in the sky. I have set fire to his palace. Should we send a tentative note, trepidant and of passive phrasing, and deliver it by footman? I throw stones. Or should we spar with our opponent, shadowboxing at reduced speed, ever careful of the rules of conduct? I strike to kill. Blood, you see, gives the banner the brightest letters."

"We oppose that," Szentellos insisted, striving against hopeless odds.

"Death is universal. And it is a message. Murder is universal, and it is the one message that cannot be misunderstood."

"It's wrong."

Thendall looked at Szentellos as if seeing a child where he'd imagined a man. "Revolution is always wrong. You are asking me to obey one law, while breaking another. That is where the true wrongness lies. Either all laws are to be ignored, or none of them are. You may choose to interpret this as an oversimplification, and yet. . . . Are we not armed? Is not the palace of the Emperor now under siege? Is not our only hope of success based upon the treachery of the men the Emperor trusted? Why do you draw so finicky a line between what you will accept and what you will not? Violence has a meaning; your words, by themselves, have none."

He turned his face away. One by one, with varying degrees of hesitancy and regret, the others did also.

∞

Lyra's daring excursion through the palace had taken her behind the sweep of the revolutionaries' attack. The battle had a fluid nature, and front lines were difficult to determine. The nobles, defending their liege and their lives, were armed with weapons they were unfamiliar with. They also had their personal symbols of command. Sometimes, those symbols enabled them to immobilize their enemies or even to turn them about to attack their fellows. Sometimes, the symbols failed, as when the revolutionaries simply opened fire on anyone they saw moving.

There were many revolutionaries and painfully few loyal nobles.

The corridors that Lyra nervously traversed were enemy territory. She was aware of this, and, to her, the draperies, the statuary, the many-hued heraldic chains, whose links were families, and the hanging crystalline lamps all seemed muted in their colors. It was as if the decor no longer existed for those who could appreciate it, and it faded under the onslaught of irreverence. Lyra went as far, in her imaginings, as to personify this fancy until she saw, or seemed to see, the art about her weeping silent tears. She fought not to weep alongside it. The palace had been alive, once, and was now dead. She gritted her teeth and sped down the weeping ways, seeking to resurrect it.

She saw the stack of corpses ahead of her, long before she was able to recognize what it was. By the time she did, she was nearly atop it. She halted abruptly and clung to Basil with strength that desperation had never before elicited from her. She'd never seen so many corpses before, except in the arena, and men sentenced to die for their crimes weren't human.

She'd seen the priest die, cut down by fuser fire in the Court of the Stone Gladiator. She'd imagined that that was the worst horror that war could hold for her, that she'd seen the worst sight her eyes would ever behold.

This was worse. Between a dozen and two dozen men lay strewn about, their wounds high and low on their bodies: black-caked, bloodless wounds. The walls bore countless scars, marking where shots had missed. The bodies were not all in single pieces. They lay atop one another, caressing each other promiscuously in still silence. Many eyes were open; many hands stretched out in frozen gestures of appeal.

Lyra shrieked, once. Basil let her. What followed, a never-ending moment of delirious grief, rage, and horror, she endured while he held her to him. His strength that she had come to love for its godlike excess of hers held her motionless. He clasped her face to his chest and her arms to his sides in easy disregard of her struggles. Her shrieks and uttered blasphemies were muffled in his furry breast. In her extremity, she bit him deeply, to which he made no response other than to look down at her. She never saw that; his eyes were wide with more than bewilderment.

It passed.

He lifted her gently and, cradling her in his arms, bore her along, turning so that she needn't see the corpses again. The journey, already dreamlike to her, grew more so with an ambiguously comforting and threatening emotional tone that she would never live long enough to identify.

In time, by using the less-frequented stairways and avoiding the lifts where revolutionary guards were posted, they came to the lower technical levels.

The decorations were no less gorgeous here, although they took on a technological aspect that was not evident above. Projected light, diffuse and of several colors, gave the floors a misty, depth-like quality, and the carpets of reflective fibers enhanced this. It was like walking on clouds above deeps that fell away forever, although the effect was only hinted at, and therefore nonthreatening. The walls likewise gave shadowy clues of wonders that shifted, moment by moment, from vistas of patterned delight to softly and randomly flowing pastel shapes. Designed to be intriguing, reassuring, exciting, and challenging by turns, even this corridor seemed, to Lyra's mind, to be world-weary and despairing. The circuits of the thoughtful computer, whose mind was deeper than any man's, surely felt sorrow at the passage of the culture that had built it.

Lyra leaped, struggling in Basil's arms. Basil stopped and lowered her to the floor.

"The computer!" she shouted, then clapped her hand to her mouth in sudden fear. *The computer! Parts of it are still alive!*

They could go no further, however: the antechamber to the computer room was guarded. Six corridors intersected here, all arriving at different, strange angles. Seven revolutionaries, armed with their fusers, maintained a watch.

There were seven of them, and she had only her Basil. But surely he was a match for seven?

She had no time to explain to him what she desired him to do; she hadn't the words, and the revolutionaries would have heard. Basil, though, seemed to know. It was almost ugly, the way his face changed expression. His alert ears swiveled back; his erect posture was lost to a fighter's crouch. Worst were his eyes. Eyes that had expressed love so fluently were now the eyes of a killer. Lyra was forgotten; she was never the object of these emotions in him. The survivor of the deadly duel in the arena now eased forward, preparing for a lunging leap.

Lyra followed him, only to hang back. The

savagery of combat was alien to her. Battle of this sort belonged on the fine sand of the arena floor, not the smoky floors of the palace. This was the closest that she had ever been to the bloody doings of a true fight.

Basil was among the seven in one bound. A great rotating swing from the waist floored three at once and disarmed another. Guns, moving slowly in the grasps of men who had never been permitted them before, swung up. Basil plucked them from hands unaccustomed to the weapons' feel. The men, their hatreds inflamed as furiously as their lifelong disdain for the slaves that were the only thing beneath them in social status, rallied themselves and moved in.

Basil began to fight. He took one man by the neck and twisted, breaking the vertebrae with one quick shake. Dropping to a squat, he kicked out, snapping another man's leg backward at the knee. He hauled another man down, then up, twisting his shoulder in an unlikely direction and dislocating it.

A fuser discharged, missing Basil by an arm's length and in no way distracting him. A trim, furry thumb entered an eyesocket and came away dripping. A powerful leg leaped up and kicked out, breaking a man's hip. An arm, scything, crushed a rib cage.

It was over in mere moments. Numbers meant less in this case than strength, dexterity, speed, and, above all, training. Basil's fighting skill was engraved into him with the precision of the computers that had molded his genes. He stood above the fallen, then straightened and flashed Lyra a happy, intelligent grin.

She darted into the control room, hoping to be able to reactivate the robots. If she could, the revolution was over.

The computer had been put out of commission by men who had no reason to preserve it for later. Much can be done with demolition tape, with pyrostruct, with hammers and with fists. The computer had been hurt badly.

Lyra, however, was the daughter of the Sultan of the Household. Shaking her head, she reminded herself of her station. *She* was the Sultan of the Household. She knew this computer. It served her.

Speaking slowly, she uttered the secret codes that activated emergency backup systems, hidden systems, secure systems.

The computer, mad before, came back to a shattered half-life, more insane yet. It still had two commands that compelled it to obedience. Serve Arcadian. Protect Arcadian.

High above, in the throne room, the two toppled stone warriors stirred. Like men awakening from having been stunned, they lifted their heads, then put their palms to the floor. They rose to their knees. They stood. Mirror images of deadly power, they held aloft their weapons.

"Your majesty," Lyra's voice came into the throne room. "I have restored some of your defenses."

Arcadian, who had never left his throne,

nodded. "Very good, Lyra." He looked about. "Very good, indeed."

"What are your instructions?"

"I have three." Arcadian's eyes sparkled. "First, destroy the revolutionaries. All of them. Every last one of them. They. . . ." He smiled and shook his head. "They have to die, you know."

"Yes, Majesty."

"Second, I have a decision I have only now made. I love you and want you to be my Empress. I've never taken an Empress, only concubines. You, before all else, have earned this boon."

Lyra's voice was shaken, as he knew it would be. "Thank you . . . thank you, your Majesty."

"Third, burn the libraries."

"I . . . I don't know what that means."

He heard the sadness in her voice. She feared to fail him. He frowned. It was strange, but he truly did love her. Arcadian and Lyra: the names appealed to his sense of meter.

"It is nothing. The computer will take care of it."

The computer already had. Throughout the vast Empire of Archive, the message flashed out, much faster than light. The weight of knowledge of four thousand years was lost.

Arcadian sat upon his throne and waited for victory.

20

They call me the Omnipath, the Master
of Misery, and they scorn me. Do they
rage at the surgeon who discovers their
illnesses? Do they whip the arithmetician
who shows them they are bankrupt?
— Trinopus
Furies Chained

In the long race from Marterly to Archive, Margaret Cliffs had an advantage. The military
ships in pursuit were not significantly faster,
although they would have eventually overtaken
the converted hospital ship that carried the
opera troupe. Cliffs, however, had the
jumpspace laser network and could coordinate
her stops in advance. The ship, which the performers had taken to calling *The Lucky Guess*,
would fall out of jumpspace above a stopover
world, and refueling shuttles would stand
ready, previously notified of the arrival. Admiral
Morgan, pressing on with better ships, lacked

this edge: he had no means of communicating his desire that the ship be stopped.

The race was not to the swift. Cliffs knew that, in time, she would arrive on Archive. She also knew that Admiral Morgan would be close behind her.

Relaying messages through Sophia's station, she spoke with Kulan Gane, who awaited them on Archive. Kulan Gane, aware of the deadline and the danger, began making her desperate plans.

Long weeks passed. The ship felt more and more like a prison. The musicians in particular chafed at the enforced inactivity; there was no space aboard the ship large enough for the orchestra to assemble to rehearse together. The Conductor and the Music Director circumvented this problem by letting the musicians practice in shifts, rotating them around as often as possible. With Cliffs' stern supervision and the Conductor's easygoing expertise, the orchestra remained a cohesive musical unit.

On Archive, counting the time and begrudging every wasted moment, Kulan Gane began her final arrangements. A symphony hall was prepared, put into good repair, polished and refurbished, and equipped with the necessary technical support gear. The manipulative machinery of publicity and promotion went into action, and Kulan Gane discovered a new talent in herself. She turned out to be a highly competent pitchman.

Steldan's original plan was set aside: all

efforts were improvised by Kulan Gane after discussion, whenever possible, with Cliffs. They ran contests, lotteries, parties and circuses, press conferences, major video presentations; they had books rushed into print; snatches of the music that Cliffs had labored for over a year on were quickly adapted and were pushed into artificial popularity.

They invented, by themselves, techniques that were older than anyone could know. The Empire had outgrown such obvious appeals to status nearly a hundred years before the discovery of spaceflight.

But, to the jaded and callous ears of Archive, the techniques were novel. Kulan Gane became a celebrity, and everyone wanted to know more about The Skeleton and the Chaffinch.

Would it be a political opera? Kulan Gane let it be known, without offending the censors or the Cultural Arts Board, that, yes, it really would be. She spoke coyly, knowing that thousands watched her on video; she *hinted* at forbidden themes.

Would there be sexual themes? Smiling with mock-innocence, Kulan Gane dodged the question. Was not sexuality itself a metaphor for the creative urge? Art and sex, she said, speaking suddenly with an extreme and pedantic precision, her face quite serious, are both motivated by the same need: to shape and to love the world.

She spoke everywhere. She dropped broad hints and sly ones. She molded the public's interest with a rare and unusual talent.

Then, with a brilliant attention to timing, she let the furor die away. The collective attention of the fickle public turned to other matters. But not all of those other matters were independent of Kulan Gane's manipulations. A series of new books caught the imagination of Archive, and the ideas spread throughout the Concordat and, thus, to all the worlds. A wave of fascination with dangerous, almost frightening, ideas billowed outward from the original home of the race. Each of the new books came from Sophia's hidden library.

One week before Cliffs' ship was scheduled to arrive on Archive, one week before the final preparations would begin for the performance of the opera, official notice finally caught up with Kulan Gane.

The Commerce Branch's Cultural Arts Board, which had demanded prior approval of the text and the music, grew tired of Kulan Gane's delays. The Communications Department of the Commerce Branch took the matter under advisement. A barrage of legal notifications descended upon her, and she was officially enjoined from making any further broadcasts publicizing the upcoming opera. Then, in a bluntly censorial move, the Commerce Branch home office denied permission for the opera to continue.

Kulan Gane filed an appeal. The appeal was set aside, awaiting further data, a move essentially the same as its denial.

The public took little notice, if any. A bright and clever idea had once again been coldly censored. It was doubtless just as well, most people concluded, for the ideas were, perhaps, too daring, too innovative. The new ideas were dangerous.

Archive turned inward again, moving along well-worn ruts so deep that only the most insightful of scholars perceived them at all.

∞

It was snowing on Archive, the year having grown old, when the converted hospital ship dropped from a dark, windblown sky and grounded on the globe that had birthed a race. Admiral Morgan, in his Destroyer Squadron, was only five hours behind.

Kulan Gane met the ship and rushed across the landing ramp. Margaret Cliffs met her and drew her aside. The troupe of musicians, actors, singers, and support personnel, in as much of a hurry as Kulan Gane had been, shot across the ramp and gazed wonderingly into the air. Not a one of them had ever been this far before; the mystery of their home called to them. They grew giddy on the cold air; they leaped and danced in the swirling windswept snow. The Conductor, seeing Cliffs in conference with Kulan Gane, frowned and took control of the troupe. Soon a conveyance slid over the landing field and gathered them in.

Cliffs and Kulan Gane stayed behind, regarding one another with warmth but, also, with misgiving.

"The project is in trouble, Margaret. The opposition has mobilized."

Cliffs snorted. "The fools. They don't even know what it is they oppose."

"No. But they fear it."

"I've come too far, Kulan Gane. I've come this far, and I won't be turned back." She sighed. "Steldan left you something."

Kulan Gane frowned. "What?"

Cliffs held out her hand and unfolded it. In it was a small, white box. Kulan Gane took it and opened it.

Inside, the red and silver symbol of command glinted.

Such an innocent device, a small gleaming emblem. Flames leaped in Kulan Gane's head, dancing behind her eyes. She stood in two places at once: a small, wiry and athletic woman, dressed in blouse and short pants, ignoring the cold of the snow, standing inside the spaceship and bent over a colorful medallion, and a giantess, standing atop the world like a colossus, her head tilted back, her heart a furnace, her hands spread to gather in the stars.

She looked at Cliffs. "Do I dare use this?"

Cliffs sneered back at her. "Use it. Or don't. I don't care. Use it, become Empress, take over the worlds, kill everyone you meet. Slay them all. *I only want my music!*"

Kulan Gane slowly closed the box over the symbol, shutting away the cold glint of total power. "You shall have it."

Cliffs nodded, then pushed past Kulan Gane, joining her people in the conveyance. Kulan Gane did not turn around to watch her go.

∞

The Praesidium of Archive met in solemn conclave. Six individuals more powerful than any others on the world — save only for one — ruled the whole of the Concordat with firm and solid control.

"Well, then," First Secretary Raymond Parke murmured, looking about the Plenary Chamber. A flat, domed ceiling arched over the circular table where the six members sat. In the gallery that ringed them in and rose up to meet the roof in the lens-shaped room, several dozen people sat in silent observation. "It seems to me that this is going to be a rather unusual meeting, notable for its . . . um . . . quietness. Do we really have anything world-shaking to discuss?"

No one answered him, and there seemed to be an icy rebuff in the silence. The five remaining members of the Praesidium were not willing to take their duties for granted.

"Admiral de la Noue has been exceeding her authority," said a slim man in a green tunic. Foreign Secretary Antonin Vissenne's face was thoughtful, not malicious. In the past, he had always been able to determine de la Noue's motivations; her recent Departmental projects were unclear to him this time, and the uncertainty troubled him.

"You can't say that in advance of a fair determination of an authoritary delegation," intoned Justicar Solme. Older than the rest, rail thin, pale and palsied, he clung to the law as he clung to life: with an unyielding, dedicated grip.

"Oh, very right." Parke held up his hands uselessly. "We'll have to take the time to get at the facts before charges can be substantiated."

"Do I have leave to bring out my facts?" Vissenne asked quietly. "May I parade forth my figures? Present my allegations? Draw up my accusations? May I — in short — have your permission to flay the Grand Admiral with indelicate questioning?"

The two remaining men at the table looked at one another and shrugged. Adrian Redmond, the dapper Secretary of Commerce, placed his hands upon the bare wood of the table, expressing a benign patience. Treasury Secretary James Wallace, less sanguine, sighed and leaned back in his chair.

Jennifer De la Noue, blonde, slender, and relaxed, even when at attention, waited for a long moment. She fixed Vissenne with her amber-eyed gaze. "Secretary Vissenne, you do not need to ask permission of the Praesidium to accuse me of impropriety. You have *my* permission. If you have uncovered something that my own investigators have not, then it is for the best of all concerned if you bring it out into the open."

Solme looked at her with cold-eyed approval. Parke smiled his puffy-faced smile that could mean anything or nothing. Redmond and Wallace shrugged again, not choosing to disagree. Vissenne nodded.

"Very well. I am referring to the power stations that you have built on no fewer than one hundred worlds." He looked at her quizzically. "Power stations? Are you now in the business of competing with the Treasury Branch in selling commercial electricity? Each station is associated — a most fascinating combination, I assure you — with a broadcast facility for video. And Admiral, Grand Admiral, there are more irregularities involved with each one of these stations than my operatives have been able to catalogue."

"My own operatives have kept me apprised." De la Noue's voice was cool. "I don't have the answers for you at this time. I'm afraid — " there seemed to be an honest apology in her voice " — that I'm going to have to invoke the military security clause of the charter. I can't tell you why those stations are necessary."

The glances that Wallace and Redmond exchanged were worried ones this time. De la Noue? The most unquestionably honest of them all, holding secrets from them? Vissenne triumphing at last? Parke looked away as if the matter were unimportant. Solme narrowed his eyes, his face deathlike, horribly unpleasant.

Athalos Steldan, de la Noue thought sadly, *you have brought me to this. Thus I find my trust repaid.*

As if her thought were suddenly made fact,

and interrupting Vissenne's next series of accusations, a messenger came hurriedly into the chamber, passed through the low, wooden partition that enclosed the Praesidium, and came around to hand de la Noue a small, handwritten note.

I have Steldan, it read. *Matters are urgent. Come as soon as you can.* It had been signed by Admiral Robert Morgan.

Redmond, who knew de la Noue the most closely, saw the turmoil in her face. The others saw only that the note had been somehow important. De la Noue stood.

"I beg the pardon of the Praesidium and ask permission to withdraw."

Parke frowned. As First Secretary, the matter fell under his domain first. If he felt any desire to compel de la Noue's attendance, he did not show it. "You may leave."

Vissenne straightened and blinked. It was *not* all right with him for de la Noue to go just yet. But the votes. . . . He smiled and shook his head. He didn't have the votes.

De la Noue left the chamber, and a nervous and ideologically divided Praesidium remained behind, unable to proceed with any but the most trivial of business.

∞

The Secretariat's Spire, tallest of the tall towers of modern Archive, was, although vast, simple in plan. In that most important of aspects, it emblematized the Concordat's huge yet straightforward mass.

De la Noue, passing outward and heading for the bank of elevators, saw Kulan Gane approach along an otherwise untenanted corridor. For a moment the sight of the woman's wild, unrestrained hair and her loose, informal clothing rankled at de la Noue's sense of propriety. But she forced herself to remember than not everyone in the Concordat was subject to military standards of attire. Nor, she admitted to herself, should they be. She passed the woman by without another thought.

The elevators dropped her four hundred meters to street level; military gravitic transport flew her up again, almost as high, and down again to the spaceport. The spaceport was built on a site considerably to the north of the ground-hugging ruins of the old spaceport the Empire had maintained. It was smaller, simpler, far less gaudy. But, like the ancient port, it was the commercial hub of civilization. De la Noue was glad her pilot knew where the landing site was for Morgan's orbit-to-ground shuttle, for she could never have found it by herself.

The aircar spiralled down to the landing field, passed precariously low over a cluster of fuel tanks, and came to a crunching halt near the grounded shuttle. De la Noue climbed out and walked stolidly toward the open air lock.

The dignity that had come intact through an awkward landing was swept away when she saw Steldan and Morgan. The two men, in their nearly identical uniforms, stood to greet her when she entered the shuttle's passenger compartment.

"Robert. Athalos." Her expression gladdened. "It's been over a year, Commodore Steldan."

Steldan, obviously ill at ease, was likewise glad to find himself with her again at last. The year had taken its toll on him, and yet she seemed as bright and healthy as ever. "Grand Admiral. I guess this is the time for me to surrender and to confess." He looked up at her, then, suddenly struck by an overwhelming fatigue, sank to a seat among the rows of acceleration couches.

De la Noue looked across to Morgan. Morgan also took a seat.

"The Commodore," he said simply, "has been acting on his own."

"As ever." De la Noue's smile faded. She turned to Steldan. "Tell me what you've done."

"I've started a revolution," he said. Then, with his shoulders bent forward, his face averted, and his voice a low, sad monotone, he told her all that he had done.

She heard him. She was predisposed to believe him. It took time and effort, on her part as well as on his, for her to accept the new revelations. After a long time, she understood. The sense of the past was new to her: a strategist, she lived for the present. History's weight was a new burden to her mind.

She had been right, many weeks ago, when

analyzing Steldan's motives. For, even after he had explained everything carefully, she found that she did not fully approve.

∞

Kulan Gane saw the Grand Admiral of the Concordat Navy walking her way down the high corridor.

Is she going to stop me? Kulan Gane thought, a tremor of fear running through her. The symbol of command that she held gripped tightly in her moist fist called out to her, almost with a voice of its own. She had had to use it only twice, to get past officious security stations. But the use of it was addictive; it was like the sweetest of sweet, sparkling wines, and the taste went swiftly to her head.

No. Don't be a fool. She's not important. The Praesidium. . . .

De la Noue was past, and the Praesidium lay ahead.

Kulan Gane took a deep breath, closed her eyes for a moment, then stared straight ahead and plunged through the doorway.

No one took any notice of her . . . at first. She pressed onward, moving closer to the wooden railing that fenced the spectators away from the Praesidium.

No. It fences them in. Anyone can see that they are hemmed by their authority. Power, for them, is as much a drug as it is for me.

Two plainclothes security officers moved to

intercept her. No fuss was made, no outcry raised. Even in an emergency, they moved calmly, like men simply walking toward the exit. Their faces stern, their bodies relaxed yet prepared for trouble, they met Kulan Gane near the wooden railing. She gritted her teeth tightly and flashed the symbol of command in their faces.

They fell back, giving her passage.

The byplay was so swift and smooth that few in the room had even noticed. Kulan Gane moved on, approaching the body of the Praesidium. One by one, then several at once, heads turned in her direction. She continued, striding directly up to the rail, then moving over it, first lifting herself up on her toes and sitting atop the wooden partition, then swiveling around and dropping her feet within. She now stood where only Praesidium members had stood. The five members present gazed at her with expressions of mingled surprise, displeasure, outrage, and fear.

Old Archive and New faced one another.

Secretary Vissenne spoke first, his voice loud and flat in the silent room. "What the hell do you want?"

First Secretary Parke, however, interposed his own question before Kulan Gane could say anything in response. His voice was, for once, precise. His eyes sparkled. "May we help you, ma'am?"

Wallace sat back, startled by the entire scene. Solme turned to face the table, showing Kulan Gane his back. He planted his fists side by side in front of him and did not, thenceforth, move. Redmond, dapper Redmond, smiled as if the whole show were a joke presented for his private entertainment. Only he, it seemed, appreciated the irony. Only he and First Secretary Parke.

"I've come to ask you a question."

Vissenne began to snap out a retort. Parke spoke first, without seeming abrupt in any way.

"Are you certain that this is the way you wish to present a request to this body? Um. . . ." His old mannerisms of hesitancy and indecision came back to him. "There are proper channels, and. . . ."

Kulan Gane swallowed. "Please, sir. There isn't time."

"How did you get in here?" Wallace asked, taking his turn to interrupt. "And are you armed? What's that in your hand?"

Shaking her head, Kulan Gane tried to smile. Her throat was painfully dry. Wallace didn't know how funny his question was, yet Kulan Gane could not laugh. Armed? She had an energy projector in one inner pocket, a spring-gun in another, and whip-wires strapped to her chest, beneath her breasts. She could kill everyone in the room, for Steldan had never taken that ability away from her. In her hand, however, she held the most dangerous of her weapons, the symbol of command. Steldan had conquered a roomful of dangerous killers with it, making nothing of their own weapons. Now, she had the power to dominate the Praesidium of

Archive and to make her ends theirs.

She did not want to command these men. She didn't want to turn them off the way Steldan had turned off the assassins back on Carpus; she didn't want to trip the master switches in their brains that would turn them into automatons. She saw them now as men: Parke, hiding his brilliance behind a facade of clumsiness and succeeding in fooling nearly everyone. Solme, utterly defiant and contemptuous, insisting on ignoring the unseemly presence of someone who had no proper business in being here. Vissenne, hot and angry, but for exactly the same reason: the due forms were not being adhered to. Wallace, troubled, but not offended, and honestly curious what emergency could compel anyone to take such a risk. And Redmond, a light-hearted man placed into a grim job, yet succeeding in making the least of the burden.

They were hers. She held them all in the palm of her hand.

She licked her lips. "Yes. Please. I'm armed. I have . . . a weapon."

No one moved; no one spoke.

Parke rose slowly to his feet and walked carefully toward Kulan Gane. "I think that we would like to hear what you have to say. Won't you hand me your weapon?"

"No!" Kulan Gane fought for control. Suddenly, she understood what was troubling her, and a sudden wave of relief came over her. *I'm a noble of Archive. My instincts, genetically bequeathed me by a man-sculptor centuries dead, are to dominate those beneath me and bend to those above.* She sucked in a deep breath. *But these men are not lords, nor are they slaves.*

Parke had stopped, still a respectful distance from her. He had seen the play of emotions over her troubled face. What he suspected — madness or some deeper, yet rational, turmoil — he kept to himself.

"Very well. We are your hostages."

"No." Kulan Gane sighed deeply. "I am yours. I have only come to beg a boon of you."

"Name it," Parke said affably. "We will take it under consideration."

"I want my freedom."

"The usual preamble to an assassination," Vissenne grumbled sourly.

"I have an opera. I want to perform it. The tickets are already sold. But the Cultural Arts Board and the Communications Department have withdrawn permission for the performance to go on."

"An opera," Parke said, his voice sounding quite dull, almost stupid.

"An opera! Songs! Music to spark the tiniest emotional reaction out of a mind-deadened Archive! How can you fear it? How do you find the *courage* to fear it?"

Redmond held up a hand and spoke softly. "Would this be *The Skeleton and the Chaffinch*, please?"

Kulan Gane blinked. "Yes." She bowed slightly toward him. "I am the opera's copro-

299

ducer."

"Who are the other producers?" Redmond seemed genuinely interested.

She would not lie to them. Victory through deceit would not be a victory, today. "Commodore Athalos Steldan and the Concordat Navy."

Vissenne leaped up, prepared to speak or, more likely, to shout. Once more Parke anticipated him and spoke with, for him, unprecedented harshness. "Secretary Vissenne. Sit. Silently."

Silence was not in Vissenne's nature, although he obeyed to the degree of seating himself and speaking in a moderate voice. "This is what de la Noue was covering up. This is the conspiracy itself."

"I don't think so," Parke said, scrutinizing Kulan Gane carefully. "No, I don't think so at all." He suddenly seemed to realize that he had been standing all this time and padded back to his seat.

"Tell us your story, please," he said.

Kulan Gane took a deep breath and explained everything. She told them of the symbol of command, a relic of their deadly past. She told them why she was able to wield that power and others could not. She told them of the assassins on Carpus, of Steldan and his covert actions.

She told them of the music, the music that made up the opera and which governmental forces so casually had silenced. Margaret Cliffs had worked for a year of her life to write that music; Steldan had sacrificed his career to let it be heard; Kulan Gane had come to the Praesidium, willing to kill or to die, to rescue the songs of an opera she believed in and which she had never heard.

"If you can censor music, then no song is safe. If you can censor thoughts, then no idea is safe." She looked about at the five men who sat in various poses of attention. Only Solme continued to defy her, turning a deaf ear to her pleas.

"Either rule me gently," she said, her voice now soft, "or I shall rule you. Either give me a few, only a few freedoms, or I must give you none. What difference is there? If dominance is what must be, then I'll be the one dominating. But, if there can be freedom, even a freedom limited by the fear that the people still have of the old Empire, then I want to be free."

Four of the six members of the Praesidium looked at her, weighing her words. De la Noue had left only minutes ago, although it seemed like an aching hour of thought. Solme refused to participate.

"How do we know you can do this?" Vissenne said at last.

Kulan Gane looked at him in dismay. "What?"

He smiled back. "I don't believe in the power of this so-called symbol of command. I don't think you are the threat you claim to be. And I don't believe it is a simple love of music that compels you to confront us."

Kulan Gane shook her head. "No. It is a simple love of liberty. And as for my power. . . ." She moved forward, passing swiftly by Vissenne, and waved her hand closely under the nose of Secretary Redmond.

Redmond looked down and froze. His eyes unfocussed. Then he cocked his head to one side and looked up at Kulan Gane. Their gazes met, and there passed a long, silent dialogue between the two. Redmond's eyes, which had been merry, were now serious. Kulan Gane's, which had been solemn, were now cold, harsh, and stern.

"Tell them."

"She can do what she says," Redmond said, his voice soft and neutral.

The discussion continued. At times the debate was furious, at times it was subdued and thoughtful. But, from the moment Kulan Gane had demonstrated her power, the issue was never in doubt.

∞

The next days passed in a flurry of preparations. Steldan and de la Noue had made their peace, although she held some private misgivings about the use of Navy resources to produce an opera. When she learned what had happened at the Praesidium meeting, her misgivings crystallized into positive dislike. Long, earnest conversations with Secretary Redmond satisfied her, although she still felt a strong reluctance. Kulan Gane made the most of the unprecedented

Praesidium reversal, and the publicity she generated made advance interest in the opera one of the highest entertainment priorities on Archive and throughout the Concordat.

∞

The day before the opera was to be shown, Secretary Redmond came to visit Kulan Gane.

"I want to see the symbol of command, please."

They met in her apartment, in a residential block near the heart of the city. Her tastes in decoration were florid, but not garish. One wall was given over to archaic weapons — whips, bows, spears, obsidian knives — and bright, artistic abstracts occupied prominent spots on the other walls.

"I have it with me. But. . . ."

"I want to see it. I have to know."

Kulan Gane shook her head. "I want to thank you for playing along with me. I . . . I didn't want to destroy your mind."

"You were sincere," Redmond said, smiling. His red hair curled from beneath his shapeless felt cap. "I believed you. I still do." His smile faded. "But I must know. Please, show me the symbol of command."

"Very well." Kulan Gane reached within her blouse and brought it forth. She held it forward. Secretary Redmond looked at it and was lost.

After a brief moment, Kulan Gane snatched it away. Redmond slowly resurfaced from the trance of obedience the symbol had plunged him into. He opened and closed his eyes as if doubting his eyesight. Then he looked at Kulan Gane.

And then he sat heavily upon one of her soft, overstuffed couches and shuddered with a quiet, gentlemanly dignity.

"I gave you no commands," Kulan Gane promised him.

"That is a very potent tool indeed."

"No!" Kulan Gane's outburst startled both of them. "It is not a tool! It's a weapon! An evil, insane weapon of domination!" She flung it to the carpet, where it winked up at them, glinting in the lamplight.

Drawing a deep breath, Kulan Gane reached into her inner pocket and drew forth the energy projector. She knelt, triggered the weapon, and played the beam of flame back and forth over the symbol. Only when the tube was too hot to hold in her hand did she let it drop. The symbol had been melted away and was now only a shapeless blot of dripping metal on the charred carpet.

Redmond looked at her. The horror on his face was mirrored in hers. They looked back at the ruined symbol.

The horror would pass. Each prayed that their freedom would not.

∞

The next day, with the six members of the Praesidium in the front row of the audience, the curtain rose upon the first performance of *The Skeleton and the Chaffinch*.

21

A rifle could be made into a flute, and
a flute, I suppose, into a rifle. It is we who
are the tools. It is we who sing and who
slay.

— Athalos Steldan
Apologia

Lyra, in the basement of the palace, struggled to
restore the computer to working order. She
knew her time was limited; this would be the
first place the revolutionaries would fight to
retake. Her best hope for survival would be to
bring at least one weapon-laden robot here to
guard her.

For the moment, however, she was guarded
by Basil. She looked up at him, expecting to see
his normally cheerful face. The voice of the
Emperor had had an unusual effect upon him,
however; he frowned, a deeply puzzled expression upon his flat face. He seemed tormented by
thoughts he could not comprehend.

"Basil? What is it?"

Basil, as silent as ever, had no way of answering. He stepped closer to her and lowered himself to his knees, looking closely at the instrumentation with which she worked.

"I'm saving the life of the Emperor," she explained patiently. "He's promised me that I'll be his bride." For a moment she swelled with joy; she clutched her hands to her breast and smiled with a stupid, happy expression. Basil watched her.

Her shoulders sagged. "No. I don't believe it. He'll never share his power with anyone. He'll never give up his concubines. He says he'll be faithful to me, but I know better." She looked at Basil and smiled sadly. "The Emperor is insane. Did you know that? He could have his way with me, any time he wants. I'm his. I don't mind being his plaything. But he won't really make me Empress. I know him too well."

Shaking her head, she reached out to continue trying to restore the computer. Basil watched her. Then, with a suddenness that startled her, he leaped to his feet and jumped around her to the doorway. The revolutionaries had arrived before the robots had. The computer, although partially operational, still lacked several vital control linkages, and she needed time to repair them. As she struggled, fighting with the controls, the computer, in its paranoid insanity, took matters into its own hands. It shut off all power to the control panel, locking Lyra out. Her hands slapped the control studs, to no avail. The computer was still alive, still sentient, to a degree, but it refused to allow her to help it.

Outside the control room, a patrol of invading revolutionaries edged nearer, determined to deny her the time. What had seemed saved was lost again. She stood, wishing that fate had fallen out differently.

Lyra knew then that she was doomed. A part of her argued for hope. She thought of sending Basil against these reinforcements. There seemed to be only seven or eight of them. Basil could defeat them as he had scattered the others whose bodies still littered the floor outside.

Or she could run, taking Basil with her, and seek the forefront of the fighting. Basil could probably shift the course of the battles. The weight of numbers was already pushed her way by seven.

She could not. It had taken everything she had, every bit of her drive and determination, to think this far ahead. She had come to the computer and restored a part of its mad mind. That had been her only goal. She couldn't muster the mental energy required to think ahead, to guide Basil up and to the battle for the throne room.

Numb, her mind now as devoid of organized thought as his was, she slumped down onto the soft floor of the computer room, and she thought of the bodies she had seen this day. Basil stood above her, watching, his expression caring.

She couldn't care any longer. She gestured

to him, and he sat beside her, soothing her, stroking her bowed head.

I was born to pleasure, she thought, the words trickling through her deadened mind. *I was born to play. And now, when everything turns serious, when the games are torn up, when the plays are disrupted, I'm useless.* Her whole life had been no more than training for the subtle joys of intrigue, of fashion, of sex, of money, of power. . . .

It had nearly been her turn, and then the game was over.

The revolutionaries found the two that way, sitting side by side on the warm floor. The patrol was only of eight; Basil could have slain them in less than a minute. But their guns were already levelled. . . . Lyra restrained him. He held her.

She was a noble; nothing could hide that. She knew what their orders were: she was to be preserved for the execution in the courtyard. Basil, though. . . .

Lyra saw it the moment the team leader did. Basil, a slave of no worth in the schemes of the revolution, was to be shot on the instant.

"No!" The cry was wrenched from her deepest heart. Basil bounded to his feet . . . and stayed there, unmoving, as his sharp mind understood her concern. His feral snarl melted into an almost silly grin. Lyra was concerned for him. His love for her was never greater.

"Go," she whispered to him. The revolutionary commander scowled, his dark hair protruding above and below his bright red headband.

He aimed his fuser. If that nonhuman slave was prepared to fight. . . .

"Go!" Lyra shouted. "Come back to me another time. Go!" Basil stood, unmoving.

"Shoot him," snapped the team leader. Fuser fire licked out, red-spitting gouts of snapping fire, moving in pencil-thin beams. Basil seemed to be somewhere else. A pattern of scorch marks marred the wall. The fire shifted; Basil was more swift.

Moving like a kite in a high wind, the most personable creature Lyra had ever known disappeared around the corner. Her final glimpse of him was of his tall, white form, his tidy and trim fur, his large, comical feet, and his ears, already turned away from her, held forward to listen for danger. Of his face, she had only her memories.

∞

Szentellos dismissed the revolutionary council shortly after his chastisement. They surely must think that he had lost. But he had not. He would yet win, although everyone would lose. Indeed, his lofty ideals for the civilization to be built upon the ashes of the Empire were already dead. His dreams were likewise dead, dead letters, utopias that would never know life.

He went, not to his quarters, as Thendall expected, but out into the streets. The fighting was mostly finished. Was the palace his? Was the Emperor dead? There was no fighting in the streets, although there was murder. Revolutionaries looted and committed atrocities less palatable, and the fires burned unchecked.

What were the others of the council doing, back in the high room he had just quitted? Szentellos guessed but could not know. Possibly they joined Thendall in a toast to the downfall of the Empire; possibly they drank to the death of the Emperor.

Did they nominate Thendall as the new Emperor? Did they divide up the power of church, spaceport, military, and palace among themselves?

Szentellos wandered, wasting time. Ahead, on a high terrace near the palace, three orbit-to-ground shuttles made clumsy, uncontrolled landings. Soldiers poured out, their weapons gripped in their hands. Szentellos recognized Petrosius at their head.

He ran. Suddenly all of his plans and schemes were of no importance. Thendall had won; the nobles must die. He ran, his lifelong dignity gone from him. He pounded up the streets, up the narrow, winding courts that hemmed him in like the alleyways in a nightmare. Up he flew, past the high gardens and vast homes of the nobles who were privileged to live in the shadow of the palace.

Ahead, the first of the shuttles bulked. One soldier stood guard. He challenged Szentellos but did not fire.

"Petrosius!" Szentellos bawled. "I need you!"

Petrosius heard. "Stay your fire, men. This is. . . ." He paused. "This is one we can trust."

He looked hard at Szentellos and saw the desperation and the misery on the man's face.

"What are you doing here?" he asked bluntly of Szentellos. The revolution was to make all men equal, but the way that a noble addresses a commoner was deeply ingrained and would require years to erase.

"The council has decided that they no longer need my advice," Szentellos puffed. He bent over, trying to regain his breath. The run had cost him, emotionally as well as physically.

"I have decided that I no longer need the council. With whom does your loyalty lie?" He looked at Petrosius and his professional soldiers. The young men, armed with weapons but without ideologies, seemed less hardened and capable than his own amateurs.

Petrosius' face sagged. "It's pretty early for a schism, isn't it?" Eyeing Szentellos, he knew, clearly, that it was not.

∞

Basil, alone, knew where to go. The Emperor received him in the throne room, looking at him with his suspicion hidden. The palace, although dying, knew what the Verna intended.

The two stone warriors stepped in front of the throne.

Basil, overtopping two meters by a head, was dwarfed by the two giant figures. Had the palace been unharmed, they would have been impossible for him to defeat. The eight men who had captured Lyra and from whom he had just escaped had done further harm to the computer. The stone warriors tried to live, to fight, but they fought like drunken men.

Basil stood only waist-high to them. He could leap, however, and his weight was not inconsiderable. He ducked in, jumped high, and wrapped his legs around the nearest warrior's chest. It was unbalanced and waved its arms in a ludicrous display. The other warrior drove in and swung its massive sword.

Basil leaped aside. Perhaps he had learned from his battle, that day in the arena: again, as then, the second robot slew the first.

Then the second one froze, its sword caught somewhere in the mechanical workings of its victim. It pulled, repetitiously, stupidly, trying to free its weapon.

The Emperor watched the show without moving.

Basil approached him, his face neutral. This was not joyous battle, nor the sweetness of love. This was the thing he had been created for. One way or another, he had always known that he would arrive here.

Refusing even to stand, the Emperor allowed him to ascend the steps of the throne.

Basil took the Emperor by the throat and strangled him dead with five quick shakes.

Then he turned, looked with ironic appreciation at the robot still drawing uselessly at its sword, and left the palace.

The day was young, the Empire dead. Basil

was not intercepted as he made his way through the city. The streets were empty. He arrived at the Arena without difficulty. The other Vernae in the chambers beneath the sands welcomed him.

He had no speech. Dynos, the oldest of them, spoke softly to him, trying to discover his aim.

"Basil? Do you wish us to fight?"

Basil looked blankly at him.

For a being so huge, Dynos' voice was small and high.

"Do you wish us to flee?"

Basil frowned and slowly nodded. The words meant nothing to him, but he understood the tone. To Dynos' instructions, the gladiators armed themselves, accoutered as for battle or parade, and issued out into the streets.

Centuries later, it would be understood by the Vernae that Basil had led them. Basil might have disagreed: it was Dynos who guided their operations. They drew to them as many of their kind as they could, collaring them when they showed reluctance, drawing them from homes, shops, streets, pens, warrens, and kennels. They arrived at the spaceport and took control of several ships.

Over seven hundred years would pass before humanity saw their descendants return. On Archive, those who had not fled were brutally killed.

Theirs were the last ships to leave the world for seventeen years.

Assembled like cattle in the slaughtering pen at a stockyard, the nobles stood huddled together, naked, men and women alike, bawling their unheeded protests, shedding their unnoticed tears.

An order was given.

There were no speeches. Fuser fire played over the lot, and the lot charred. No one saw Lyra in the crowd. No one saw Thendall. The stink of their burning flesh was like that of food burning over an open grill: hideously savory, nauseatingly appetizing. They charred, and that was more or less that. A mercy crew waded out into the heap and used hand fusers to dispatch anyone who had been unlucky enough to survive. Those who watched turned away, feeling awkward and guilty, empty and quite lonely.

Loneliest of all was Szentellos, the one to whom they all owed their victory. They'd dreamed of following him in triumph down the city ways. Today, however, he had stepped down from his post at the head of the revolutionary council.

It didn't matter; the council was four-fifths dead now. Thendall had never understood, even as he stood with his peers, burning, dying, that the death of the nobles was not something he should have demanded. But not even the trick that had saved Petrosius, casting aside any claims to his noble title, would have saved Thendall. He had made a greater error. He had

314

not been fully committed to the death of the Empire and the casting down of all Emperors. He had, in his greed, dreamed of supplanting Arcadian, the star-kindler, and ruling more wisely in his stead. The revolution was a deeper matter than that and would no longer abide that kind of rule.

Thendall had the revolutionary council behind him. Szentellos had the revolutionaries.

But who will follow a man who sends his allies to the pyre?

Szentellos strode off, powerless now in a world he'd toppled and faceless, nameless, in a world that he would not be permitted to help rebuild. No one remarked upon his passage.

He would live to see the light fade and the reason turn to madness. His single voice of protest would be drowned out in the reign of chaos.

Two years later, when matters were still unsettled, he was not invited to sign the document known as the Concordat of Archive, and his opinions were not sought.

A year before his death, he finished his *Regrets*.

"History's wheel has broken the spirit of our race."

22

Life is the thing we love.

— Achorus
The Skeleton and the Chaffinch

Nothing in the production of *The Skeleton and the Chaffinch* was traditional. Cliffs, in her desire to outrage established custom, had gone beyond mere avant-garde experimentalism and had used the most positive of classically derivative forms: metaphor.

The show began early, a blaring crescendo of music crashing through the theater, cutting through the murmured conversation of the members of the audience. The house lights snapped off abruptly; the curtain flew up; the music continued from its brassy entrada into a shocking, limping march. The stage, although brightly lit, was bare of singers. Scenery had been constructed, a minimalist setting that sketched in the lines of a quaint country village of more than a thousand years past. Pastel blue drapes slanted down from a dingy grey building, and a well stood alone at the right of the stage. The scene was a small market square, deserted, unnaturally, in the bright light of day. Beyond, to the right, the scenery hinted at a desert or dry plain.

The music grew softer but more ominous, and the march deepened its emphasis on the offbeat as if the music heralded the appearance of a monstrous, alien army, slouching tiredly forward. Just when the music seemed about to reach a climax, just when the tension seemed as if it could not be twisted any tighter, the music ended, the way it had begun, in the middle.

After three beats of silence, a ragamuffin bumpkin in loose, bucolic clothing ambled carelessly onto the stage, his shoulders and arms flopping, his legs fluid, his overlarge feet never quite stumbling.

The audience, shocked and relieved, laughed loudly. The clown turned to them and put on a sad, forlorn face.

"Yes, you laugh at a bumpkin." The technique of an actor addressing the audience was not new to Archive, but it nevertheless jarred. The bumpkin faced them down, bending forward, shading his eyes with his hands, glaring at the audience thoroughly. Then he stood, made an impossible little leap, and clacked his heels together in midair. The music took up with a variation on his entrance march, and he strolled across the stage in a magnificent pantomime of affronted dignity. The rest of his speech would be unheard.

Athalos Steldan, in the darkness of the rows of orchestra seats, seventeen rows back and well off to one side, forced himself to sit unmoving. Most of the other guests wore evening wear of a greater or lesser degree of formality; he sat stiffly uniformed. Ahead of him and to the right, somewhere, de la Noue watched the opera, not knowing what it had meant to him, not understanding the cost. He had won only her grudging permission to continue, and, when she had learned of Kulan Gane's actions in front of the Praesidium, she had been sorely angered. It had taken the calm words of Secretary Redmond to win her approval. Steldan looked for her in the audience, using the wan light that reflected from the scenery and stage lights. Was that her, a head of blonde hair gleaming in the sea of heads? Was Admiral Morgan with her?

A young Navy enlisted man walked with great anxiety down the rightmost row, looking back and forth. Steldan saw him and wondered. Before long the messenger had found who he was looking for: de la Noue. He pushed carefully through the press, bent to whisper in her ear, and then, vastly ashamed, made his careful way out of the theater.

That, Steldan smiled, was so very like de la Noue. She would want to be kept abreast of developments, no matter what the occasion. Steldan had once been like that himself.

With a pang, he realized that he still was. For, instead of watching the opera and enjoying its music, he found that he was more intent on watching the audience. Were they absorbing the message? Would they learn the one thing they most needed to learn from it?

He forced himself to watch the stage.

The Skeleton had appeared, a symbol of death, most unmistakably, and yet played by a young, slender man. He wore no makeup and was dressed in a quiet white garment, the pants tight about his athletic legs, the blouse loose and pleated, the small cape fluttering behind him. The point was driven cruelly home, however: he seldom moved. Most of his performance — and it lasted for almost the entirety of the opera — involved him standing motionlessly in artful poses. When he did move, a translucent projection of an actual human skeleton appeared beside and behind him, and it moved in the same way. When the two were in their new pose, the skeleton faded. Cliffs' music was keyed to these movements, and the slow dissolving of the projected image was accompanied by a series of appoggiaturas which lent the music a hollow, empty sonority.

The plot of the opera, like the plot of all operas, was subsidiary to the music. The skeleton sought to discover the reason for his death and, thus, the reason for his life. The town came to life about him, and he spoke with the citizens. A farmer explained that life was only a matter of feeding and being fed. A merchant answered his inquiries with a fascinating and humorous patter song dealing with the way that wealth is acquired by the buying and selling of commodities.

"Are you only a middleman?" the skeleton asked.

"Of course," the merchant responded, "but I am a wealthy one."

The skeleton left the man and wandered over to the well, trailed by his truly skeletal shadow. The latter was clean and gleaming white, the polished curves of the bone showing the true beauty of death. Insubstantial, it hinted at the comfort enjoyed only by the dead. Through it, the outlines of the buildings and the market could be seen.

A soldier told the skeleton that the secret lay in killing before one was killed. A woman hinted, shyly, that giving birth to more young lives outweighed the cost that must finally be paid by dying. A judge argued that, if, during the course of one's life, one bettered the world, then that life was ultimately a benefit to all other lives.

"You put thieves and scoundrels to death, then?" the skeleton asked, and, when he lifted his head, a dim skull behind him was also lifted.

"Of course." The judge stared at the skeleton intently. "And I let philosophers live — in exile!" Frowning in his barely suppressed wrath, the judge stamped away.

The house lights came on then, and the curtain began to lower. The skeleton stood, then knelt, his motion paralleled by his ghostly alter ego. His stance was one of pleading, and he faced the audience as if imploring them not to leave, not yet. Although he held this pose for the few seconds it took the curtain to descend, this time the bones beside him did not fade away but, also, knelt, beseeching the audience for a help they could not offer.

A twenty minute intermission had been ordained. Steldan, dazed, rose from his seat and wandered out into the theater lobby with the rest of the crowd.

There, beneath the high globes of light that decorated the large, mirrored lobby, he found Grand Admiral de la Noue, standing by Admiral Morgan.

De la Noue looked up and smiled thinly at Steldan. "I'm impressed by the music," she said, shaking her head. "But I have to ask you. Is it worth it?"

Steldan sighed. "My career is ruined. My loyalties have been tested to the uttermost. But, yes." He looked at her, no longer ashamed. "This music has been worth it."

"I'm going to try to save your career, Athalos." De la Noue glanced at Morgan, who plainly disapproved. But the two of them had settled the matter earlier, and Morgan was not one to disagree with his superior in front of witnesses.

"Is that possible?" Steldan asked, his voice full of wonder. The scenes just passed played again through his head. The skeleton spoke for him, surely, when he asked, again and again, his hopeless questions. *What is my life to mean, now that my life is ended?*

De la Noue's smile broadened and grew sincere. "Athalos. You are now what you always have been. A Commodore in the Concordat Navy is the same as an undersecretary of commerce or a practicing intern in an emergency hospital. You're a servant of the people. You told me that you wanted this opera to free the human race. But you won't be free yourself, will you?"

"No, ma'am." Steldan faced her bravely. "I never will be."

Her smile faded. "I received a message during the first act. The Vernae, off in the stars they've claimed, are leaving. They've finished building an armada of gigantic, unarmed spaceships, and they're simply leaving." She looked at him. "Is this your doing?"

"It is, but it wasn't my intention. I wanted us to live in peace with them."

"They came from our past," Morgan said, his voice sudden yet mild. "Where are they bound?"

"They are leaving, then? Are they going away forever?" De la Noue found it difficult to comprehend. "We've scouted the cities they've vacated. No one remains. But what could cause such a migration?"

"They cannot live with us," Steldan said. The sadness he found at this news combined with the sadness he felt from the music and message of the opera. It was, for the moment, more than he could bear. He turned away.

"Athalos," de la Noue's voice, soft and almost musical, recalled him.

"Yes?"

"The Black Book assassins. You said that

322

they are no longer able to be killers. Is that the truth?"

"Yes."

She looked at him. Her smile was ironic. "Then you did what I asked you to do, only four years late. You disbanded the Black Book. And was it ever used in the intervening years?"

"Never. Never once."

"No lives have been lost." She stepped closer to him. "All other crimes can be forgiven, Commodore." She placed a hand on his shoulder. "Let's go back inside. I want to see how the opera ends."

She guided him to Morgan's seat, and he, still dazed, wasn't aware of it happening until he sank down to sit by her side and realized that Admiral Morgan had withdrawn, doubtlessly to assume the seat Steldan had earlier occupied.

The second half of the opera began in a more traditional way: the lights dimmed, the curtain rose, and music started up.

The Chaffinch was played by an actress made up in a costume of brilliant blues, her face shaded by a small, tight-fitting hood. She appeared on stage, and the light, almost dance-measure music that introduced her rose, lightheartedly, to the ceiling of the vast hall. The skeleton, seeing her, frowned and stepped back into a corner.

The chaffinch had a simple message: life was song. And the soprano voice with which the singer had been blessed gave ample demonstration of that happy theme. She sang runs, warbling back and forth between difficult notes and notes even more difficult until it strained credibility to think that a human throat could emit such complex music. Her song was of daylight and the clouds above. It was of nighttime and the terrors of bird-catching beasts. It was of love found, love lost, love regained; it was a song of hope, never foresworn.

Following that was the centerpiece of the opera. Achorus' ancient words, written centuries ago, before the troubles were foreseen that would lead to the collapse of the eternal empire, had been adapted brilliantly by Margaret Cliffs. The duet, lasting no less than eighteen minutes, was a canvas for voice and orchestra that bordered on the impossible. The skeleton stood still, save for a very few shifts of posture at which times his companion of bones would shift with him. The chaffinch was never still, pirouetting and posturing, dancing all the time she sang. Both of the singers were athletes; both needed to be.

The message of the duet was simple: it was an exhortation to all who listened: die.

In essence, that was what they sang. Die. "Go thou, and die in thy time."

Hidden behind the message, subtly woven in with the slow words of the skeleton and the quick words of the chaffinch, was a denial of that dire compelling. They did not affirm life; had not the skeleton already proven that to be useless? They did not celebrate living. The hidden message in their music, their stance, and their tireless voices was this: die, for to die one must have lived.

During this long duet, Steldan lost all awareness of de la Noue beside him. He forgot where he was, and, indeed, he forgot who he was. He was up on the stage; he surrounded the two singers and saw them from every angle. The music filled him, and, for the first time in over a year, he knew that he was happy.

Die. He knew he would, in time. It was only that he had something to do, first. Like the farmer, he had meals yet to eat and meals yet to serve. Like the merchant, he had deals yet to arrange. Like the soldier, he had people to kill. Like the woman, he had lives to nurture and children to raise and to protect while they grew. Like the judge, he had a world that needed to be made better — a hundred thousand worlds, all in need of human judging.

No one lives forever; no one ever completes all of his life's jobs. Like the skeleton, Steldan knew he would someday die. Like the Chaffinch, he would live the years remaining to him in the best way he could.

A musical denouement and artfully manipulated subplot ended the opera, and, at the very close, the bumpkin came out again, sneering haughtily. He still lived, he still stumbled his way across the world. The skeleton and the chaffinch flanked him, and the three stood abreast, facing the audience. The skeleton moved his arm very slightly, and his projected twin, a skeleton in truth, appeared in the very spot where the bumpkin stood. The bumpkin stepped forward, turned about, and waggled his fingers in the blank holes of the eyesockets of the pale, grinning skull.

When the curtain came down, he was left standing outside it, facing it, his back to the audience. Slowly he turned around, goggled in pop-eyed astonishment at his exposure, and burrowed under the curtain, his elbows and knees flailing.

The audience, expecting anything but that, laughed and then began to applaud the performance.

Steldan took a deep breath and rose unsteadily to leave the theater.

Epilogue

Kulan Gane and Athalos Steldan sat side by side on a couch, looking over a pile of readouts that gave the demographic breakdowns of the viewing audience who had watched the opera by transmitted image.

"We reached only eight per cent of the viewers," Steldan sighed. "We've failed."

"There are a lot of things to watch, Athalos."

"Of those who watched," Steldan went on, "how many watched it all? And how many understood it? And of them, how many will dare to think about it, even for a moment?"

"One in a thousand." Kulan Gane took Steldan by the shoulders. "You only want one person in a thousand. You want results, don't you?"

Steldan grimaced. "Of course, but. . . ."

Kulan Gane laughed and moved over to seat herself rudely in Steldan's lap. "You wanted results overnight. You wanted to wake up this morning and find the universe completely altered." She kissed his forehead. "Why didn't you just use the symbol of command and compel the changes you wanted?"

He had no answer; she knew his mind as well, if not better, than he did.

"Have we had word from Sophia?" he asked, embarrassed by the overly intimate way that Kulan Gane was using him.

"Oh, yes. She's convinced, using her superior abilities at estimating mass trends, that we've done the right thing."

Steldan laughed. "Well, I was sure of that much at least. Will we have had any effect?"

Kulan Gane kissed him again. "A small one. Sophia said that the superficial effects will be obvious immediately. The lasting ones, if they are to arrive at all, will take a few years. She said it would all be easily seen by those who know how to look."

"We'll live to see it."

"We'll live to see it begin," she corrected him. "The full impact will take centuries to arrive."

"And what about Margaret Cliffs?"

"I talked to her this morning."

"What is she going to do?"

Looking down at Steldan, loving him now more than ever before, Kulan Gane laughed at his simplicity.

"She's going to write another symphony. It will be her fifth." She looked up. "Do you think anyone will hear it? Maybe we ought to arrange matters ourselves. . . ."

Steldan extricated himself from her increasingly friendly embrace. He stood, paced a bit, then paused at a safe distance.

"No." He pointed a finger at her. "This time, she's on her own."

**Tales of the Concordat
by Jefferson Swycaffer**

The story continues in...

VOYAGE OF THE PLANETSLAYER

The People on the *Planetslayer* are just following orders. What they're doing is for the good of mankind, after all.

The world known as Kythe-Correy is potentially capable of supporting human life, but the planet's present ecology is poisonous. So before it can be colonized, the *Planetslayer* must be brought in to do its work.

Taviella-i-Tel and her crew would rather not be here — but when the government tells you what to do, you do it. Similarly, the scientists aboard the ship are obliged to observe and record the "cleansing" of Kythe-Correy. Not all of them are in favor of the mission, but they are all duty-bound to see it through...

. . . Or are they?

EMPIRES LEGACY

The crew of the merchant ship *Coinroader* has been to a lot of unusual places and seen a lot of strange things — but nothing so extraordinary as a planetoid that shouldn't exist. There it sits, visible and violating the laws of physics.

Taviela-i-Tel and her crew are entrepreneurs, and laying claim to this strange space station and its secrets could be the break of a lifetime.

Walking a tightrope between the promise of great new discoveries and the threat of death, they go deeper and deeper in search of full knowledge of *The Empire's Legacy*.

Fantasy adventure from

GORD THE ROGUE™ Books by Gary Gygax
$3.95 each

Sea of Death
Night Arrant
City of Hawks
Come Endless Darkness
Dance of Demons

The Legend Trilogy by David Gemmell

Against the Horde	$3.95
Waylander	$3.50
The King Beyond the Gate	$3.50

Skraelings by Carl Sherrell	$2.95
The Last Knight of Albion by Peter Hanratty	$3.50
The Book of Mordred by Peter Hanratty	$3.50